# THE
# DARK

MICE

For my parents

# THE
# DARK
# PORTAL

## Book One of
## THE DEPTFORD MICE

## Written and illustrated
## by Robin Jarvis

MACDONALD YOUNG BOOKS

First published in Great Britain in 1989
by Macdonald & Company (Publishers) Ltd
Reprinted in 1990, 1991 (x3), 1992 (x4) and 1993 (x2) by
Simon & Schuster Young Books
and in 1996 by Macdonald Young Books
51, Western Road
Hove
East Sussex
BN3 1JD

British Library Cataloguing in Publication Data
Jarvis, Robin.
The Deptford Mice,
The Dark Portal,
I. Title
823'.914 [F]

ISBN 0-361-08548-6
ISBN 0-7500-0628-5 Pbk

Typeset in Palatino by Tek Art Ltd
Printed in Great Britain by
The Guernsey Press Co. Ltd, Guernsey, Channel Islands

# CONTENTS

# THE MICE

ALBERT BROWN
Loving father and devoted husband. Albert is a commonsensical
mouse, not usually given to rash actions.

ARTHUR BROWN
Fat and jolly, Arthur likes a scrap but always comes off worse.

AUDREY BROWN
Tends to dream. She likes to look her best and wears lace and
ribbons. Audrey cannot hold her tongue in an argument, and
often says more than she should.

GWEN BROWN
Gentle wife of Albert and caring mother of Arthur and Audrey.
Her love for her family binds it together and keeps it strong.

ARABEL CHITTER
Silly old gossip who gets on the nerves of everyone in the
Skirtings.

OSWALD CHITTER
Arabel's son is an albino runt. Oswald is very weak and is not
allowed to join in some of the rougher games.

PICCADILLY
A cheeky young mouse from the city, Piccadilly has no parents
and is very independent.

THOMAS TRITON
A retired midshipmouse. Thomas is a heroic old salt – he does
not suffer fools gladly.

WILLIAM SCUTTLE or 'Twit'
Twit is a fieldmouse visiting his mother's sister Arabel Chitter.
Twit is an 'innocent', and does not have a bad word to say about
anyone.

ELDRITCH and ORFEO
Are brothers, and as bats see far into the future. Bat advice is a
very dangerous thing to seek, for they tell you only fragments of
what they know.

THE GREEN MOUSE
A mysterious figure in mouse mythology. He is the spirit of
Spring, and of new life.

# THE RATS

### MADAME AKKIKUYU
A black rat from Morocco. She is a fortune-teller who wanders around selling potions and charms to gullible customers.

### FINN
A sly old worker – one of his ears is missing, but he doesn't miss much.

### FLETCH
A dirty old rat with bad breath and spots on his nose.

### ONE-EYED JAKE
A popular rat who is threatening to oust Morgan from office.

### JUPITER
The great dark god of the sewers. He lives in the dark portal and possesses awesome powers. All fear him.

### LEERING MACKY
A rat with a terrible squint. He and Vinegar Pete are old cronies.

### MORGAN
The Cornish piebald rat who is Jupiter's lieutenant. Morgan trusts no-one, and does all Jupiter's dirty work.

### SKINNER
A rat with a mousepeeler strapped onto his stump of an arm.

### SMILER
A strong giant of a rat who works in the mine.

### VINEGAR PETE
This rat never smiles. His face is always sullen and he and Leering Macky mutter to themselves.

# THE GRILL

When a mouse is born he has to fight to survive. There are many enemies – owls, foxes and of course, cats; but mice suffer far more at our hands. I have heard of a whole family of kind, gentle mice, wiped out by eating poison – four generations gone and only the baby left because it was too small to eat solids.

Mice are all descended from rural families and they remember their traditions wherever they live. They honour the green spirits of the land as Man once did and every spring they hold a celebration for the awakening year, calling to the Green Mouse to ripen the wheat and see them safe.

In a borough of London called Deptford there lived a community of mice. An old empty house was their home and in it they fashioned a comfortable life for themselves. People never disturbed them with traps, and because all the windows were boarded up they never even saw a cat.

So they dwelt there quite happily. In the winter they would visit the building next to theirs where a blind old lady lived and eat from her pantry. She never minded; her nephews always brought cakes and chocolates so there was too much for her alone. The mice never took more than they needed anyway. There were also berries on the trees that hugged the house and some of the younger mice would venture outside to pick them. The only blight on their carefree existence was the sewers – or rather the rats that lived in them. Cut-throats and pirates the lot of them. Thin and ugly, a rat would smack his lips at the thought of Mouse for dinner. He would kill, peel and, if he was a fussy eater, roast it. Not that the rats ever came out of the sewers – they had enough muck and slime down there to keep them happy. No, what worried the mice was the Grill.

This fine example of Victorian ironwork was in the cellar of the empty house. Beyond it lay a passage that led straight to the sewers. It nagged on the mind of every mouse. The Grill, with its leaf pattern of iron was all that divided them from the bitter cruelty of the ratfolk and their dark gods. All the mice in the Skirtings knew of the Grill. It was the gateway to the underworld, the barrier between life and death. Only whispering voices would discuss the sewers in case strange forces were awoken by their mention out loud. The mice knew that deep below ground, beyond the Grill, was a power which even the rats feared. No-one dared to name it in the Skirtings – it was enough to still any conversation and bring a sudden, sober halt to merrymaking.

And yet the Grill seemed to draw mice to it. In one corner there was even a tiny hole edged with jagged rusty iron which a mouse could just squeeze through, if he was foolish enough to want to do so.

One such mouse was Albert Brown. He could never afterwards understand what had compelled him to do such a crazy thing but through the Grill he had gone.

Albert had a wife called Gwen and two children, Arthur and Audrey, so you see he had everything to live for. He was happy and his family was content. There was just no reason and he kicked himself for it. With a shudder he remembered the warnings that he had given his own children: "Beware the Grill!" He had never been brave or overtly curious, so why did the Grill call to him that spring morning, and what was the urge to explore that gripped him so?

# 1

## THE ALTAR OF JUPITER

The sewers were dark, oppressive and worst of all smelly. Albert had gone quite a way before he shook himself and suddenly became aware of where he was. Quickly he stifled the yell that gurgled up from his stomach and raced out of his mouth. Then he sat down and took in the situation.

He was on a narrow ledge, in a wide, high tunnel. Below him ran the dark sewer water. Albert cursed the madness that had gripped him and sent him running into danger.

"Yet here I am," he thought ruefully and wondered how far he had come. But he was unable even to recall how long ago he had left the Skirtings. Alone, in the darkness, Albert sat on the brick ledge trying to quell the panic that was bubbling up inside him. He pressed his paws into his stomach and breathed as deeply as he could.

"Got to get out! Got to get back!" he said, but his voice came out all choked and squeaky and echoed eerily around the tunnel. This frightened him more than anything: the rats lived down here. Around the next corner a band of them could be waiting for him, listening to his funny cries of alarm and laughing at his panic. They might have knives and sticks. What if they were already appointing one of them to be the mouse-peeler? What if . . .?

Albert breathed deeply again and wiped his forehead. The only thing to do was to remain calm: if he succumbed to fright then he would stay rooted to the spot and the rats would surely find him. He stood up and set his jaw in determination. "If I stay calm and use my wits then all I have to do is retrace my footsteps and return to the Grill," he told himself.

\* \* \*

It was many hours later when Albert sat down on yet another ledge and wept. All this time he had tried to find his way out, but up till now he had been unable to recognise anything that could tell him he was on the right track. What hope had he of returning to his family? He sighed and wondered what time of day it was. Perhaps it was another day altogether? Then he remembered and hoped that it was not. The Great Spring Celebration was today, and he would miss it. He would miss the games, the dancing and the presentations. Albert groaned. His own children, Arthur and Audrey were to be presented this year; they had come of age and would receive their mousebrasses. Today was the most special day in their lives and he would miss it. Albert wept again.

Then in his sorrow he put his paw up to his own mousebrass hanging from a thread around his neck.

It was a small circle of brass that fitted in the palm of his paw. Inside the golden, shining hoop three mouse tails met in the middle. It was a sign of life and an emblem of his family. Albert took new hope from tracing the pattern with his fingers – it reminded him that there were brighter places than this dark sewer and he resolved to continue searching until he found home or death.

Along the ledge he walked, his pink feet scarcely making a sound. Carefully he went – aware of the dangers, keeping close to the wall and the wet brick. Suddenly he heard a faint pit-a-pat from around the corner. Something was approaching.

Albert turned quickly and looked for a place to hide, but there was only the bare wall and no escape. His heart beating hard, he pressed himself against the bricks and tried to merge into the shadows. Albert held his breath and waited apprehensively.

From around the corner came a shadow – it sprawled over the ledge then flew into the darkness of the tunnel. Albert gasped in spite of himself when the shadow's owner finally emerged. It was a mouse.

All his fears and worries melted and he was left with such relief that he hugged the stranger.

"Gerroff!" said the mouse, struggling. Albert stood back but continued to shake the other's paw.

"Oh you've no idea how glad I am to see another mouse," Albert said.

The stranger breathed a sigh of relief.

"Me too, though you gave me an 'orrid fright pouncing on me like that. I'm Piccadilly. Wotcha." He took his paw from Albert's and pushed back his fringe. "Who're you?"

"Albert," was the reply. "How did you get here?"

Piccadilly then told him his story while Albert looked him over. He was a young mouse, a little older than Albert's children because he already had his mousebrass. He was also grey, which was unusual in the Skirtings, and he had a cheeky way of speaking. Albert put that down to Piccadilly's lack of parents: they had been killed by an underground train.

Piccadilly had been involved in one of the food hunting parties in the city when he had lost his comrades and, like Albert, strayed into the sewers.

"And here I am," he concluded. "Mind you, where that is I'm not sure."

3

Albert sighed. "Neither am I, unfortunately. We could be under Greenwich or Lewisham, or anywhere really ..." His voice trailed off and he looked thoughtful.

"Anythin' wrong Alby?"

"Yes, and less of that sauce!" Albert scratched an ear and looked seriously at the young mouse. "Apart from the fact that I shall miss my children's mousebrass presentations, as yet I've seen neither hide nor tooth of any rats down here, so it's only a matter of time before we run smack bang into them."

Piccadilly laughed. "Rats! Slime stuffers! Are you afraid of them?" He paused to hold his sides. "Why, I'll handle them for you grandpa. A few bits of well chosen chat from me will get 'em runnin'."

Albert shook his head. "Around here the rats are different. They're not the feckless bacon rind-chewers that you have in the city, Piccadilly. No, these are far worse. They will eat each other, let alone us. They have cruel yellow eyes and they are driven by a burning hatred of all other creatures."

"I'll drive 'em!" Piccadilly scoffed. "Ain't nothing different Alby, rats is rats wherever!"

Albert closed his eyes and lowered his voice. "Jupiter," he whispered. "They have him."

The young mouse opened his mouth but no cheek came out. "In the city we've heard rumours of Jupiter," he stammered at last. "The great god of the rats, lord of the rotting darkness ... is he here?"

"Somewhere" Albert replied unhappily.

"Are the myths about him true then?" continued Piccadilly. "Has he two great ugly heads, one with red eyes and the other with yellow?"

"No mouse has seen him," said Albert, "but I don't think that the rats have either – I've heard he lives in a dark hole and doesn't come out. I'll wager Morgan has seen him though."

"Who's he?"

"Oh Morgan is his chief henchrat, and slyer than a bag of lies. He does most of Jupiter's dirty work."

Piccadilly looked around him. The dark seemed to press in on him now. "So the rats are more cruel here then?"

Albert nodded. "Do you think we ought to find a way out?" he said.

They set off together, searching the tunnels and exploring deep into black places. Paw in paw, the two mice found comfort in each other's company; but both were terribly afraid. All they could hear were steady drips and every so often a *sploosh* sound in the sewer. Sometimes they had to turn back when the smells got too bad and made their whiskers itch. Then a tunnel would end abruptly and they had to retrace their steps back to the last turning point.

The sewer ledges were treacherous, the gloom hiding every kind of trap: holes, stones and slimy moss. Albert and Piccadilly went forward very carefully and very slowly.

Way above them the new moon of May climbed the night sky and only the brightest stars could be seen above the orange glare of the city lights. Albert's family were unable to sleep, worrying in their beds.

"Another dead end!" said Albert in exasperation. Piccadilly ran his paw over the wall that blocked their path and rubbed his eyes.

"Do you think we'll ever get out?" he asked quietly.

The older mouse could see even in the murky darkness that Piccadilly's eyes were wet and already he was sniffing a little. Albert took his paw and they sat down. "Of course we will! Why, I've known mice in worse pickles than this come out tail and all. Take Twit – now there's an example!"

"Who's Twit?" asked Piccadilly.

"A young friend of my children – must be your age though – got his brass you see: an ear of wheat against a sickle moon."

"He's one of the country mice then?" said Piccadilly, brightening a little.

Talk of the outside and the chance of a story cheered his spirits. Albert was quite clever and tactful.

"Yes, a fieldmouse Twit is, and the smallest fellow to wear the brass that I've ever seen. In the dead of winter he came to the Skirtings to visit his cousin."

"In winter, with the snow an' all?"

"Snow and all," said Albert. "A terrible journey he had and many unexpected happenings on the way." He paused for effect.

"Foxes, owls and stoats he met. 'Suave is Mr Fox,' Twit told us. You have to be careful of him – 'Old Brush Buttocks' he calls him."

Piccadilly laughed. "Twit's an odd name," he mused.

Albert nodded. "Comes from having no cheese upstairs, if you understand me."

"And hasn't he?"

"That's a tricky one: first sight yes, but then no." Albert sucked his teeth for a while. "If I had an opinion and the right to tell it," he said eventually, "it would be that Twit is an innocent. He's forever thinking of the good: he's not simple – no – or else he'd never have made it from his field. No, I think it's something which other animals sense and they leave him alone. In the nicest possible way Twit is . . . green, as green as a summer field, as green as . . ."

"The Green Mouse," Piccadilly said.

"Exactly! Now that's a better thing to think of. The Green Mouse in his coat of leaves and fruit."

"I think I would like to meet Twit," Piccadilly said.

"If we ever get out of here, that is."

"Oh he and Oswald are a pair indeed."

"Oswald?"

"Twit's cousin."

"Tell me about him," Piccadilly asked.

"Another time," said Albert, getting to his feet; he had suddenly become aware of their position and how vulnerable they were. The darkness seemed to close around him.

"On your feet lad. Time to go – and let's make this the last stretch, eh?" He pulled Piccadilly up. An uneasy fear was growing in him and he did not want the younger mouse to sense it.

They started off again. Piccadilly ran his paw along the bricks as they went. "I suppose it's all a bit of an adventure really," he said. "Ought to make the most of it." Then he stopped and cried out.

"Alby! I think I've found something here. Come see, there's a small opening in the brickwork."

Albert peered into the hole that Piccadilly had found. The air was still and strangely lacking in all smell. Albert twitched his whiskers and tried to catch a scent that would give them a clue to what lay beyond. There was nothing.

The hole was deeper and blacker than the darkness they were used to, but what choice did they have? At least it would be a change. They were bored with wandering around on sewer ledges; and they could always come back if this turned out to be yet another dead end.

The opening was just big enough for them to squeeze through. Once inside they found that they were able to stand quite comfortably, although the pitch dark was unnerving and they often stumbled over unseen obstacles.

Strange thoughts came to Albert as he led the way, holding tightly to Piccadilly's paw. He felt that they were crossing an abyss, descending into a deep black gulf. He was unable to make out the paw in front of his face, and in the raven darkness his imagination drew images before his eyes: visions of his wife Gwen, and Arthur and Audrey, forever beckoning yet always distant. Albert despaired and held his grief, nursing it in silence.

Following blindly, Piccadilly clung on to Albert's paw. He had never experienced a darkness like this before, not even in the tunnels of the underground in the city. This was a total dumbfounding of the senses; he could see nothing, he could smell nothing, and even sound was muffled by the suffocating night. He tried not to think of the sense of taste, as he had not eaten for a very long time. The only thing left to him was touch and he was kept painfully aware of this every time his toes banged against stones and fumbled over rough plaster. The dark seemed to have become an enemy in its own right, a being which had swallowed him. Even now he felt he could be staggering down its throat.

Albert's paw was the only real thing. The pain of the stones and the passage walls were confused – vague contacts that made him giddy.

They had not spoken for a long time and Piccadilly wondered whether Albert had been replaced by some monster that was leading him to an unknown horror. This thought grew and turned into a panic. The panic seized him fully and became icy terror. He began to struggle from the paw which now seemed to be an iron claw dragging him to his doom.

Then he was free of it and alone. All alone.

The initial relief rapidly turned into fright as he felt the unknown engulf him, isolating him from all that was real. He could not contain his anxiety much longer. The panic was almost bursting him. He closed his eyes but found there the same darkness, as if it had seeped into his mind.

"Piccadilly?" Albert's gentle voice floated out of nowhere and the fear fell away. "Where's your paw? Come on lad, I think I see a point of light ahead."

It was a dim, grey, rough shape, where the passage came to an end and they made for it gladly.

"Trust in the Green Mouse Dilly-O. I knew we'd be all right."

At the end of the passage they peered out, blinking. In front of them was a large chamber with numerous openings leading off into the darkness. Along a ledge nearby two candles burned. The mice remained in the tunnel until their eyes became accustomed to the light.

Between the candles was a figure, crouching in an attitude of subservient grovelling. It was a rat.

He was a large, ugly, piebald creature with a ring through his ear and a permanent sneer on his face. He had small, red, beady eyes that flicked from side to side all the time.

The two mice pressed themselves further back inside the passage, their hearts pounding. The rat had a stump of a tail with a smelly old rag tied around the end. He swung it behind him with an ugly unbalanced motion.

It was Morgan – the Cornish rat, Jupiter's lieutenant.

Although Albert was dreadfully afraid, he strained to see what the rat was doing. It seemed as if Morgan was humbling himself before something. Looking beyond the orange tip of the candle flame Albert could see an arched portal in the brick, and there, blazing in the shadows, were two fiery red eyes, impossibly large and equally evil. Albert put his paw to his mouth as the awful reality dawned. He and Piccadilly had marched into the heart of the rat empire. They were within whispering distance of the altar of Jupiter.

Albert hoped that no-one would catch scent of Piccadilly and him, yet he dared not move for fear of making a noise. He remembered the "peeling" procedure and shivered. Piccadilly did not need to question the identity of those burning eyes: the powerful evil force that beat out of them was enough to tell him that this was Jupiter.

Morgan lifted his head and spoke into the shadows, his voice thin and cracked.

Albert strained his ears to catch the words but it was difficult. Jupiter's voice was soft and menacing, it both soothed and repelled.

"And why has the digging been delayed?" he asked from the dark.

Morgan bowed again. "Lord!" he whimpered. "You know what the lads are like, 'What for we doin' this?' they do say, an' 'Gimme a mouse.' Fact is – they'm bored, an' right cheesed off. They want action – an' now." The rat looked up and squinted in the glare of the fiery eyes. "One quickie like – grab'n'dash – with a bit of skirmishin' in the middle." He licked his long yellow teeth.

"My people must do all I ask of them," Jupiter said flatly. "Do they not love me?"

"Oh in worshipful adoration Your Lovely Darkness, more than they love themselves."

"Nevertheless, I have asked for one simple task to be undertaken and all I hear is incessant whining. I fear they have little affection for me." The voice rose a little and a sour tinge crept into it.

"Never, Your Magnificence! Why else would they bring you their tributes: the cheddar biscuits – nearly a whole half packet last week; and that bag of rancid bacon! It fair tore their hearts to part with it but they did. All for your love, Great One! For your greater glory, oh voice in the deep."

Morgan wrung his hands together for the finishing touch and hung his head for extra emphasis.

"Love!" Jupiter spat with scorn. "They do these things from fear." The soft voice snapped, filling the large chamber. The eyes narrowed but lost none of their fire.

"I am Jupiter! I am the dark thought in their waking hours, I invade their dreams and bring horror! I am the essence of night, the terror around the corner, the echo behind! They fear me!"

Morgan threw himself on the floor. The candles flared and flames scorched the chamber roof.

Piccadilly shrank against the tunnel wall. This was their chance to escape, but fascinated by the scene before them the two mice remained frozen.

Jupiter continued. "You do well to prostrate yourself before me," he told Morgan. "Perhaps you forget my power and hope to blind me with the honeyed words that ooze from your deceitful tongue. Remember your place as my servant!" The candle flame suddenly spluttered and turned an infernal red so that Morgan appeared to be bathed in blood.

"Oh Master spare me!" he squealed and buried his snout in his grimy claws. "They conspire and grumble, and I am caught in between. What can I do?"

The candle flames dwindled in size and returned to their normal colour.

"Send two or three of the troublemakers to me. They shall serve me here in the void, on this side of the candles. Tell the other conspirators that I hear their grumblings – my mind stands beside each one of my subjects."

Morgan rose and waited for permission to leave.

Jupiter spoke again.

"Better still, bring them all before me. A demonstration of my unease should quell their

11

mutinous hearts. I will give them the goal that they desire for their work. Leave me."

The rat bowed and scurried into one of the openings that led off from the altar chamber. The two eyes retreated into the black recess and disappeared. The voice, however, could still be heard faintly as Jupiter talked to himself and went over his plans.

Piccadilly tugged Albert's elbow. "Let's go now," he hissed, "while we can." But Albert was still looking beyond the candles, trying to pierce the shadows.

"What's he up to?" he asked softly.

"I don't care and you shouldn't either," whispered Piccadilly. "It's all rat stuff – nothing to do with us – some mucky scheme or other – sewer business."

"No lad," said Albert taking a step forward. "There's some terrible evil here and it will affect us all – rats, mice and the world beyond." He looked at the young mouse yet did not see him, for his thoughts were far away. He felt an awful doom creeping up on him which he knew he would have to bear. He looked up quickly. "I must hear him. You stay here."

Piccadilly was horrified. The older mouse crept out into the altar chamber and passed the first candle until he was beneath the dark portal. His paw cupped his ear as he listened to the designs of Jupiter.

Piccadilly paced around inside the passage. Was this mouse cracked? Any minute now a whole army of rats would come pouring into the chamber. He scratched his head and looked over to Albert. Albert could obviously hear the rat-god, and what he heard was clearly not good news.

The look of disbelief on Albert's face turned to one of complete shock. Piccadilly tried to warn him but

only a strangled "squeak" came out. It was too late. Albert felt a terrible pain in his shoulders as they were gripped in sharp claws.

Morgan had him and would not let go.

"Ho, My Lord!" cried the rat. "See what I, Morgan have found – a spy!"

Piccadilly saw Albert swinging by his shoulders where Morgan still held him tightly.

"Alby!" he shouted and ran from the tunnel.

"Another spy!" Morgan snarled.

Albert wriggled in the rat's clutches as hundreds more gushed into the chamber. Above he could hear Jupiter returning. He had no hope of escape. Morgan's hot, foul breath was on his neck.

"Piccadilly! Don't even try," he shouted. "Run as fast as you can." Albert twisted and tore at the mousebrass around his neck. "For Gwennie!" he called and threw the charm to the young mouse.

"Don't dither, lad!" he called, then turned his attention to Morgan. "I bet you don't know what his nibs has got in store for you! You're all going to catch it hot!"

Piccadilly clung to the mousebrass, his heart pounding in his mouth and his feet like dead weights. The teaming force of rats rushed towards him, and Piccadilly ran.

"Don't look back, Dilly-O. Tell Gwennie I love her!"

Jupiter's voice suddenly boomed in the confusion. "Catch that mouse and bring him to me!" Cries and whoops came from the rats enjoying the chase. "Now," Jupiter turned to Morgan, "deliver your spy – I shall peel him myself."

As Piccadilly ran blindly in the dark passage, over the tumult of the pursuing enemies, he heard Albert cry out – then no more.

Sobbing as he fled, Piccadilly clenched the brass tightly to his thumping breast.

# 2

# AUDREY

Audrey ate a meagre breakfast; her appetite was small today. Idly she nibbled on a cracker, and thought about the day ahead. It was to be a busy day in the Skirtings. The preparations for the Great Spring Festival were already being made. With her head resting on one paw she sighed. Her brother, Arthur, had gulped down two helpings and hurried away to join in the making of the decorations. Audrey was not in the mood. Where was her father?

It had been a whole day and night since Albert had disappeared – no-one had seen him slip through the grating so nobody knew where to start looking.

That morning, Gwen had woken the children as usual and tried to put a brave face on things. When Albert was mentioned she would pause and explain that he was probably on a foraging jaunt and would bring them a wonderful present each. But Audrey had heard her mother weeping in the night: her heavy sobs had kept her awake and now she was tired and miserable.

"Come on Audrey," her mother said. "A big day for you, you must eat." Gwen Brown had a matronly figure that spoke of a comely beauty in her youth. Her fur was a rich chestnut and her hair a curly brown. Today, however, the usually bright hazel eyes seemed dim – her face looked worn and her shoulders seemed to droop.

"I'm not hungry, Mother," Audrey said and pushed the food away. "When will Father come back?"

Gwen sat down next to her daughter and cradled her head in her arms. "He's never been away this long," she admitted. "Perhaps you and I ought to prepare ourselves for grim news – or none at all." She stroked Audrey's hair and held her tightly.

"Today I get my brass." Audrey looked into her mother's eyes, "I'll be a grown mouse." She paused and fingered the brass that hung around Gwen's neck. It was the respectable sign of the house mouse – a picture of cheese formed in the yellow metal. "Mother, do you know what my sign will be?"

"No my love, no-one knows – not even the Mouse in the Green who gives it to you. It is your destiny. Whatever you receive, it will be right for you."

"Then I hope it isn't like yours," Audrey remarked. "I don't want to settle down and be a house mouse forever."

"Well, that's just what you are, my love," said Gwen. "Now go and help Arthur and the others decorate the hall while I clear away."

Audrey left the table and wandered into her and Arthur's room. Sitting on her bed, she took a pink ribbon from around one of the corner posts and tied it in her hair so that the top of her head looked as if it was sprouting.

She had delicate features – almost elfin. If you could imagine a fairy mouse that would be Audrey, although she would not have thanked you for remarking upon it. Her eyes were large and beautiful; her nose was long, and tapered into a small mouth fringed by long whiskers which she was careful to keep free of crumbs – unlike her brother, who always seemed so messy.

Audrey missed her father terribly: she was closer

to him than to her brother.

"Why aren't you here?" she cried violently. She felt angry at him for being away. It was a new feeling and she was ashamed of it. But where was he? She had looked forward to this, her big day, for so long – but now, without her father, it meant nothing.

*     *     *

All the mice were outside the Skirtings, decorating busily. From the garden they had brought in bunches of hawthorn blossom and leafy branches – "White for the Lady and green for the land spirits," they cried as they weaved them into garlands. In one corner were the chambers of Summer and Winter. Each year these were cleaned and dusted and decorated for the mousebrass ceremony. Today those with brasses were working in them, but no youngsters were allowed in.

A pair of old maids were sewing brightly coloured favours onto the leafy images of the Oaken Boy and the Hawthorn Girl. Three stout, sweating husbands had heaved the maypole into the centre of the hall, and already ribbons had been attached to the top of it for the dancing.

Into the chambers strode Master Oldnose carrying a strange straw framework – he was quickly followed by Twit, greatly excited and struggling with a large bundle of leaves and blossom.

Arthur was having a grand time. He was in the middle of it all hanging up boughs of flowering hawthorn. The scent of the blossom had always excited him, for its sweetness signalled the end of the bleak months and heralded the beginning of summer.

Oswald Chitter was trying to help him but mostly he was just getting in the way.

"Could you pass me that pin please Oswald? Ooch!" Arthur sucked a sore finger and the row of branches which he had just put up fell down.

"Oh dear, I'm sorry."

"Never mind, Oswald," Arthur sighed.

Oswald was an albino runt – which meant that there was no colour in him at all, except for his eyes which were pink. It also meant that he was so weak that he often found it difficult to join in some of the rougher games. He was, however, very tall – perhaps too tall for a mouse. He was painfully conscious of this and was apt to stoop – much to his mother's annoyance.

"What sort of brass do you think you'll get, Arthur?" he asked.

"I don't know, probably nothing too exciting."

"You never know what the Green Mouse has in store," Oswald said eagerly. "I can't wait for my turn and it's still a whole year away."

"I don't know about the Green Mouse," Arthur replied, "but I saw old Oldnose go in there with a bag of clinky things before."

"Ah, but that's just him," the other protested. "He's only standing in for the Green Mouse."

"He does make the brasses though."

"Does not!"

"Oh yes he does! I've seen him in his workroom hammering and polishing them."

"Maybe, but he doesn't know who gets what! It's just lucky dip and it always works; they always match the right person – so there must be something in it."

Arthur finished pinning up the hawthorn. "Come on," he said. "Let's try and find Twit."

Oswald shook his head. "Cousin Twit went in with Master Oldnose – but here's your mother and Audrey."

"Uh-oh," warned Arthur, "I spy *your* mother advancing."

Mrs Chitter had seen Gwen Brown arrive and made a beeline for her.

"My dear," she breathed, "how you must be grieving."

Audrey frowned. She did not like Mrs Chitter at the best of times.

"Grieving for what?" she asked stubbornly.

Oswald's mother blundered on. "Why your darling father of course – absent now for so long." She held out her paw to console Gwen Brown.

Audrey looked at her mother. Her eyes were moist again. What was this silly mouse trying to do?

"I'm sorry Mrs Chitter, but Father has not been away for that long really, so there is no need for anyone to mourn – I'm certainly not going to," said Audrey fiercely.

"As you say dear, you know your own heart I'm sure." Mrs Chitter twitched her whiskers, embarrassed for the moment, then Arthur and Oswald joined them. "Ah boys, I was just saying."

"Oh Mother," Oswald interrupted, "have you told Mrs Brown what you heard last night?"

Mrs Chitter brightened – a new field of tittle-tattle had been opened for her. "Why no! Gwen, you can't have heard can you? That travelling person is back – you know that awful rat woman with the shawl who came last year – the one with the foreign name."

Arthur pulled Audrey away. "Good," he said. "She'll gabble on about Madame Akkikuyu for ages – it might take Mother's mind off things."

"She's an insensitive, stupid nibbler!" fumed Audrey. "Just listen to her twittering. How Mother stands it I can't fathom. If it was me I'd shove her down a hole and jump on her silvery head. It's all right – she can't hear me. Just wait till Father gets back!"

Arthur looked at his sister. "Audrey, he's been

gone too long. I love him too but he isn't here is he? Today of all days, he would be here. You know he wouldn't miss this for the world."

"He'll be here," she said, "I know he will."

Then everything was ready; the garlands were all in place, the maypole erected and the chambers of Summer and Winter were pronounced complete. Twit had organised a small trio of musicians with himself on the reed pipe, Algy Coltfoot on the whisker fiddle and Tom Cockle playing bark drum. Together they struck up a merry tune and from out of one of the chambers came Master Oldnose. Normally he was tutor to the young ones but today he was the Mouse in the Green. He was inside a straw framework which he had covered in leaves and blossom, and here and there little bells had been hung, which tinkled as he danced. As the Green Mouse he masqueraded amongst the gathered mice and chased the young ones. Everyone clapped and sang. The celebrations had begun.

Gwen Brown was pulled into a corner by Oswald's mother. "Well, she is gifted you know," she continued. "She has a crystal in which she can see things, and she sells love philtres and all sorts of potions and medicines. Normally I would be the last mouse to go within smelling distance of a rat but she isn't one of the sewer kind you know, she's a foreigner and they're different, aren't they?

"Anyway," the gossip continued, "maybe you should consider going to see Madame Akkikuyu yourself Gwen. Well just think, she could tell you where your Albert has got to."

"Oh I don't know," said Gwen. "I've never had dealings with the ratfolk and I have no desire to start now, thank you."

"Well it's a shame because she isn't the sewer type, as I've said," persisted Mrs Chitter.

"No really, if I wanted to know the future I think I would rather speak to the bats."

"Oh pooh, and come away with half a dozen stupid riddles that neither you nor anyone else can make sense of. Not me, thank you!"

\*       \*       \*

Audrey stood on the edge of the mouse gathering. She glanced at her friends enjoying themselves but did not feel like joining in. Arthur was dodging Oswald's clumsy steps. The musicians played faster and faster. Even Mrs Chitter tapped her feet. Mouse tails were swaying everywhere like pink corn. Twit looked up from his piping and caught Audrey's faraway look. When the jig ended he passed his pipe to Algy Coltfoot, much to everyone's dismay.

"Give us another!" cried one.

"Yes, 'Eglan and his Lady Love'," called another.

"No, 'The Suitor's Dance'."

" 'Old Mog's Drowning'."

All these requests Twit fended off politely, saying that he needed to wet his whiskers and that Algy could play well enough. There were still some grumbles, though these ended abruptly when Master Coltfoot began "The Riddling Bats".

"Good day!" Twit's voice broke into Audrey's thoughts.

"Will you join in the dance?"

"Pardon? Oh sorry, I was thinking of something else . . . What did you say?"

"Will you be joinin' the dance?"

Audrey declined. "Later perhaps."

"Well, there's the games yet to come and then the givin' of the brasses."

Twit seemed taken by a sudden idea and a quick grin flitted across his face. Making a brief "excuse me" he ran into the middle of the dancing mice.

In spite of herself Audrey could not help smiling at

Twit's little russet gold figure nipping in and out of the swaying dancers. In a moment he was standing before her again and in his paw there were two small silver bells.

"From Master Oldnose's Green Mouse finery," he explained. "I thought maybe you might like 'em." Twit blinked shyly as he gave the bells to Audrey.

"Oh thank you Twit!" she exclaimed. "Why they are lovely! Listen: the sort of sound stars should make."

Audrey would have hugged Twit but his ears had turned scarlet. He nodded quickly and ran back to Algy and Tom.

Audrey reproved herself. Her father was missing and that was all as far as she was concerned. Somewhere he was safe and trying to get back to them. She must not mourn too soon or she would be as bad as Mrs Chitter. Audrey decided to enjoy the day.

Twit took over the piping.

"Oh look," Mrs Chitter nudged Gwen Brown. "Audrey has joined in at last."

When the dancing was over the older mice retired breathlessly. "The maypole!" shouted the younger ones and Audrey's voice was amongst them.

With a ribbon in their paws the mice children danced around the pole weaving in and out, plaiting them as they went, until it was covered in a sleeve of interlaced fabric. Laughter came in gales and the older ones were roused to call for the next game.

With much giggling the two old maids brought out the leafy images. These were life-size; a boy mouse made of oak leaves and a girl from hawthorn. Favours had been sewn on lightly so that they could be ripped off easily. Then all the children were blindfolded, and at a given signal they joined in a mad scramble and fought for a scrap of the material.

Arthur wrestled with unseen bodies in his path, unable to find a piece. Oswald, however, found one first of all – he always knew where to find things – it was like a sixth sense to compensate for the rest of his freakishness. Presently, Audrey won hers after a brief struggle with her own brother, although neither knew the other. When all the skirmishes were over and the favours had gone Arthur removed his blindfold and stared blankly at the leaf images – he was the only one not to have found anything.

"Shame!" laughed Audrey.

Everyone wondered what would happen next. Their excitement was simmering and the murmuring chatter constant. Master Oldnose signalled to the musicians and they began a solemn tune.

"Come to the Green Mouse ye who are ready and receive his bounty and your destiny," he called to everyone with great ceremony. "But . . ., er . . ., one at a time, please," he added.

So Master Oldnose disappeared into one of the rooms, whilst several mice circled the area quickly and manned the curious levers and strings that surrounded the chambers.

Audrey sat next to her mother and waited for her turn to enter. Gwen squeezed her paw. "Are you nervous, love?"

"No Mother."

"Good. This is a great day for you and Arthur. I am so proud of you both."

\*　　　\*　　　\*

Arthur stepped into the first room, grinning nervously. Inside, it had been decorated to represent the bleak winter months and the hardship that they brought. Grim, grotesque masks hung from the ceiling. Mournful paper ghosts flapped noisily from dark corners. Streamers, invisible in the gloom, dangled down and touched him, and skeletons reared up and moaned, rattling chains. Arthur loved it. He knew that outside the mice were pulling strings, wailing down tubes and operating sticks. But when something flapped unseen past his face he still jumped back and gasped. Then he laughed and plodded through the gnashing cardboard cat's mouth and entered the second room.

This was the chamber of Spring and Summer. Smiling faces beamed benignly from the floor, fresh blossom garlanded the walls and heady scent filled the air. On one side there was a large golden image of the sun that blazed brilliantly. Above his head, corn dollys hung amidst various samples of cheese and grain. At these Arthur gazed, wondering if he could reach any of them. But a stern voice called to him.

"Master Arthur Brown. Why have ye come?"

Arthur collected himself quickly and replied correctly. "To receive that which is now mine by right and to call down upon me my destiny."

"Be it great or small, tall and dangerous, meek and futile?"

"Let it be as the Green Mouse wills it."

"Then roll away the sun," demanded the voice.

Arthur stepped up to the golden picture of the sun and rolled it to one side. Beyond stood Master Oldnose, resplendant in the Green Mouse costume and surrounded by small candles.

He looked out from the leafy cage. "Take it Arthur," he said, holding out a black bag.

Arthur closed his eyes and picked out the first brass he touched – as was the custom. When he opened his eyes he gasped in surprise.

"Why, it's like my father's," he said, pleased.

"The sign of life and your own family," nodded Master Oldnose.

"Good one that – reliable."

"Three tails together," Arthur agreed. "Thank you."

"Well go on, tell your sister she's next and don't touch any of that cheese on your way out."

*     *     *

Audrey admired her brother's mousebrass when he showed it to her and once again wondered what hers would be. Eagerly she entered the first room.

As her eyes grew accustomed to the dismal light, she could see the masks painted with evil faces all around her. A faint wind seemed to be stirring them and as she looked their eyes turned to her.

There. She heard a laugh. Audrey knew that there were mice outside having fun working the strings and rods, but that laugh was unlike any voice that she had ever known. It was thin and sneering.

For some time she stood by the entrance, unwilling to go any further. Gradually the noise of her friends died down – but not into silence. Rather, it was as if she had drifted far from them and although they were still rowdy, the distance between them was too great for them to be heard clearly.

Audrey tried to get a grip on herself. "This is ridiculous," she told herself. "Something is very wrong in here."

A strange, cold blue light rose around her. What was happening? The masks seemed to hang lower now, the faces almost animated. Yes, they were moving in horrid scowls and greedy twists, the various mouths writhing. Audrey was surrounded by them; they pressed in closely blinking their pale, narrow eyes and licking pointed fangs. She could feel the breath from them beating upon her face.

"Stop it!" she wailed and waved her arms madly.

Something touched her.

The streamers that Arthur had felt were twig-like hands to Audrey. They clawed at her hair, raking her

26

head with sharp nails.

Voices called her name, telling her to go back; the masks gathered in front mouthing threats and barring the way.

Audrey knew that this was more than just her imagination. Little figures darted in and out of the shadows; starved creatures which pinched her painfully when they ran past. A cold wind was blowing incessantly now – winter was howling in. It battered and gripped her with a malevolent chill until she shivered and trembled.

"Go back," the voices in the gale called.

"Return!" the mouths hissed.

Audrey would not listen. She had seen countless eyes watching her from the darkness – eyes that were hungry.

This was the heart of winter – the lean time when stomachs are empty and wolves go ravening. Audrey shivered as the wings of midwinter death unfolded around her. The demons of the cold were there with her in the darkness. She could feel their bite.

She was their prey.

Audrey ran.

Ahead was the entrance to the chamber of Summer, suddenly revealed in the bitter gloom. She flung herself through the doorway.

Sobbing, Audrey rubbed the bruises on her arms and legs. Then she became aware of warmth – the cold had gone and new life seemed to wake in her.

Audrey looked up. Before her was the painted image of the sun. Its surface dazzled her and walls of heat came from it. All around Audrey sensed growth. Green things were sprouting; she felt the joy of unfurling leaves stretching themselves and revelling in their newness. Buds swelled up and burst, exploding into rainbows of blossom – cherry, orange, apple. Their sweet scent filled the air.

Audrey was astonished. Everywhere glowed green like the sun through the leaves. Blossoms fell in a snowstorm of multi-colours and fruit took its place, expanding and growing quickly. Apples puffed up and shone red and green, pears filled out sensually and hung heavy and ponderous on the branches. Acorns and hazel nuts browned in the sunshine before dropping to the floor. Audrey could see whole fields of grain rippling like strange yellow seas. Was she dreaming? How could this be happening?

The green light was all around now, and her thoughts turned to flowers, their lives dependent on the sun, all faces turned to it. Under Audrey's feet she felt them growing; daisies, marigolds, dandelions – all sun symbols bowing their beautiful heads to the greater one.

And when Audrey felt drunk with it all a voice commanded.

"Mistress Audrey Brown. Why have ye come?"

"To receive that which is now mine by right and to call down upon me my destiny," she replied.

"Be it great or small, tall and dangerous, meek and futile?"

"Let it be as the Green Mouse wills it."

"Then roll away the sun!"

Audrey touched the blazing image – it was not hot but seemed to be made of the purest gold that had been burnished like a mirror. Gently she pushed and the sun rolled to one side.

There stood Master Oldnose, his face a picture of bewilderment. He stared beyond Audrey at the living green landscape and his mouth fell open. He tried to speak but all that came out was a strangled squeak. He looked down at Audrey, disbelief all over his stricken face. And then he changed.

Suddenly he was not there. Only the leafy costume remained – and that began to writhe and grow as life

28

gripped it. The costume sent out branches and blossomed.

Audrey stepped back as it grew. It had a light of its own, rising in the sap, glowing, feeding the leaves until they shone like lamps and the blossom as wheels of spinning fire.

Then two eyes formed above her and smokily a face manifested around them. It was old and fierce, kind and noble. Upon the brow was a crown of leaves and wheat.

It was the Green Mouse.

Audrey fell to her knees before the majestic figure, but try as she might she could not take her eyes from his. They spoke of countless centuries of life; they were a deep green, and yet within that green were many greens. The green of new life burnt brightly there but was flecked with the dull hues of graveyard mould: death is never far from life, the eyes told her.

The mass of growing greenery was his coat and it moved with him, now shimmering with the light of life. The blossoms fell in fiery rain and strange fruits took their place. At first they were small and round yet as they opened and swelled they became all manner of different shapes. All were yellow. They were mousebrasses.

Audrey gasped and the face smiled at her. Then a green hand appeared from the coat and plucked a brass from the leaves.

"Take it Audrey," said a deep, rich voice.

Half-afraid she raised her paw to take the gift but withdrew as she saw it glitter magically. The face before her smiled again, and the green fur wrinkled on the forehead. But Audrey was frightened.

"I dare not," she whispered reverently. "On my life I dare not take it."

Audrey felt an arm close comfortingly around her shoulders.

"Do not be afraid, Audrey my love."

She jumped up and looked around – that was her father's voice!

"Where are you?" she cried, taking a step back. But an invisible arm guided her gently back to the Green Mouse.

"Take it and wear it always," Albert's voice told her.

"But Father, I can't see you. Where have you been? We've missed you so much!"

"The mousebrass, Audrey."

"When can I see you?"

Albert's voice grew faint. "I promise you will see me before the end, my darling child. Now, the Green Mouse is waiting."

Audrey looked into the eyes of the Green Mouse once more and took the mousebrass.

\*     \*     \*

"That's funny," said Master Oldnose. "I don't remember putting one of those in the bag."

Audrey stared at him. The Green Mouse, the light – everything had gone and all was normal. "Sorry?" she managed at last.

"Your cat charm! Don't remember that'un."

Audrey looked at the mousebrass in her paw. It resembled a cat's face with narrow eyes and whiskers. Confused she turned around. "But my father was here with the Green Mouse."

Master Oldnose tried to calm her down. "Now, now, it's all the excitement of the day; last year Algy Coltfoot thought he saw pink rats jumping the moon. Your dad isn't here lass. You know that don't you?"

Audrey glared at him angrily. "But don't you remember anything?"

"No I don't. Now go and show your mum what you've got. Oh, and send in the next one."

So Audrey left the chambers, positive that her

30

father was alive somewhere. But how could she get to him? Who would know where to find him?

*   *   *

"Oh that is lovely darling," said her mother when she saw the mousebrass gleaming around her neck.

"Oh, yes, the Anti-Cat charm," joined in Mrs Chitter. "Haven't seen one of those for a long time. Not very useful around here though is it?"

"Mrs Chitter," Audrey began. "What were you saying about Madame Akkikuyu before?"

"Well now, if she isn't the best fortune-teller around these days – knows all sorts of things – uses cards or the crystal – whatever you prefer."

"And have you been to her?"

"Er . . . well personally, if that is what you mean, as in 'have I spoken to her?' Well – no. Although others have told me of their experience with the famous diviner of the future."

"Where do you think she will be now?" Audrey tried to sound as casual as she could.

"Ah, child you have me there. I'm afraid you missed your chance: she was in the garden last night, but by now she's probably taking a short cut to her next venue – through the sewers."

"Beyond the Grill?"

Mrs Chitter nodded wisely. "Yes, on the other side, where none here dares to venture, I'm afraid. Oh look Gwen – the children are painting the side of the grottos. You missed out there, Audrey. What is Arthur depicting? Oh my, good gracious – a rat with two heads, eight legs and three tails. I don't think I've ever seen anything so horrid – you ought to watch that boy Gwen. What's he writing under it? Can you see, Audrey?"

"Jupiter," she replied.

# 3

---

# THE
# FORTUNE-TELLER

The moon was high when Audrey slipped out of bed. Carefully she dressed, anxious not to wake Arthur. She yawned sleepily and tied the pink ribbon in her hair. In the moonlight the silver bells looked like small blue globes. Audrey picked them up gingerly and they made no noise. She slipped them onto the end of her tail and moved silently out of the Skirtings.

In the dark the hall was a different world. Tall shadows covered the walls altering them into areas of pale moonlight and black caverns; deep shade and soft moonglow. Audrey could not tell the solid objects from the illusions.

She noticed that all the decorations had been cleared. Audrey was glad of that. She remembered the hateful masks and nameless horror of the cold. Crossing the hall Audrey took deep breaths and dug her nails into her palms. The long shadows of the banister rail scored her path with deep diagonal stripes.

For a moment she paused: the entrance to the cellar reared before her. It was a great door with peeling paint – the first gateway to the Grill. Audrey looked around nervously, every instinct told her to go back. "Beware the Grill", she had always been told and "Trust no ratfolk!"

The door was ajar. Even the moonlight seemed afraid to cross the threshold. It was a deep dark beyond.

"Come on," she told herself. "That fortune-teller is the only hope I have of finding Father." At this, Audrey bit her lip and went down into the cellar. Descending the stone steps she was surprised to find that there was some light: a strange yellow haze was filtering from a hole in the ceiling from the street above.

The cellar was strewn with large wooden crates, weird objects and rolls of musty smelling paper. Around the far wall a space had been cleared. Audrey stared at it in silence. Gaping like an open mouth was the Grill.

In the gloom she took in everything. The iron leaf pattern and the rusted corner, just as she had always heard it described by her elders as they spoke in hushed tones around the winter fires. On the wall surrounding it, strange charms were scrawled – simple protections against the sewer folk painted long ago by brave and frightened mice. Then to one side of the Grill she saw a fresher piece of artwork: a picture of the dreadful two-headed Jupiter. Audrey smiled ruefully. Arthur must have been down here.

Somewhere, beyond this portal lurked this dark and evil god. His power seeped through the sewers like the water they contained.

Suddenly she looked up. Without realising she had walked right up to the Grill. She shook her head. What uncanny forces drifted through the Grill to tantalise the unwary and cloud the judgement of the wise? Once more Audrey thought of her father alone and lost. She crouched down and crawled through the rusted gap.

\*         \*         \*

Madame Akkikuyu revived herself with a draught of some coarse liquor she had brewed herself. She threw back her head and slowly swallowed. She felt it burn all the way down her throat. It had been a disappointing few days. No trade, no pickings. She hoped her next venue would prove more profitable. Still, a few more potions on display might be a good idea.

Madame Akkikuyu unloaded her pack, wondering what to boil up. Her herb pouches were nearly empty.

"Ach," she muttered, "not much here, not much. Poor little mouselets need something for their health. Potions make them strong, make them happy," she laughed. "Make them a little bit dead sometimes too."

She was a large black rat, a traveller, trading anything for anything. She had voyaged from Morocco on a cargo ship when she was a very young rat maiden and now she wandered around dealing in potions. Madame Akkikuyu loved to put on a show for her customers. A tattooed face adorned her right ear and a red shawl with white spots covered her shoulders. She took out her pot and filled it with sewer water. "Ah the powers of the elements – fire and water," she said, taking a sip from the pot and licking her teeth. One of them had been broken long ago when a love philtre had gone terribly wrong and her client's bereaved father had driven her away with stones.

She had no magic – just a rudimentary knowledge of poisons. Of course she pretended to all her customers that she had "the gifts", but it was all a fake. But how she longed and how she dreamed! Power and knowledge of evil things were what she had always craved but never possessed. She had come to accept that she was nothing but a third-rate phoney and it rankled.

Akkikuyu heaved the pot onto one of the pipes that ran along the ledge. She never knew how it worked but long ago she had discovered the secret of undying flame. With her knife she poked and struck the pipe until a vapour hissed from the puncture. Humming softly she struck two stones together and the sparks ignited a blue flame.

"Very good," she muttered. The rat waited for the water to boil as she hunted in her bags for leaves and powders. "'Twill do," she said, examining a peculiar dried object, and threw it into the pot. As she searched Akkikuyu brought dreadful things to light. Shrivelled frogs' feet, the head of a kitten drowned at birth, a lark's heart wrapped in paper and a rabbit's eye stuck through with pins. She never cared what went into her pot. She didn't drink her own potions.

She poured some yellow powder into the water and took a long bone from her untidy knotted hair. With this she gave the mixture a vigorous stir.

Thick mustard coloured smoke issued from the pot. She sat down satisfied and left the pot to simmer for a while.

She liked the sewers. The dark did not frighten her – nor did Jupiter's rats. She threw a good punch and always had her knife in her belt. She had given many a hard time in the past so they generally left her alone.

She fumbled in a bag and took out some peanuts and half a soggy biscuit. She chewed as she contemplated her next venue. "Maybe Greenwich I should try," she thought aloud. "The young bushy squirrels will be awake now. Yes, I remember they like fortunes told there. But be careful Akkikuyu. That old one, she is wily wise and snoopy smart." The rat smiled unpleasantly and thought how nice a squirrel tail would look wrapped around her shoulders. "Hmmmm, there I shall go," she decided.

Akkikuyu leaned back on the sewer wall and sighed. It was time to rest. She yawned and closed her eyes. A long march lay ahead and just for the moment she was comfortable. One more swig of liquor and she was at peace with the dark, listening to the echoes in the sewer. The water running below, the steady drips falling – a quiet cool place. Slowly Madame Akkikuyu drifted off into sleep, pleasant and deep with rich, restful, wicked dreams.

She awoke gradually, her long whiskers twitching. Somehow the air was different. Akkikuyu opened one eye and grumbled. Something was approaching. She could hear soft footsteps.

"Not rat," she calculated, "too soft, too nervous – ah, mouselet maybe! All alone too. But why? Mousey no belong here. Maybe come to visit Akkikuyu. How brave, how venturesome," the rat chuckled, "and how stupid."

Audrey saw a blue flickering glow ahead. She had not gone far but it was enough to tell her about the sewers: the treacherous pools of slime and the awful smells. She had been expecting to see hordes of rats swarming around down here – but somehow the empty loneliness was worse. The source of the blue light was around the next corner. Audrey had no idea what it might be. Was it Jupiter? In all the stories she had heard he could breathe fire. There was also a terrible smell, like something bad cooking. She stopped and wondered if she dared turn the bend to see what it was. Perhaps it wasn't too late to turn back.

"Do not fear me!" a loud thick voice called to her. Audrey jumped in surprise. "Come around, let me see you mouselet."

"Is that Madame Akkikuyu?" Audrey stammered, standing quite still.

"Ah, a girl mouseling! How daringly brave you

are, how desperate your need must be!"

Audrey peered around the corner. Madame Akkikuyu stood behind the bubbling pot. The light of the fire flickered and danced over her and through the haze and smoke she seemed to shimmer. She looked like a being from another world.

"I am Akkikuyu," she said. "You have journeyed here through peril to seek me."

"Why yes," said Audrey. "How did you know?"

"I am Akkikuyu," the rat repeated. "I know many of the secrets the future withholds from others."

"I want to find my father. I don't know where he is," Audrey ventured.

"Not so fast Miss Mouselet! Akkikuyu needs payment to pierce the shadows." The rat scrutinised Audrey keenly.

"I have nothing," the mouse replied.

Madame Akkikuyu came forward and touched the mousebrass. "Pretty dangler do nicely for Akkikuyu. Keep cats away, yes?"

Audrey stepped back. "I can't give you that," she said. "I must wear it always, I've been told to."

"Ach!" snorted the rat. "Must pay or papa stay put." She reached into a bag and pulled out the kitten's head. "Your dangler save you from this cat maybe?" She waved the horror in Audrey's face.

"Oh poor kitty head – ward off many things, dark dreams and fear of water. Is pretty yes?"

Audrey shook her head. "It's horrid, take it away."

Madame Akkikuyu laid the grisly thing aside. "No like poor Tiddles. Ha, he keeps me company. Akkikuyu lucky to have him." She paused and sucked her teeth. "What else you have? Don't want ribbon and frilly lace – no use."

Audrey's heart sank. This was her only hope and she could feel it slipping away. What could she give this rat? Madame Akkikuyu interrupted her thoughts.

"What are these dingle dangles?" She pointed at the silver bells on Audrey's tail. "Akkikuyu could find use for them."

Slowly Audrey took them from her tail and sadly handed them over.

Madame Akkikuyu greedily snatched the bells and quickly buried them in one of her bags. She turned back to Audrey.

"Now come. Akkikuyu show mouseling many things."

Audrey watched apprehensively as the rat sorted through her bags. She brought out a pack of yellowing cards and sat down. She lay the cards on the ground and fanned them out. "Sit down here mouselet." She tapped the floor next to her.

Audrey approached but sat opposite. Madame Akkikuyu stared at her through narrowed eyes. "So your father is lost. Itchy feet does he have?"

"He just disappeared," said Audrey, obstinately returning the other's stare.

The fortune-teller scanned the cards and waved her arms. "Dark things surround you my mouselet, if you continue your searches."

She eyed Audrey's lace and ribbons.

"Your momma care for you?"

"Yes she does."

"I don't think she know you here. Right now she worried 'long with your brothers and sisters."

"I have no sisters," Audrey said. She strained to see the crude drawings and mysterious symbols on the cards.

"Hmmm," the rat resumed, "the cards tell me much."

"About my father?"

"Patience mouselet, your papa long way off, needs time to find. Ahh, I see a boy for you."

"I only want my father!"

Akkikuyu coughed and picked up the cards. She had lost interest in this pestering mouse and decided it was time for some professional vagueness. She would tell her some story to get rid of her. "I get the crystal. Nothing is hidden from Akkikuyu when she crystal gazes." The rat searched in the largest bag and brought out a glass globe. "My crystal!" she said reverently.

It was her most precious possession. Audrey looked on in admiration. The swirl of colours in the middle suggested all kinds of strange powers.

Madame Akkikuyu placed the crystal on a special plinth hauled from another bag and stroked the cold smooth surface with her claws. She was pleased: the mouse was awed and a little frightened. A little showmanship to accompany the story and she would soon get rid of her.

"I look into the crystal," she said solemnly. "The clouds of the infinite are clearing. Reveal the secrets of unknown places to me, oh crystal!"

Madame Akkikuyu bent over the globe and looked into its depths. She threw a quick glance at Audrey, who was staring breathlessly into the crystal. Then she resumed her act. She blinked and was about to invent something when she gasped.

The colours in the glass were moving, dancing in rainbow flames. Flickering shapes darted around the globe until they formed strange patterns and then pictures.

There was the altar of Jupiter, the candles burning high and two fiery eyes blazing from the black portal. Before them a vast army of rats bowed down. Then Akkikuyu saw the army marching, for there was war and the globe filled with blood. The visions continued. The rats filled her view, fighting, murdering and plundering. Then, suddenly in the heart of the crystal, something shone – a bright clear light stabbing through the other, vile images. It was Audrey's mousebrass and she was following it. The rats became obscured by her, trampled under her small pink feet.

The globe fell into darkness. But Akkikuyu could see that the visions had not finished. She saw night. Tall stalks of grain swayed under a full summer moon and in the sky a night bird swooped and wheeled. Unnatural things walked under the stars and spread fear over the earth. And suddenly, there was fire. Raging, all-consuming flames scorched inside the crystal and seemed to leap out at Akkikuyu, blinding her.

The rat staggered back as if hit by an unseen blow. Her face was drawn and haggard. Audrey gasped.

"Did you see? Child did you see?" Akkikuyu asked frantically.

"No, what happened? What did you see? Was it my father?"

Akkikuyu breathed thickly for a time. Never before had she experienced true clairvoyance.

"Your father is dead," she croaked eventually.

Audrey shook her head defiantly. "It's not true!" she cried. "You're lying. You can't see the future. I have no sisters and my father isn't dead!" Audrey beat her fists against the black rat.

"Leave me. Go!" Akkikuyu snarled and threw the mouse from her. "Your pappa is no more. Believe that!"

Audrey bit her lip to stop it trembling. She did not believe the fortune-teller. She turned and ran.

Madame Akkikuyu let her go. She was confused – the memory of her visions had startled her. What was she to do? She felt sure that they were all true. Was this to herald a new time for her? She turned back to the crystal and looked at it suspiciously. She poked it tentatively as if it were a sleeping snake. It did not move. She took it in her claws once more and gazed into it. All was dark. No matter how she tried

no more visions came. Slowly the rat raised her eyes from the globe. Perhaps it had something to do with that mouse. Akkikuyu put the crystal into one of her bags and slung it over her shoulder. She set off to find Audrey.

*     *     *

Audrey had run a long way. Her heart thumping and her body racked with sobs, she had to stop. She leant against the brick wall and tried to catch her breath. Why should she believe Akkikuyu? She was certain her father was alive – she had heard his voice. Why did everyone think he was dead?

Audrey had been breathing hard. She suddenly realised the noise she was making. Down in the sewers that was a big mistake. She covered her mouth with her paw to muffle the sound but it was too late. Someone *or something* was coming.

Audrey stood stock still, too afraid to move, hardly daring to look. Whatever it was, it was getting nearer. Through her half-closed eyes she couldn't see much. Perhaps it would pass by without seeing her. Lowering her eyes she saw that below the ledge on which she stood was another. Perhaps she could jump down onto that – it didn't look too far. It seemed her only chance. Audrey dashed out of the shadows, pushed past the figure and jumped off the ledge.

Piccadilly let out a howl of fright. He had been walking with his head down, keeping a look out for slippery patches, when without warning he received a sharp dig in the stomach from something rushing by him. He crumpled up as the wind was knocked out of him. Turning quickly, he was just in time to see Audrey disappearing below the ridge. Piccadilly dragged himself to the edge and called out.

"Hey! What do you think you're doing?"

Audrey stopped. The clear high voice belonged to

no rat. Turning, she saw the young mouse leaning over the edge, looking down at her.

"That hurt, you know," Piccadilly said.

Audrey sauntered back. "Serves you right for sneaking around."

Piccadilly grinned. "Frighten you, did I?"

"Certainly not! I did think you were a rat, but I wasn't scared," she pouted.

Piccadilly sobered. He had managed to outrun the rats, but only just. They were not his favourite topic of conversation at the moment. He put out his paw to help Audrey back up.

"Thanks," she said when she stood on the top ledge once again. "What are you doing down here anyway?"

"Trying to get out," Piccadilly answered grimly. "And don't talk so loudly!"

"I haven't seen any rats since I've been down here," she said, "apart from that fake fortune-teller."

Piccadilly shook his head. "Well I have and believe me, they're terrible."

Audrey looked at this mouse. She had never seen a "grey" before. Yes, she liked him, apart from his silly fringe. "Where are you from?" she asked.

"The city. I'm Piccadilly by the way."

"Audrey Brown," she smiled.

Piccadilly's face fell. The change was so dramatic that Audrey thought he had seen something dreadful behind her. She turned but there was nothing.

"If you're Audrey Brown then I suppose this belongs to you," he said slowly and took a mousebrass from his belt.

Puzzled, Audrey took it and gasped. "Where did you get this? It's my father's."

"Albert told me to give it to Gwennie, but . . ." his voice trailed off sadly.

"Why? When did you see him?"

Piccadilly looked away. He didn't know what to say.

Audrey was shaking. "Well?"

The young mouse looked directly into her eyes. "He gave it to me just before . . . before he was captured." There was a silence, "I'm so sorry Audrey, I think your father is . . ."

"No he isn't!" Audrey wouldn't let him finish. She didn't want to hear that word again. "The rats took him and you ran away, didn't you? You turned tail when he needed your help."

"That isn't true – it's not how it happened at all. He told me to go. There was no hope of saving him."

Audrey glared at him. "I hate you! You're a coward. You left my father with the rats. Well, he's not dead. I heard him yesterday afternoon."

"Yesterday?" Piccadilly tried to reckon the hours. "But that isn't possible, Audrey. I was with him all yesterday."

"Look!" Audrey snapped, "I don't know why you're saying these things but we're going to get back to the Skirtings and we'll see what my mother thinks of your lies." She set off along the ledge.

Piccadilly ran after her. "Why won't you listen? Albert was taken because he overheard Jupiter's plans – I only just got away."

"I don't believe you."

"It's true," protested Piccadilly. "He told me to trust in the Green Mouse and . . ." He wiped his eyes as the memory brought back the fear and grief. "How could he have let that happen to Albert? I hate the Green Mouse!" he cried. "He doesn't exist."

On the ledge below, Madame Akkikuyu listened with interest – especially to the part about Jupiter. She was sure the lord of the sewers would be grateful to know the whereabouts of this mouse. Madame Akkikuyu smiled widely and licked her long yellow teeth.

# 4

# THREE IN THE DARK

Deep in the sewers Madame Akkikuyu crept along a ledge towards the altar of Jupiter. Below her the dark swirling water was disturbed by the leaking of an ill-fitting sluice gate set into the wall and operated by heavy chains. The fortune-teller stepped around one of the candles and looked up into the deep dark portal. She was about to call to the god when Morgan sprang out behind her.

"What do you want here, hag?" he hissed.

Akkikuyu sniffed at him. "I come to speak with the great one, not you, Stumpo."

Morgan grabbed at her. "No one talks to 'im 'cept me. Now go on, you old baggage."

"Oh you spotted stump," she laughed. "How long you remain chief lacky? I wonder." The fortune-teller narrowed her eyes. "I have news for the great one, news of your blunderings. Dare you stop me?"

Morgan snorted with contempt. "Where do you get your news, maggot-face?"

Akkikuyu lowered her voice and spoke with reverence. "It has been revealed to me in the crystal. Much have I seen."

At this Morgan scoffed. "Don't come the phoney here, ducks. It won't wash. I knows what you were 'afore you got too old an' ugly. Now 'op it!"

A great rumbling interrupted them.

"Now you've torn it, you old witch," whispered Morgan fiercely. "He's coming!"

From the portal above, the rumour of Jupiter's approach sounded loudly in their ears and two fiery points blazed out of the shadow.

The piebald rat fell on his face. "Oh Great Glory," he stammered.

"Why have you disturbed my rest?" said Jupiter.

Morgan trembled. "No, not I, Dark Majesty. 'Tis this witch lump 'ere. She come a-pokin' an'-a-nosin'. Shall I have 'er 'ed separated from 'er shoulders – nice an' gradual-like?"

Throughout all this Madame Akkikuyu stood proud and erect. Now she spoke.

"Oh Lord of All," she began and bowed with more grace than any would have given her credit for. "This day I have seen in my crystal things which I cannot pretend to understand."

"Shut it trollop!" squawked Morgan.

The flaming eyes burned brighter.

"Leave us, Morgan," Jupiter said.

"But My Lord! Oh Prince of the Dying!" exclaimed the rat. "She is nowt but a fake, why she used to . . ."

The voice from the dark growled at him and Morgan left the altar quickly, swinging his stumpy tail after him.

"And now, Akkikuyu," Jupiter continued in a sweet but menacing tone, "tell me all."

Madame Akkikuyu swallowed hard and told everything that she had seen in the crystal – the empire of rats with Jupiter at their head dominating the world; the young mouse-girl with the shining ornament; and then the overheard conversation with Piccadilly.

To all this the darkness in the portal listened, savouring every word. Finally Jupiter spoke.

"Akkikuyu, I believe all you saw will come to pass,

but these mice must be removed from the tale. Can I trust you with the task?"

"Yes, I no fluff it like master-no-tail."

"Excellent," Jupiter continued. "Yet I sense there is more you would ask of me."

She bowed once more.

"You are wise, Great One. As I, Akkikuyu have said, so shall I do. I pledge my loyalty."

"And yet?"

She took from her bag the crystal.

"This do I offer unto you for your service, My Lord – only today was I allowed to use it properly. How much more would I like never to need it again."

Jupiter laughed, a horrible high jarring sound. He saw what she was driving at.

"So that's it. Morgan merely wants power but you desire much more. You seek some of my magic! Even now I feel the lust for it in your blood. Ha! I fancy you would make a more efficient lieutenant than he when the time comes. Yes, it amuses me. I accept your crystal, but only when you deliver unto me the girl Audrey *and* Piccadilly shall I invest you with some of the black powers.

Akkikuyu stood back and bowed.

"As you have willed so shall it be," she said and was granted permission to leave.

On her way out she met Morgan. He snatched at her by her bag straps.

"Don't mess with me," he warned her. "He may have a new toy in you for the present but as soon as he's bored, you're for it – I swear."

Akkikuyu looked at him coldly.

"Your time is over, Stumpo. You not flavour of month any more. I shall not fail him."

Anxious, Morgan shook her.

"He needs me to get the lads to do his diggin'. He needs me."

Akkikuyu brushed him away from her.

"Soon I take your place," she goaded. "You best make plan to flee."

She turned her back on him and continued on her way. Morgan watched her leave, the remains of his tail beating angrily on the ground.

"Oh I got plans, true enough," he muttered. "Just don't get in my way, witch!" and he spat venomously.

*       *       *

Arthur turned over. The early morning rays of the sun were slanting in across his bed. He mumbled and tried to regain his sleep. For a while he lay there breathing softly, waiting to slip back into his dreams. It was no use: he was wide awake. Arthur opened one eye.

It was a bright morning outside, one of those rare, beautiful Mays was just beginning. He opened the other eye. Arthur stretched and scratched, then stretched some more. He looked over to Audrey's empty bed. She was up early, he mused. He got out of bed and stood in the sunlight. The disturbed dust floated in and out of the rays giving them a solid appearance. The warmth on his face made a refreshing start to the day.

Arthur liked being up and about early; it was just the waking up he found difficult. It was unusual for his sister to be up before him though. Audrey liked to stay in bed and "think about things" as she put it. He had no idea what these "things" were. She was dreamy, everyone knew that. Arthur wondered where she was. Leaving their room he went in search of breakfast.

"Hello Mother."

Gwen smiled at him.

"Good morning. Any sign of Audrey getting up?"

"But she already is. I mean when I woke up she

wasn't in the bedroom," Arthur said.

His mother stopped preparing breakfast. "Well where can she be? She hasn't had a thing to eat."

Arthur shrugged. "You know what she's like, Mum. What's for breakfast?"

"Arthur please, before you eat anything, go and find her."

"Oh Mum," he began, then he saw how upset she was. "All right – just wait till I do find her. I'm a growing mouse, I need breakfast, even if she doesn't."

Arthur made his way out of the Skirtings.

Oswald and Twit were in the hall when he came out.

"Morning Arthur," greeted Oswald. "Isn't it a glorious day? Cousin Twit thinks he might venture outside today and I might go with him."

"Have you seen Audrey this morning?" Arthur asked them. They shook their heads.

"If that isn't just like her, the silly ass, wandering off without a word to anyone."

"Maybe she'm gone outside herself," suggested Twit. "Perhaps we should look for her there." Arthur agreed.

The three friends crossed the hall and went into the kitchen of the old house.

The floor was covered in smooth linoleum but it was not so polished as to make them slip. Where the floorboards joined the foot of one wall there was a gap and through this the mice would sometimes venture into the garden. In the winter the passage had to be plugged to prevent a terrible draught whistling throughout the Skirtings. It had only been unblocked the day before for the boughs of hawthorn to be brought in and the paper with which it had been stuffed was scattered untidily about the entrance.

"Have you ever been outside before?" Arthur asked Oswald.

The other shook his head.

"You know I haven't."

Twit looked up at his cousin. "You don't have to come if you ain't willin'" he said generously.

But Oswald dismissed all thoughts of staying behind.

Arthur had only been out once himself and that was with his father in the autumn when there were no leaves for enemies to hide behind. "Of course," he said wavering on the edge of the passage, "we don't really know that Audrey came this way."

Arthur wasn't really worried about his sister. He thought she could be upstairs somewhere and they would find her later. For the moment he was enjoying the thrill of adventure without a serious thought to any real danger. The three mice knew that the garden was safe enough if they were careful. Arthur didn't really expect Audrey to be out there, but hunting for her was a good excuse to explore with his friends.

So through the passage they went, happily scaring each other in the dark and then they were outside. Instinctively they dashed for cover and ran into the tall grass.

Strictly speaking it was more of a yard than a garden, with a concrete area in the centre. But with long neglect nature had taken over. The brambles had thickened, the nettles had grown tall and the hawthorn had spread freely. Now there were cracks in the concrete and green was poking through. The garden was a wild place.

Oswald blinked his pink eyes in the bright light. They were weak and pained him.

Nevertheless it was very exciting to feel the breeze through his whiskers and see the abundant new growth of spring all around him. The scent of the hawthorn blossom was so beautiful that he held his breath for some time.

Twit was in his element. He had been cooped up in the Skirtings for most of the winter and it was not natural for him. To be out under the sky was a great tonic, and now he seemed to come really alive. He found a stalk of cow parsley and in no time had shinned to the top. There, amongst the starry white spray of flowers, he stayed motionless, his thoughts returning to his field. Once more he was surrounded by golden stalks of corn, nodding and swaying their heads like pale flames. Twit touched his mousebrass, an ear of wheat against the sickle moon. An ache was born in him. How he yearned for his home, his life in the country! He broke out of his reverie and looked down at his friends. Silently and sorrowfully he acknowledged the call of the country. He knew that soon he would have to leave and return home. Slowly he began to climb down. The sun picked out the gold in his fur and it shone as he descended.

"That's a good trick," Arthur called up to him. "Do you think you could teach me?" Twit laughed as he thought of Arthur's stout frame clambering up a grain stalk.

And so the happy mood had returned to him. Twit was a simple sunny-natured mouse. He did not let things trouble him for long.

The three mice quite forgot that they were supposed to be looking for Audrey. Twit showed them the curly scrolling of worm casts, and the creatures that lived under damp stones. Oswald squealed as a large shiny black beetle ran over his tail.

After a while they lay exhausted on the ground. Oswald was panting heavily and shielded his eyes from the sun with the scarf his mother had made him wear that morning.

Oswald really was the cuckoo in the Chitter's nest. It was as well that Mrs Chitter was such a "good body" or there might have been unpleasant speculation on his origins. He was so tall and, well, rattish. But no-one was ever cruel enough to say so – it would have hurt him deeply. When he had regained enough breath he asked, "Is this what it's like in your field, Twit?"

"Not much. The field she'm bigger, the corn do be higher," said the fieldmouse.

"And the sun?"

"Oh she'm the same," and they laughed.

They could have stayed out there much longer but a rumble came from Arthur's stomach and that settled it. Back they went.

Once they were in the kitchen Oswald was able to open his eyes properly.

"It must be dinner time now," Arthur said crossly. "I can feel my empty stomach flapping around. Wait till I see Audrey. I bet she's had hers already."

But Audrey was not at home and Mrs Brown was very worried now. She embraced Arthur when he came in, fearing that he too had disappeared.

"Suddenly my family is vanishing," she said unhappily. "First Albert and now Audrey. I don't know what to do."

Arthur calmed his mother down and started to think about Audrey seriously for the first time. He knew that although she was dreamy she wouldn't miss two meals. Where could she have got to?

Gwen Brown busied herself by preparing dinner. Twit and Oswald stood shyly to one side until she spotted them.

"Oh I'm sorry boys," she apologised. "Would you like to stay?"

The two mice politely refused, saying that Mrs

Chitter would have some dinner ready for them and that they could ask about Audrey on the way. So they departed and Arthur told them he would see them later.

"We haven't tried upstairs yet Mother," he reassured her. "She'll be mooching around up there somewhere."

He ate his breakfast and then started on his dinner.

\*     \*     \*

When Arthur met Twit and Oswald later they had already asked all the families around the Skirtings with no luck. So they began upstairs. For some reason the mice on the landing always acted superior to those below. "Sniffy" Arthur called it and if truth be known Mrs Chitter had always wanted to live there. Yet despite this they were all very sorry to hear of Audrey's disappearance and gave all the help they could in the search.

"You know," Arthur said after a time, "there is one place we haven't looked: in the cellar."

Oswald was alarmed.

"But you can't go down there, Arthur you daren't!"

Twit was interested. He had heard all the stories of the Grill from the elders and recalled how they would shiver in their skins when they told warning stories of it. Even his mother, Mrs Chitter's sister, had taken tales of the sewers out to the country with her and made up lullabies to sing to him when he was a babe. The fieldmouse's eyes were sparkling now.

"Oh yes let's go. It'll be good."

But Oswald was worried.

"Nobody, but nobody, goes down there! Arthur don't!"

"It's all right. It's not that bad, I've been before," said Arthur not a little boastfully. "Besides, we really have looked everywhere else for her."

His mind was made up and Twit was eager. Oswald trailed behind them putting forward well-reasoned arguments, but they did not listen. They gathered some stout sticks "just in case" and headed for the cellar door. But Oswald's legs trembled when they reached the great object. He had never wanted to pass beyond it.

"I'm not going," he said flatly.

"Suit yourself," replied Arthur, "but don't tell anyone where we are."

"I promise. Oh you'll be in such trouble. Twit, you really shouldn't."

"Look, just make sure no-one sees us go in and keep a lookout. If we're not back soon, well, don't come after us."

"I won't, don't worry."

Arthur looked at the door.

"Well, see you Oswald. Come on Twit." He passed through into the darkness and Twit made to follow him.

Oswald was in a terrible state. He felt an awful coward just standing there, but he was desperately afraid of the cellar and the Grill. In frustration he looked about him. Would he see his friends again? He cursed his own failings and was about to wish them well when he heard footsteps, and with them the affected cough of Master Oldnose. All his fear, all his nerves were suddenly switched off by the need to be out of sight. To be caught here was the worst thing possible.

So Oswald pushed Twit in front of him and dashed through the door. He stumbled, tripped and flew through the air, knocking his cousin over. Together they tumbled down the steps, bowling Arthur over in the process.

Three bruised mice lay in a tangled lump at the bottom of the cellar steps. The first to move was Arthur.

"You thumping great nit!" he fumed at Oswald and staggered to his feet, shaking the dust off his shoulders.

Oswald groaned.

"I'm sorry, but Oldnose was coming. Oh Twit, are you all right? What's the matter?"

"He's laughing," said Arthur.

Twit took control of himself.

"I'm all right. I took no hurt, I landed on Arthur's belly."

"Ha, ha," said Arthur dryly.

Oswald stood and looked about him. The musty smell of the damp paper rolls made his nose wrinkle. The cellar was cluttered with tall wooden rods and large crates. They wondered what some of the objects were for. Oswald took a step forward and gasped.

"Arthur! Help something's got me."

Arthur turned to look and tutted.

"It's only your scarf on a nail! Come on, be serious. AUDREY!" he called.

"Not so loud!" hushed Oswald.

Twit wriggled into small spaces and searched the inside of the paper rolls but there was no sign of Audrey.

Oswald stood before the Grill. From the deep sewers a draught stirred his fur. He swayed slightly, mesmerised by the power that flowed from the darkness. Shadows and enchantments lay behind the grating. A chill slowly crept under Oswald's skin from the base of his tail up to the top of his neck and made him all goose pimply.

Gradually the Grill gathered the other two before it.

They gazed long at the iron leaf pattern, tracing the curling and sprouting foliage around and around until they found that they were all staring at the rusted gap in the corner.

"'Tis a remarkable thing to be sure," remarked Twit. They all sensed the grandeur and menace of it.

"You realise that if Audrey isn't here or anywhere in the Skirtings . . ."

"No, Arthur, not through there," began Oswald, but his words failed him as the teasing, tantalising force of the Grill worked in him. Soon he found himself nodding in ready agreement. Without another word the three mice stepped through the Grill and were swallowed by the darkness.

\*     \*     \*

The sewers never changed, always dark, always slimy – always grim.

Oswald's spirits were very low. He knew what his mother would say if she could see him there – her cries of alarm and shrieks of dismay would ring in his ears for weeks, yet he felt that he would rather be in the Skirtings suffering them than down here in the darkness.

Twit peeped around Arthur who was in front of him. The tunnels branched out endlessly.

"I never thought it was like this," said Arthur. "So dark and damp."

They progressed in this way for some time, each clutching their sticks and cautiously looking from side to side, trying to remember the way back. Arthur led, with Twit behind him and Oswald bringing up the rear. All they heard were echoes, and the rush of the sewer water. There was no sign of Audrey.

"Shall we call for her?" suggested Arthur.

"Please don't!" Oswald replied. "Think of all the dark slimy things that will come at us out of the walls. Nasty slithery horrors."

But Twit was not to be put off. He cupped his mouth in his paws and called out "AUDREY" as loud as his little voice would go. The call echoed along the tunnel, distorting strangely as it went. Then there was silence.

"Oh Twit," Oswald wailed, "you've done it now!" And he was right.

Immediatley there was a howling and a whooping. Out of the darkness, a pack of three rats came rushing towards them.

"Run!" cried Arthur. The mice bolted along the sewer ledge, half-running, half-slipping. Oswald kept letting out little squeals of fright.

The rats were used to the sewers and they were swifter. Twit looked back. They were gaining.

He had never seen anything so dreadful in his life. The rats were large and ugly. One had a patch over one eye and clenched a sharp steel point in his claw; another gnashed his broken yellow teeth – he was doing most of the whooping, gleefully enjoying the chase; but the last, Twit noted with horror, had one of his claws missing and in its place, bound tightly to the stump, was something that made the fieldmouse squeal like his cousin – a peeler.

"Ha!" cried the rats.

"At 'em lads."

And, "I bags the fat one."

Arthur realised that they would never be able to outrun them.

"We've got to turn and fight," he called to the others.

"What? How?" squeaked Oswald.

"Use your sticks!"

So, when the mice reached a corner in the tunnel they turned and faced the enemy, brandishing their sticks as menacingly as they could. But where were their pursuers?

"Maybe they've gone," suggested Oswald.

"No, they're playing with us," said Arthur. "Watching and waiting for a chance to leap out when we're not expecting it."

There was a loud laugh and the rat with the eyepatch leapt onto a brick behind them. He waved the sharp steel over his hideous head. Arthur swung out his stick, but the other was too quick, dodging here and there whilst the mouse tried in vain to hit him. Then the rat struck out – he jabbed Arthur in the arm and then cut his ear. The mouse gritted his teeth and winced at the pain, blood trickling from the wound in his ear. He changed the stick over to the other hand and continued.

Twit was having problems of his own. Over the side of the ledge a claw had appeared followed by a great ugly rat head. The fieldmouse raised his stick and then dropped it as the rat brought his other arm over the edge, revealing the peeler. Twit shrank further back against the wall while the rat advanced.

Oswald was jumping up and down in dismay. He saw that Arthur was tiring and that his wounds were hurting. He knew that the rat with the eyepatch would soon finish him off. He froze in horror and blinked his albino eyes at the mousepeeler in front of his cousin. Then the third rat came behind him and Oswald was seized.

The mouse leapt in terror, then kicked and flailed his arms around so wildly that the rat was taken aback for a moment, and before he knew what was happening the snarling creature was left holding nothing more than a green scarf.

But Oswald had nowhere to run. The three friends were cornered. Trapped with a rat on every side and the wall at their backs, the mice knew that this was it. Arthur's stick was sent flying out of his hands and resistance was over. Oswald covered his face.

"What a catch!" said Skinner. "Let's make a 'bloody bones' of them."

"Beats digging any day," cackled One-Eyed Jake.

The third rat laughed. "A 'raw head and bloody bones' just for us – not for Him. I'm not goin' back there lads, never."

"Nor us – kill 'em and let's have done."

Skinner edged forward, licking his teeth as he decided who to slaughter first. The mice could hear the juices stirring the rats' bellies into action, squelching and gurgling horribly inside their dirty skins.

Twit closed his eyes. He had been chosen.

"How's this for a pretty coat," Skinner jeered.

The fieldmouse waited for the first blow.

Suddenly all was confusion. Skinner was knocked off the ledge and sent spinning into the water below. Something leapt onto Jake's back and bit deeply into one of his ears so that he cried out and dropped the steel point.

The three friends stood amazed as a strange grey mouse picked up the weapon and charged after the rat with the broken teeth who turned and fled. At the same time Audrey – for she it was – clung onto Jake's neck and gripped his ear with her teeth until he too ran.

She sauntered back wiping her mouth.

"Yuk," she said, "rat tastes horrid."

"Come on," urged Piccadilly, "let's go while they're still surprised."

So they ran, Oswald leading the way because he remembered it best.

There was no time for talk – no time to explain. Arthur had a score of questions to ask. What was Audrey doing down here and who was this grey mouse? He had to wait until they were all in the cellar once more before he began.

Audrey fended him off firmly.

"Look Arthur, I went to find Father. No-one else seemed bothered."

"That's not fair, Audrey," Arthur snapped back. "Have you thought of Mother in all this? She's been going spare."

Audrey glared at him.

"I had to go, I had to try. Why does everyone think the worst when someone goes off?"

"Because they care, you silly ass!"

There was a pause. Oswald coughed uncomfortably.

"Oh look Audrey," sighed Arthur shaking his head sadly, "you've got to realise once and for all that Father must be dead."

There was that word again. Audrey turned cold.

"This is Piccadilly. You'd better hear what he has to say," she said.

Piccadilly felt awkward. He said "hello" to everyone and then added, "Do you think I could see Mrs Brown please? I really don't think I could say this twice."

Arthur agreed that it could wait and that they had better dust themselves down before they left the cellar. It was while Audrey was straightening her collar that she noticed something was wrong. Her mousebrass was not around her neck. She had lost it in the sewers.

# 5

## THE RETURN

A silent, tense group climbed the cellar steps and crossed the hall, passed into the Skirtings and gathered in front of Mrs Brown. Gwen rushed forward and hugged Audrey desperately. Her daughter held on tightly. Arthur gave Twit and Oswald a quick look; they understood and slipped out silently. When Gwen had made sure that Audrey really was there she wiped her eyes and scolded her. Audrey took it quietly, sorry to have caused so much worry. Eventually she said,

"Mother, this is Piccadilly – he has something to say."

This was his cue. Piccadilly cleared his throat and began. Gwen Brown listened patiently and Audrey watched as her mother serenely accepted it all, her eyes dry and her face calm. Audrey did not understand.

When Piccadilly finished he handed over Albert's mousebrass. "And the last thing I heard him say was that he loved you," he added finally.

Arthur covered his eyes with his paws.

"Well I don't believe him," Audrey said flatly. "It's obvious he ran away when Father needed him."

Gwen clutched the mousebrass next to her heart. "Audrey," she said softly, "it's over and I want you to promise – you and Arthur – that you will never

ever go into the sewers again."

Audrey knew that her tone meant no nonsense and she made the promise.

Then she remembered her own mousebrass and crumbled inside. How was she to get it back?

Gwen Brown prepared tea. Piccadilly was famished and went at everything that was laid before him heartily. Even Audrey managed something though she pretended to pick at her food.

"And you Piccadilly," said Mrs Brown when they had all finished, "what of you now? You say you have no family and the city is a long way off. Will you stay with us? You would be more than welcome."

Before he could answer Audrey muttered something and left before she was excused. Her mother let her go.

"Best to get it out of her system, although she won't be happy till she knows he's gone and cries for him."

Arthur said his sister was potty but eyed Piccadilly cautiously. Like Audrey he too had never seen a "grey" before.

"If you'll excuse me I think I'll see how Audrey is," said Piccadilly. "She blames me for everything."

"That's her hard luck and don't you take no notice," said Arthur. But the grey mouse went to find her anyway.

*       *       *

Gwen Brown stood where she could see the outside. The moon was rising; it had been a weary day. Arthur put his good arm around her. She had bandaged his ear and bathed his wounds.

"Are you all right?" he asked gently.

She smiled and nodded.

"I knew it was coming," she said simply. "One feels certain things, Arthur, when two are very close.

I knew that first night that my Albert wasn't coming back."

Arthur gave her a slight squeeze.

"I wish Audrey would realise it," he said.

His mother agreed.

"I'm sure she will get around to it. Poor Piccadilly! Audrey can be very cruel – be nice to him, he's been through a lot."

"I will. You know I think I felt it too when Father went away."

Gwen Brown took his hand.

"Just because he isn't here anymore doesn't mean we shan't talk about him. He was a fine mouse, a loving father and a good husband. We loved each other very much. The fact that he is dead won't end that love: I will always love him and what he felt for me will never change – it will always be there for me." She breathed deeply but there was no sadness in her eyes.

"Go and find your sister, Arthur; it's time for bed. You must all be very tired. I'll make up a bed for Piccadilly here."

Arthur left her.

Gwen held Albert's mousebrass lightly in her hand. She looked out at the stars and thought of him. When they were young, she had had many admirers but it was the unassuming Albert whom she had chosen. They had laughed together and he had courted her in the garden beneath the blossoming hawthorn. She had worn the flowers in her hair and he had kissed her. Under this same moon they had sworn undying love for each other.

It was a beautiful night. If anyone had been there to witness it they would have seen a strange thing happen to Gwen Brown. As she stood undisturbed in the moonlight, erect and lovely, it seemed as if the care of years fell away and she was young again.

Gazing out beyond the stars her remote eyes chanced down to her paws.

For as they held his mousebrass she felt that familiar touch on her arm and an unseen palm closed for a tender, precious moment over hers.

"Farewell," she managed to say.

\*     \*     \*

Audrey had found Twit and Oswald in the hall. They greeted her and asked after her mother.

"Oh she's fine," she replied, "only . . ."

Twit raised his eyebrows. "Be there some other thing worryin' 'ee?"

She nodded and blurted it all out.

"It's my mousebrass. I've lost it. It must have come off in the fighting. You'll think I'm mad but strange things happened when I went into the grottos yesterday – I saw the Green Mouse himself! And when I took the brass I heard Father tell me never to part with it. Now I don't know what to do. I'm sure it's frightfully important."

Twit and Oswald were taken aback. Oswald wondered if Audrey was quite well: visions of the Green Mouse were not common in the Skirtings.

Nevertheless, a mousebrass was important.

"I don't know how we can help," he said.

"But we'd like to," added Twit.

Audrey smiled at them gratefully.

"I knew you would," she said. "But the thing is, I can't go back down there. I had to promise Mother."

Oswald gasped. "Oh surely you weren't thinking of going back into the sewers Audrey! Wasn't once enough?"

"But that's where it is," she insisted. "What am I to do?"

Little Twit blinked and shuffled his feet. He looked up at her and said timidly, "I'll go back in there for you."

"Oh would you? That's marvellous." Audrey was delighted.

Oswald knew that he could not refuse: he too would go down there. He gulped loudly.

"If Twit goes, then I ought to as well," he said at last. "Besides, I'm the only one who can find it, aren't I?"

They all knew what he meant. Oswald's albino blood made him sensitive to lost objects. He had a divining rod shaped like a spindly catapult and with it he had found many things believed lost forever. He went to fetch it.

"I'm glad Oswald is a-comin'," said Twit. "I ain't too sure of the way."

When he returned Oswald said hurriedly, "Mother's on the rampage: she wants to know where we've been and asked me where my scarf was. I'd forgotten I left it down there."

They crossed to the cellar door and were about to pass through when Piccadilly surprised them.

"Hello Audrey," he said. "I've been looking for you."

"Well I don't want to see you," she answered rudely.

Then he saw what they were doing.

"Where are you going?"

"It's her mousebrass," said Twit. "Got lost in the scufflin', it did."

Piccadilly didn't like it. He had seen far too much of the sewers to want to go near them again.

"Please Audrey!" he exclaimed. "Don't go."

"I'm not going," was the curt reply. "I made that promise to Mother. Twit and Oswald are going." She paused and added, "They're not afraid."

Oswald wasn't so sure about that but the accusation stung Piccadilly – he knew more about the tunnels than they did and realised the danger.

"But two's enough," said Twit hastily. "Only needs two of us."

Audrey stared at Piccadilly – a hard stare that seemed to say, "Go on, prove you're not a coward, go with them!"

The grey mouse battled with his fears. He remembered vividly the altar chamber and could never forget Albert's last cries. There truly had been nothing he could have done, yet he felt that he should have tried.

"All right," he said, "I'll go instead of Oswald."

"But I've got to go," said Oswald miserably. "We won't find it without dowsing for it."

"Then instead of Twit," said Piccadilly. "Now don't argue, you said yourself it was a job for two."

Reluctantly, Twit agreed and they descended the cellar steps. At the Grill they stopped for a moment. Audrey hesitated: she knew she was wrong. Twit tugged at his cousin's elbow and wished them all luck.

"May the Green Mouse watch after 'ee," he said.

"Fat lot of good he is," laughed Piccadilly. He looked at Audrey and said forcefully, "Keep your phoney Green Mouse. I don't need him," and he slipped through the grating.

"Oh my, oh my," squeaked Oswald, "he oughtn't to say such things." He looked woefully at Audrey and Twit. He had never expected to pass beyond the Grill once and here he was twice in one day.

Audrey felt wretched making them do this for her.

"I'll stay here and wait for you," she said.

"Oh my," was all Oswald could manage as he wriggled through the gap.

Twit and Audrey were left alone in the cellar. She bit her nails and felt guilty and afraid.

"They be fine," assured the fieldmouse. "Cousin Oswald, he'll find it in a trice an' there ain't no-one who'll know the way back better'n he."

Still Audrey knew she had been unforgivably selfish and wished they had not gone.

*     *     *

In the sewers Oswald held his divining rod in outstretched arms.

"Does that work?" asked a sceptic Piccadilly.

"Oh yes, every time."

They set off, Oswald leading the way, the rod giving an occasional twitch.

The two mice did not know that at that moment in the chamber of Jupiter news of their escape had reached Morgan's ears from the rat with the broken teeth. Gingerly Morgan approached the altar. Jupiter had to be told. He looked up and saw that the eyes already blazed out of the dark portal. Morgan abased himself before them.

"You have news," said the voice.

"Oh My Lord, word is those mice bandits escaped."

Morgan hid his face.

Jupiter's voice boomed out of the blackness.

"Is there nothing I can trust you with, you spotted simpleton?"

Morgan blocked his ears against the deafening roars.

"Send the best of your scurvy lads. I want those mice here!"

Morgan crawled away to give the orders.

*     *     *

Piccadilly felt a little better than he had done the last time he was in the sewers; Mrs Brown had given him a good meal and now he had a chance to show Audrey he was not a coward. It might even let him rest easier.

The tunnels were familiar to him now; the wet brick arches, the strange slimy moss which grew in

69

the dark, and the turgid water that swilled around below. He wondered if anything lived in it – what fish would swim in the muddy currents? Perhaps no fish at all, but scaly toad monsters with big pale eyes sightlessly groping in the dark, hunting for food. Piccadilly pulled himself together and rebuked himself severely – thoughts like that led to panic. Oswald was concentrating on Audrey's mousebrass, picturing it before him, recalling every detail. The image was translated through his veins, travelled down his arms and entered the wood of his divining rod. It searched for the brass, jerking in agitation whenever they took a wrong turn. Oswald was an accomplished dowser.

"Is it far do you think?" whispered Piccadilly.

"Shshsh. You'll spoil my concentration. Actually I can't tell – it's quite odd."

Suddenly Piccadilly gave a cry of discovery. "Look look," he called. "It's a scarf!"

Oswald lowered the rod. "That's a relief anyway," he said. "Mother hates it when I lose something she's made."

He picked the scarf off the floor – it was slightly damp but he wound it round his neck just the same.

"This is the place where the rats got us," he said. "Audrey's brass must be here somewhere. Have a look will you."

They searched everywhere. Piccadilly even felt in some slime for it but the mousebrass could not be found.

"Do you think it could have fallen down there in the water?" he asked.

They both looked over the edge and gazed at the black stream below.

"Oh dear we'll never find it in that," Oswald despaired.

Piccadilly wiped the mud from his paw.

"It's no use – it's totally lost," he said.

Oswald had to agree. He shook his head when he thought how unhappy Audrey would be. They were about to return to the Skirtings when the divining rod gave an almighty leap.

"Oh my!" exclaimed Oswald. "Piccadilly look, we're not done yet. The mousebrass can't be in the water, it must be down that tunnel. Come on." He dashed off, darting into a tunnel they hadn't been down before.

"Hang on Oswald," said Piccadilly. "We'll get lost if we don't stick to the same route. Oswald come back!" he called. "OSWALD!" But Oswald was too far ahead to hear. Piccadilly ran after him.

\* \* \*

Audrey waited anxiously in the cellar with Twit. They found it difficult to speak about their departed friends. Dread and guilt weighed heavily on Audrey's mind – what had she done?

Twit sat on the ground, his head cradled in his paws and his knees tucked under his chin. He knew he shouldn't have let his young cousin go down into the sewers. He tried to hum a little tune but the mood stifled it. He looked at Audrey and smiled weakly.

So preoccupied were they in their thoughts that the two mice did not sense the change of air flowing from the Grill or detect the muffled movements of body against body on the other side.

Audrey sat down and sighed. The picture of Jupiter that Arthur had painted seemed to leer at her; she had had enough of faces that grinned at her and turned her back to it. Now she was directly in front of the rusted gap, unaware of the plans being made behind the ironwork.

A voice called her name in the hall. It was Arthur looking for her.

"Can you fetch him, Twit?" she said. "I said I

would wait for them here."

Twit got to his feet and climbed over the rolls of paper till he reached the cellar steps. He was really too short to tackle them himself and his struggles to clamber up them brought the shadow of a smile even to Audrey.

In between the iron leaves of the Grill indistinct forms advanced and then beady yellow eyes blinked greedily in the dark.

When he reached the top step, Twit looked down at Audrey sitting next to the gap and then squeezed through the door.

Arthur was wondering if he ought to try the landing when Twit came to him.

"Oh hello," he said. "I'm looking for Audrey again – and that Piccadilly."

"She'm in the cellar," said Twit.

Arthur was furious.

"What's she doing there?"

Twit explained about the missing mousebrass and how Piccadilly and Oswald had gone to look for it.

"But they've been gone a while now," he ended sadly.

"We really can't have this," protested Arthur crossly. "If she lost it then it's her own fault and she's got no right to make Oswald and that 'grey' go looking for her."

He strode down the hall and barged through the cellar door.

"Just you listen to me Audrey!" he yelled, but she was not there.

# 6

# VISITORS IN THE ATTIC

There was no sign of Audrey anywhere, but Arthur and Twit guessed at once where she had gone. They knew nothing of the brief desperate struggle that had taken place moments before and how, overwhelmed and defeated, Audrey had been dragged through the Grill by sharp, snatching claws. Arthur thought the worst of his sister.

"She's gone back in," he gasped in disbelief. "She vowed to Mother she wouldn't and yet as soon as she's on her own what does she do? Ups and goes back down there!"

Unpleasant thoughts began to form in his mind. He thought how dishonest his sister was. Every little thing which irritated him about her was magnified unreasonably in his mind. He remembered any slight selfish act, recalled every small meanness. He was experiencing just one of the powers of the Grill: a wicked sorcery which turned friends into enemies and curdled innocence.

Arthur's face turned sour and his plump, cheerful head became ugly with hate.

The humble charms daubed in great faith around the Grill were not strong enough to protect him.

Arthur sneered.

"She can go to rot down there," he spat in a voice that was not his own. "I hate her and her precious ribbons and lace. Stay down there Audrey, we're better off without you!"

Twit was astonished. He had seen the change in Arthur's face and it scared him. Some blight had stricken his friend and he was at a loss what to do. For a moment the little fieldmouse stammered and dithered, hopping about in a terrible state. Finally he jumped up and, giving Arthur a sharp slap, dragged him away.

Why the enchantments had no effect on the fieldmouse is not certain. Perhaps it was his own simple nature that saved him. Twit had never had an unkind thought about anyone and never held grudges, so the dark magic had nothing to work on. The spells broke against his natural defences.

At the foot of the cellar steps he paused. Pulling a bulky housemouse when you are a tiny fieldmouse is not easy. Arthur was breathing strangely – like someone coming out of a fever he swayed and spoke thickly.

"What was that?" What did I say?" He winced, ashamed at the memory of it. "Twit, I didn't mean any of it – those things. Audrey's not bad. What was I saying?"

Twit had calmed down. For a moment there he had thought his friend was going mad.

"You sit down Arthur," he soothed. Arthur followed his advice, landing with a hard thump on the floor. "I reckon 'tis some nasty 'fluence comin' out of yon grating."

"It was awful," spluttered Arthur. "I had all these horrible pictures of Audrey in my head and they just got worse until I really wished she'd come to a sticky end down there. I'm so sorry Twit, you don't think a wish like that could come true, do you?" He looked helplessly at the fieldmouse.

"'Tweren't your fault," Twit assured him, "that

tricksy Grill been up to mischief."

Eventually Arthur felt better but was not keen to venture near the Grill again.

"I don't really think she would have broken that promise," he decided. "Audrey has got some common sense for all her dreaminess. But if she didn't go wilfully . . ." he trailed off miserably.

"Should we go down after her?" suggested Twit. "I could rouse Algy and maybe old Tom; a few others might be persuaded to help."

They considered this but knew that no other mouse from the Skirtings would dare pass through the Grill. They would rather jump into fire and have done with it.

"Then that do leave only us," said Twit glumly.

Arthur sat with his head in his hands. He had to decide what to do. Should they follow Audrey and break the promise to his mother? What would they come across down there this time – a whole army of rats perhaps? Arthur had always thought that things became easier when you came of age but it wasn't turning out like that at all. He felt very unprepared for this responsibility. If only his father was there he could ask him – but that was how this all started. Albert was not there and Arthur had to grow up fast to take his place in the Brown family. His mother had had enough worry and strain that day, he could not turn to her. Whom could he ask for advice? Arthur did not believe strongly enough in the Green Mouse to pray to him. Audrey had gone to that ratwoman Akkikuyu, Arthur remembered, but who else was there? Then he had it. The bats.

Those strange creatures in the attics. They had supernatural powers – everyone knew that. Sometimes you could ask them for advice: Master Oldnose did it once.

Arthur cheered up considerably. "Twit," he

announced, "I'm going to visit the bats. They'll know what's going on and what I should do."

Twit's eyes opened wide – he had never even seen a bat before. They were secret animals who wrapped themselves in mystery. A tingling thrill went through the fieldmouse. He longed to meet them and his whiskers quivered with excitement.

"Oh yes Arthur, I'd dearly love to go a-greetin' the bats."

Arthur turned to him. "Oh no, I'm sorry but they only allow one visitor up at a time, please understand, Twit."

Twit was disappointed, but knew there was nothing to be done about it. Arthur had to go alone.

They climbed the cellar steps.

"How do you get there, Arthur?" Twit asked.

"There's a passage under the stairs in the hall which leads to a space between two walls. There are bits of junk stickin' out all over them right to the top, easy really, just like a ladder."

"All the way to the attics?"

"That's right."

"I reckon there's a handsome view from up there. Can you see out?"

"Well I suppose there must be holes in the roof for the bats to get in and out."

Twit tried to imagine what it would be like to see all the buildings from on high. When he had arrived in the Skirtings months ago, it was the dead of winter and he was too cold to pay much attention to the scenery. At home in his field he had climbed an oak tree once and marvelled at the view then. He wondered at the possibilities here.

By this time the two mice were in the hall. Arthur crossed to the stairs.

"The opening is here somewhere," he said, lifting a corner of the carpet. "Good job Oswald's not here

– it's bound to be full of spiders down there."

Twit thought of his cousin somewhere in the sewers. "Don't be long, Arthur," he whispered.

But Arthur had already found the hole. It was obscured by webs and fluff. In disgust he cleared them away, sending spiders scampering back to the shadows. As he prepared to lower himself he took Twit's paw.

"I'll be as quick as I can – I promise, and then we'll know what to do. I'm sorry you have to stay here." He gave the small paw a last squeeze and was gone.

Twit leaned over the hole to see him but there were so many webs and dust bundles down there it made things extremely difficult. Then he made out two bright round eyes blinking up at him.

"I didn't think it was such a big drop," Arthur's voice drifted up to him. "Good job there's so much dust and stuff to land on. See you soon."

"Good luck," murmured Twit.

Poor old Twit. He felt so lonely – everyone had gone. First Oswald and Piccadilly, then Audrey and now Arthur. He wondered if he would see any of them again.

The fieldmouse sat at the brink of the hole, his light spirits thoroughly subdued.

What a world this was, he thought to himself. Little had he realised when he left his field what lay in store for him.

A cloud that had hung about the moon now sailed clear. The moonlight flooded through the cracks in the boarded-up windows. Silver beams filtered down, spreading in a tide of ghostly splendour across the hall. Once more it was a playground for the night.

The little mouse was lit by the soft, shimmering moon rays. He tipped his head to one side and the light glimmered through his ears.

Twit sighed. Far away his parents would be sleeping under the stars, and that same moon would hang brightly over his field. Twit thought of his parents and smiled. The story of their love affair had been a scandal in the past but now it was a romantic tale loved by the younger mice. Twit knew it off by heart; perhaps even now it was being told by old Todmore, the storyteller of the field.

Twit went over it in his mind to ease his sudden homesickness.

\*     \*     \*

"Elijah Scuttle was a fieldmouse," old Todmore would begin, "respectable and simple. He loved feeling the sun on his back as he sat at the top of a barley stalk keepin' a look out for enemies. Only one night when the blackberries had been too long fermentin' and he was slightly dizzy with it all, an owl came swoopin' out of the sky, all quiet-like and snatched him off the ground."

Here old Todmore would gaze dramatically at his open-mouthed audience.

"High the bird carried him, cackling to itself and poor Elijah dared not look down. Far they flew until Elijah shouted, 'Hoy owl, where you takin' me?'

"Now birds, as we all know, don't talk much and few can get sense out of them."

"Well, this owl cocked its flat head down at Elijah, dangling there in his talons and he gabbled, 'Fooood fooood – dinner for meee an' the missus – ooooh lovely mooouse grub!'.

"'Oh lawks!' said Elijah an' many another exclamation not fittin' for your ears.

"Then he had the sense to bite the dratted bird hard on the ankle.

"How it hooted! It hooted and howled so much that it plum let the fieldmouse go. Down he dropped, wondering if it had been such a good idea, that bite

– when SPLOOSH! Water swallowed him.

"Elijah struggled and splashed, feelin' only then how deep that owl had dug his talons into him. Well, as luck would have it there was a piece of wood a-floatin' in the river and he made for that . . . What's that? Yes, he landed in a gert river – anyways onto this wood he hauled himself, all shakin' and wet through.

"Terrible cold he was and faintin' too, them being awful painful wounds on his shoulders like.

"Well, next he knew it was daytime an' he was a-shiverin' an' coughin' but worse of all there weren't no country no more. On either side of the water there were buildin's an' smoke an' such – well somehow Elijah paddled his raft to the bank and stepped on land. He didn't know how long he were in that swoon but he was mighty hungry – 'Oh woe', he cried in the strange place and roamed about for near on a week steadily gettin' in a sorrier state. His wounds went all pussy an' started poisonin' his blud. One day it got so bad that Elijah just gave up and crashed down in some poor excuse for a garden.

"Well his shoulders being what they were and his fever a-racin' he were all done in – a goner he was. Then, as the Green will have it, out came two city mouse sisters – Arabel and Gladwin.

"'Look yonder,' cried Gladwin, prettier of the two, 'poor young fieldmouse,' and ran to aid him.

"This stuck-up Arabel said, 'Leave him – 'e's ded an' maggoty.'

"But her kind sister she found a flutterin' heartbeat and made snotty Arabel help her indoors with him.

"That Gladwin she were all carin' and tended to his wounds. Real rotten they were but she stayed up all night till the fever passed. In the mornin', Elijah opened his eyes and saw her fast asleep next to him – her paw in his. Right there and then he fell straight in love with her – him a fieldmouse and she a city mouse. Fever do strange things.

"Well this Gladwin she were willin' to wed Elijah but her dad wouldn't hear of it. He didn't want his daughter wed to a fieldmouse an' ranted about the disgrace an' shame she were bringin' on him. Everyone seemed against them so one night they ran off together an' eventually Elijah came back to his field here with his bride. We'd all thought he was dead months back! Greatly shocked we all were. Well upshot was they settled down 'ere, an' you know yourselves how nice Mrs Scuttle is an' she soon forgot her city ways. Happy they lived from then on and as time went by they were delivered of a son."

The moon fell on Twit's face. He looked like a small silver statue. Sadly he recalled the end of the story.

"William Scuttle he was called, although you all knows him as Twit. Yes, him with no cheese upstairs, poor young moon-kissed lackwit that he is."

Here the audience would laugh and old Todmore would caution them.

"Now don't you go lettin' this tale turn your heads. City and country don't go together, and he's the proof of it – always 'appens, mark you well young 'uns."

Twit's eyes were moist at the memory yet he still felt he should return home soon.

Then he thought of the bats again and wondered if Arthur had reached them yet. Suddenly, with a resolution foreign to him, he swung his short legs over the side of the hole and dropped down. The dust flew as he landed with a bump. Great choking clouds of it billowed out and spiders, annoyed at this second disturbance, ran to protect their eggs.

Twit scrambled to his feet. To follow Arthur without him knowing was the plan. With a bit of luck he might be able to overhear what was being said with the bats.

The passage under the floorboards was very dark but it wasn't damp or smelly like the sewers. Old abandoned cobwebs dangled down, thick with dust. They brushed over him in a horrid tickly way as he pushed ahead.

There were traces in the dust to show where Arthur had gone and Twit followed them.

For a while he tracked the footprints until a rush of cold air met him so abruptly that he stopped and wondered what it could be. He sniffed his small web-covered nose. He could smell the night air. Cautiously he groped around until he found a sheer brick wall. High above, pale moonlight shone through the occasional gap and revealed to him the giddy heights of the wall. This he would have to climb if he hoped to get to the attics. Twit began to search for the first rung of his ascent.

\* \* \*

Arthur heaved himself up one more level. He was nearing the eaves now. What a climb it had been; his arms ached madly. He let out a grateful sigh, knowing it couldn't be much further. Arthur's esteem of Master Oldnose soared; he had no idea the boring old fuddy-duddy had this sort of thing in him.

He rested for a moment and rubbed life into his muscles then stretched his arms and massaged his shoulders. There was a cool, steadying breeze wafting around him – it whispered experiences of the night, of closed buds and unseen clouds scudding across the sky. The tiles were loose on the roof and here and there a star could be seen stabbing through with frosty light. Arthur felt sure it was the last leg of his journey. He hoisted himself to his feet, taking great care to balance properly with his tail. The fall was too dangerous for any mistake to be made. The next support was above him: Arthur reached up and gripped the wooden strut firmly, then pulled himself up and swung his tail like a pendulum to counterbalance his weight.

There. He had managed it. One more stage upwards: two more clambers would do it. Already he could see the opening to the attics.

When he reached it he lay on his back and stroked the beam beneath him thankfully. He tried not to think how difficult it would be to get down again.

There was an unusual calm in the attics. An atmosphere of expectancy hung in the air. Arthur picked his way around under the rafters, hopping from beam to beam.

A sweet incense hovered thickly about him. He felt truly as if he had entered another realm. Hushed and tranquil, even the noise of the street was muted. The attics were silent and reverent, nothing disturbed their peace; nothing except for Arthur. He tried to walk as quietly as possible but it wasn't easy. He shuddered at the din he was making and looked about him for any sign of the bats.

"Hello?" he murmured. There was no answer; all was still. Maybe the bats were all out flying in the night. Should he continue?

Arthur tried again. "Hello?" Nothing.

What an odd place it was with the sloping beams and lofty ceiling. It was all new to Arthur. He marvelled at the sight. Thick solid rafters rose from the eaves and met at a great beam overhead.

Arthur felt it was like being in the belly of a huge animal and the rafters were its ribs. Not far away the outline of the chimneys could be discerned faintly.

Arthur decided to try to reach them: maybe the bats were on the other side.

Something tugged him along, something more wholesome in feel than the power of the Grill. A wave of excitement washed over him as he reached the chimney and peered round it.

This part of the attic looked like a great hall of kings. High and magnificent, the rafters soared into the darkness above. Yet there was one lying broken and askew.

Arthur stared up at it. The roof had been broken in the rafter's ruin and through the open space he could see a cluster of stars in the midnight sky.

A dark shape on the rafter stirred unexpectedly. It shifted its position then settled down again. Arthur gasped – it was a bat.

The mysterious creature was perched high on the rafter so that Arthur had to tilt his head right the way back to see him.

The bat's head was hidden in his great folded wings. Only two tall pointed ears could be seen behind them.

Arthur gave a slight polite cough.

There was a dry rustle as the bat raised his head. Above the tips of his wings it reared and Arthur noticed that the ears were set on the side of a noble, fox-like face. The light of the stars came down to rest on the bat's brow in an aura of knowledge and wisdom. Haughtily the bat gazed down from the rafter and scrutinised the mouse keenly.

Arthur stammered greetings, trying to remember the correct formal introductions you must use with bats.

"A hundred felicitations I offer thee," he said, hoping this was right. "May I present myself, Arthur Brown, a cousin in the links of creation. Mouse of the Skirtings. Most humbly do I beseech thy help."

Suddenly it occurred to him that this was in fact the correct etiquette when dealing with foxes. Arthur blushed to his ears and bowed hastily.

The bat eyed him with large black orbs, which

sparkled beneath the stars.

Arthur fidgeted in embarrassment.

"I am Eldritch," declared the bat. "You are late, Master Brown." Arthur apologised, uncomfortable at being expected. Then he said, "I am here for a purpose, oh Eldritch."

The bat stretched and yawned. He unfurled his wings, then in a mocking, mellifluous tone said mysteriously:

"I see a mouse, young and fair. Her brass is lost, and so is she; ribbons and lace adorn her."

"That's Audrey – my sister," cried Arthur. "Where is she?"

Eldritch glared at him for interrupting, and then continued: ". . . ribbons and lace adorn her, but into heathen darkness is she dragged. Oh where is she the fatherless? Whose eyes are red at her going? Who will save her from the half-blind? With brutal partners shall she dance; from bloody temples and through the ash of the dead does her fate lead her." Eldritch stared at Arthur for a moment and then whispered, "Only the spinning, shining circle can save her from the fiend below."

The bat paused and looked into the heavens. "Orfeo approaches," he said.

Arthur stood at the edge of the starlit area, wondering what the bat had been rambling on about. And who was this Orfeo? He could see no-one else in the attic and he heard nothing. Arthur was puzzled.

For a full three minutes he stood in silence. Eldritch continued gazing upward at the stars. Suddenly a shadow flitted outside, cutting off the starlight. Then, as Arthur watched half-fearfully a second bat entered through the hole and alighted silently next to the first.

"Salutations Orfeo," greeted Eldritch.

Arthur noticed how similar the two bats were in appearance.

"Hail Eldritch," the newcomer returned. "Is this the company we sought?" He stared at Arthur imperiously.

Eldritch yawned again and replied in a bored, dry tone, "It is the one but not the other."

"Then our time is wasting here – you, Master Brown," Orfeo rapped out sharply. "You would seek council of us, my brother and I? Well, listen and may you have your fill for an age and more when we are done."

Arthur clasped his paws together, fearing what they would say. Bats are only interested in themselves and unless something amuses them they do not care for the drudgery of petty lives. They can give or withold information as the fancy takes them – but all of it is true, however undesirable it is to hear. This is what Arthur braced himself for.

Eldritch began:

"Threefold the life threats. How shall he be vanquished? By water deep, fire blazing and the unknown path. Remember brown mouse, pain and horror stalk the summer fields in straw clad form. When noon is hot and corn is gold, beware the ear that whispers, Master Brown, and shun the darkness. Through fire into fire, break not the sphere and let the demon out."

Eldritch raised his skin-webbed wings and gathered them about his face until he was a crouched, cowled figure and said no more.

Then Orfeo began, intense and urgent:

"Look to the mouse with bells on her tail – she who made the doll. Through ice and blizzard will hail great doom. However sweet the bell may sound, stray not into the fog, for bitter spears shall rain. Who is the mouse without the brass? What silver shall she wear if all survive the dark months?"

Orfeo closed his eyes of jet. They had both finished with Arthur.

"Depart Master Brown," they said as one.

Arthur shook himself. What a load of twaddle, he thought. He wouldn't be able to remember any of the stupid riddles. He could not understand why they felt they had to cloak their advice in them. Arthur thanked the bats courteously and bade them farewell.

Eldritch regarded his retreating figure and called after him, "If any live through the winter, Master Brown, look to your own children – of what stuff will they be made?"

"Beware the three," added Orfeo.

Slowly Arthur walked back to the eaves, trying to piece together the ridiculous bat advice. He abandoned the attempt, and dismissed the bats as crazy. An interesting but wasted journey – they had not helped him at all.

*       *       *

If Arthur had not been so intent on these thoughts, maybe he would have noticed the small figure hiding in the shadows, watching him with bright round eyes. But Arthur did not notice and with renewed efforts began the climb down once more, muttering angrily to himself.

From the dark corner Twit emerged. He had lain hidden for a short while – afraid to interrupt the bats' discourse. Now Arthur had left, Twit was unsure what to do. He knew he should follow his friend, but Eldritch and Orfeo had greatly impressed the little fieldmouse. The dramatic gestures they made with their wings captivated him and he dearly wanted to see more of them. From his corner he watched them and then brought himself up sharply. *They* were watching *him*!

Eldritch had one eye glaring out from behind his wing curtain, but Orfeo was staring directly at him. The fieldmouse gulped.

"Come forward witch husband," demanded Orfeo.

Eldritch stirred in his wing cocoon, "Step out, friend of the trapped mouse," he said, finally raising his head.

Twit meekly shambled towards them. "I be sorry if I offended 'ee by lurkin' there," he ventured to say, "but I was desperate to lay eyes on you – ain't never seen a bat before."

The brothers looked at each other with an odd smirk on their faces.

"Into the light, childless one," they encouraged. Twit obeyed, entering the circle of starlight. He looked up at them perched high above.

"Noble mouse!" laughed Orfeo.

Eldritch tossed his head and said darkly, "When troubles stir and passions rouse whose paw will you take to save all?"

"And when your bride returns home why are you not by her side?"

Orfeo was enjoying himself.

"Beg pardon, but I ain't got no wife," Twit informed them.

"This is he, this is the one," cried Orfeo delightedly. "The simpleton, the cheeseless mouse," he gurgled with amusement.

"Hey you ain't got no right to go a-callin' me that, bats or no," the fieldmouse interjected. "You ain't got no manners for lordly folk, that's certain."

Orfeo and Eldritch laughed all the louder. "Ah, but you are precious to us."

Twit eyed them uncertainly. The bats puffed up their furry little bodies and strutted along the rafter, waving their wings pompously.

"Yes, you are the seed that will bear all our fruit."

"We need you, witch husband."

Twit put his paws on his hips and shook his head crossly. "As I said already, I got no wife and I've no mind to take a witch to meself. What fer I do a daft thing like that?"

Eldritch clapped his wings together for silence. They made a leathery dry, rasping sound. "Quite – you are not as addled as others make you Master Scuttle. Come brother, make no jests at our guest's expense. I fear we now displease."

He looked sternly at Orfeo but there was still that odd twinkle in his eyes.

Twit cleared his throat.

"Well that's all right," he said. "You don't have to go a-sayin' you're sorry. I've had folk laugh at me 'afore an' I reckon they'll not stop now."

The bats winked at each other, drew themselves up to their full height and dived off the rafter. For a moment they flew over Twit's head and the fieldmouse watched them dart to and fro. Then they flitted down to him, seeming very grave and serious. They pressed round him closely and put their open wings about him.

"Hear not the scorn of others," said Orfeo.

"Not many are as brave and true," continued Eldritch.

"When horror stalks your field you shall win through."

"Despair not in the long lonely years."

They hugged Twit tightly as if trying to console him for some hurt that was yet to come.

The fieldmouse struggled, embarrassed by their embraces. He wriggled his arms and flicked his tail about.

"Now what are you a-blatherin' about?" he asked, his small voice muffled by bat wing.

"I can scarce breathe with you so tight round me."

He disentangled himself from the two brothers and gasped for breath.

"You'll do me in at this rate," he said crossly.

"Forgive us master," they said and bowed formally, draping their languid wings on the ground in dainty apology.

"He needs air," declared Orfeo.

"Fresh air," cooed Eldritch and that strange smirk lit his furred fox-like face.

"Now come, Master Scuttle, I believe you enjoy visiting folk. Is this so?"

Twit nodded. "Truly that's how I come to be in the city – to pay a visit to my mother's kin."

Orfeo smiled broadly showing a fine row of neat white teeth, "Verily and how much of this grand city have you yet seen?"

Twit admitted that he hadn't seen anything.

Eldritch appeared shocked and dismayed, then his forehead crinkled as he glanced quickly to his brother. "You must attend to this Master Scuttle, while there is yet time," he said. "Let us rectify the situation and pay for our bad manners."

"We shall give you air," cried Orfeo gleefully.

Twit scratched his head. He wasn't sure what the bats were up to.

"Come, come," they both said.

"Where to?" he asked nervously.

Orfeo clambered onto Eldritch's shoulders and pointed to the sky. "Into the night," he called down. "Let us show you the world as it should be seen – from the air."

Twit blew a raspberry. "What me? I can't fly like you." He wondered if they were making fun of him again.

But the bats persisted.

Eldritch raised one eyebrow and said casually, "Is

it not in your blood to fly?"

"Beg pardon?"

"Did your father not fly once?"

"Why he did, as a matter of fact – with an owl."
Twit suddenly realised their meaning and a slow grin
spread across his face. "It were one night when my
old dad was . . ."

"No time for that," sniffed Orfeo. "No dull family
histories here, if you please."

Eldritch made himself ready. "This will not be as
painful a journey, Master Scuttle. Just hold up your
paws."

Twit reached up into the air.

The bats began to flap their wings and rose
elegantly upwards. They each gripped a tiny pink
paw in their feet and beat their wings harder until
the dust that lay on the beams around them was
disturbed and swirled about the fieldmouse's feet.
Up went Twit exclaiming in wild delight.

"Hold tight, Master Scuttle," shouted Orfeo.

With graceful and easy movements the bats
carried Twit higher and higher, until they were out
of the hole in the roof and into the night air.

# 7

# THE MIDSHIPMOUSE

Twit dangled beneath the two bats as they flew up into the darkness. He could not believe his eyes. They left the red chimney pots behind them and soared higher still, leaving the old empty house far below.

The night air streamed through his fur, making him wriggle with delight. It was a wonderful sensation to feel nothing under his feet and his tail hanging in empty space.

"Oh my," Twit sighed. The stars above were so beautiful. The two bats carried him through wispy clouds, which felt like fine damp mist. For a while his tail trailed in them leaving a long thin smoky wake behind.

Orfeo looked down at him. "Observe the night, Master Scuttle, you are a part of it now. We move in our element but only by permission of the Lady of the Moon. It is she who tempts us out, enticing us with tender, shadowy caresses. All who move in the clear night feel her presence."

"Patience brother," cut in Eldritch. "Master Scuttle desired to view the city. Look now, mouse of the fields, it is below you."

Twit lowered his eyes away from the stars and his mouth fell open.

All around and beneath them lay a glittering sea

of light. The great city of London sprawled magnificently in all directions, an incomparable, matchless slumbering creature, bejewelled and dangerous.

It was impossibly large for a tiny mouse to imagine. Twit just breathed in wonderment like a fish gasping on land.

The bats wheeled in circles, chuckling to one another.

"It's luverly," Twit managed to say at last. "Perfect."

At this the brothers laughed loudly. "Not perfect, Master Scuttle. Come see." They dived. Down they went, past the flat roofs of slim blank tower blocks and through the tops of trees. They reached a weird buzzing orange light on the top of a tall post and Twit had to kick away the moths that fluttered like ghosts around him.

"We will take you to the dark side of the city," explained Orfeo. "In the night the ferae roam."

"The what?" asked Twit.

"The feral creatures – wild, hungry and frightened."

They flew over a road where great glaring engines hurtled along at a frightening speed. The bats skimmed some garden fences and Twit received a splinter in his tail.

A hollow clang clattered nearby.

"What was that?" asked Twit.

"It is the feral cats," said Orfeo.

And Twit saw thin skulking animals that might once have been cats scavenging in dustbins. Forlorn and ravenous, they tore open bags and spat at each other in their fight for food. The fur on them was thick and dusty, their tails were bushy and their whiskers were more like bristles.

"Do you know others of this untame breed in your

field Master Scuttle?"

"Well no, there ain't nothin' like that, they'm so scrawny," shivered Twit.

"The city makes them so."

Twit noticed with alarm the green hungry eyes turned to them as they flew over. The mournful wails scraped into the night air.

"The tune of the dark," uttered Eldritch. "Come, more to see."

They soared up once more and Twit was grateful to be out of sight of those pitiful creatures scattered below.

Up they went over houses and derelict shops.

"See the feral man," said Orfeo.

The fieldmouse stared down. Amongst the deep grass in the middle of a rough area of wasteland lay a crumpled figure. His hair was long and matted, dirt soiled his skin and clothes and an empty bottle was clenched tightly in his hand.

With slow movements he raised his shaggy head and Twit noticed with alarm the same desperate soulless look he had seen in the cat's eyes. A miserable, melancholy sound came up to them. Twit shuddered and the bats flew by. On they went into the night. Gradually Twit became aware of a faint musical sound; it had a quality that tugged his heart and made him catch his breath.

"So you can hear that," said Eldritch. "It is to be expected."

Twit strained his ears to listen. It was so sad and lovely. There were no words to the melody – just continual tones of deep yearning and loneliness, desperate and urgent.

"Who is it that sings?" asked Twit. "They'm so sad, why's that?"

"The night hears everyone," said Orfeo, "you heard the cries of the cats and the howl of the man.

The night collects the sounds of the heart and we who ride beneath the moon hear it. Sometimes still and peaceful, sometimes roaring and angry – tonight it is despondent and despairing. Listen to the heartaches Master Scuttle and grow wise. And thank your Green Mouse that you were blessed with your simple wit."

It seemed to Twit that they were flying in a sea of music; music which eddied around them in soft, sad waves. It was a sound that the fieldmouse never forgot although he could never explain it to anyone else.

Then as they spiralled higher the wind rushed into his ears filling them until they were numb and Twit heard the music no more.

Deptford passed below them: the cramped estates, the old buildings with grimy windows and sagging lintels. A bright neon cross flickered outside the mission and on the gateposts of St. Nicholas' Church at Deptford Green two stone skulls grinned up at them.

Three small silhouettes glided before the moon. They had come to a quiet, squat power station with one tall chimney. The bats circled it twice.

"Not your story, Master Scuttle," cried Orfeo.

Twit saw the shimmering ribbon of the Thames on their left, snaking around the docks. They cleared the power station and passed on over a scrapyard.

Great iron posts and springs encrusted with orange rust stuck sharply out among the heaped piles of discarded rubbish. Tall skeletal cranes straddled the refuse and the bats flew through their lattices.

Deptford was behind them; ahead lay Greenwich.

"What's that down there?" Twit asked as they passed over an unfamiliar object.

"A ship to sail the high seas," answered Eldritch.

Before Twit had time to consider the strange, spiky thing it had been left behind. They swept along over beautiful white buildings, their many windows and pillars reflected in the calm river. Soon Twit saw a wide parkland drawing near. Within it was a green hill crowned by bulbous buildings and ancient trees.

"And what are they?" he asked.

The bats flew around the observatories, and swooped low over the domes. Twit's feet caught a golden weather vane and sent it spinning round frantically.

"This is where the stars are studied," boomed Orfeo. "They search for answers far out in the deep heavens."

"When at their feet the Starwife knows all. Wise fools!" snorted Eldritch.

Twit wondered who the Starwife was, but the bats seemed to be slowing. Not far off lay Blackheath and the fieldmouse could see the vast expanse of flat grassland. But his companions refused to go any further.

"Back," they cried, "we must return."

Actually Twit was glad. He was awfully cold, for the wind bit right through his fur. They made haste and veered away from the hill.

"This has been splendid," he thanked them.

Orfeo looked at him oddly with that strange smirk on his face.

"I tire," he said. "Who could have thought that a small mouse would weigh so?"

Eldritch agreed. "This burden wearies me also. Shall we release him?" he asked casually.

Twit heard them and trembled. "Don't drop me," he squeaked, "I'll smash to bits."

The bats flew out over the river. "A softer landing Master Scuttle," they laughed.

The fieldmouse saw their reflection in the dark

water. "No, I can't swim – I'll be drowned."

They dived down, pulling up just before Twit hit the water, and continued along with his tail skipping on the surface. Twit did not enjoy it. He could feel the bats laughing, their chucklings spread down their legs and their feet jiggled in amusement.

Twit felt sick. The water rippled underneath him, and now and again the bats would drop a little so that his toes were dunked.

"I don't like this," he called up to them.

"What shall we do with him?"

"He cannot swim."

"What better time to learn?"

They lowered him suddenly. Twit lifted his legs up to his chest but his bottom skimmed the river. He chanced to glance over his shoulder and saw the wobbly shape of a large fish approaching rapidly. He squeaked even louder.

The bats laughed again but soared from the river leaving the fish to clap its jaws together on empty air.

The illuminated glass dome of the Greenwich foot tunnel entrance lit them from beneath as they wheeled over.

"Oh where shall we deposit our baggage?" sang Orfeo.

"He belongs to the fields, put him in a nest."

They circled round the old ship they had passed earlier. It was the Cutty Sark. Under the fierce face of the figurehead they darted and then spiralled upwards through the rigging, flitting around the main mast until they reached its topmost point. Then they let go of the fieldmouse and flapped off, laughing loudly.

Twit fell.

For a moment he was wriggling wildly in mid-air, the ground rushing towards him.

"This is it," he thought.

Then a gasp was thumped out of him as he hit the main mast. He was winded but still managed to cling onto the timber.

The Cutty Sark has no sails to adorn her three masts, and in the moonlight she was a stark, ghostly memory of what she had been. Her rigging was like a dark web spun by a vast black spider.

Twit lay on the mast struggling for breath, clinging to the ropes for dear life. Finally his breathing eased and he dared to look down.

He was teetering on the brink of destruction.

Twit closed his eyes and shook his head. He had thought that the bats were friendly but all the time they must have been laughing at him – just like everyone else. No, not everyone. He knew that he had friends and that thought comforted him.

The wind blew his whiskers this way and that. It carried the deep green smell of the river to him and once again his stomach turned over.

The fieldmouse surveyed his position. He knew that he had to get down somehow. He thought about it carefully, collecting his thoughts slowly. Perhaps he could shin down the mast: but it was so sheer and wide that this idea did not appeal. In the end he decided to climb down in stages, crisscrossing the rigging; he could pretend the ropes were just long barley stalks.

Twit made his way carefully to the end of the yard-arm where a rope began.

He clambered onto it, taking it firmly in his paws and winding his tail about it. He began the descent.

With even his small weight the rope swayed and bobbed about. But Twit was an expert and deftly managed the feat. Soon he was on the next level and began again on another rope. It was not long before Twit stood on the deck of the ship.

He ran gladly to the side, happy to have something

solid beneath his feet at last. He scrambled up the side of the deck and peered over.

The Cutty Sark was in a long concrete trough supported underneath and round the sides by many iron struts. Twit could see no way of leaping from the deck onto the edge of the concrete. It was too far and besides, at the top of the trough a high rail penned the ship in. He looked down as far as he could.

From a hole in the side a great chain issued and fell to the ground where an anchor was attached and rested on the trough floor. He wondered if he could scale down the hull of the ship and reach that chain. At both ends of the concrete grave were steps: he felt he could manage those.

Twit swung himself over the side. Luckily there was a decorative panel immediately below which carried the ship's name in gold relief. His small pink feet could get a purchase on it. He grabbed the "C" and worked his way down. At the base of the letters was a ledge overhanging the rest of his ship. Twit squirmed around. If he could just reach ... He stretched out his legs. Below him were two ropes that led to the bowsprit under which the figurehead glared out. He caught the ropes and scrabbled about, ready to swing down onto the next border where a gilded scrolling of leaves and vines glinted coldly in the moonlight.

"Mercy on me!" Twit hurled himself forward.

"Ow!" came a startled voice. "What's that?"

Twit regained his balance. He had thrown himself against something soft.

A beady orange eye blinked at him. "Clear off, clear off. My roost, my roost," said the voice angrily.

A scraggy, feathered head poked out of the shadows: it was a tatty pigeon.

It jerked its head.

"My roost, my roost," it repeated.

Twit looked at the bird. It was thin. Its beak was blunt and its feathers dirty. There were scabs around its eyes and Twit winced as he noticed its gnarled, mutilated feet.

"I'm sorry," he apologised, "I didn't know you were there."

He felt sorry for the scruffy bird. Its voice was filled with fear and nervousness.

"Clear off! My roost!" It seemed to be talking to itself now, trying to reassure itself. The bird shivered and twitched, shifting its weight from one mangled foot to the other.

Twit could never understand birds. Few could speak and none could maintain a conversation without drifting off into mindless food talk or the merits of mud in nest building.

Twit excused himself, apologising once more to the jittery pigeon. He left it to its mutterings. Slowly the bird pulled in its ruffled head and closed its dry, sore eyes against the wind.

The fieldmouse crept along the golden carvings. It was a long way down. His progress was slow even with footholds. He pressed himself close to the gilt where it ended in a flourish of curling fronds. On his left was the hole where the chain left the ship but a metal ridge across his path prevented him from reaching it. The chain was just too far away. He leant over as far as he could and groped into the hole, hoping there were no more pigeons hiding anywhere ready to peck him. The recess seemed to go a long way back. Twit wondered if he could make it to the chain if he jumped really hard.

He braced himself, tensing his whole body, judging the distance.

"Ahoy!" shouted a deep voice.

Twit looked around but could see no-one.

"Ahoy there! In here!" it called again. The voice

seemed to be coming from inside the hole. Twit blinked and stared: two eyes approached – it didn't sound like or appear to be a pigeon.

"You're in a spot, matey." A thick, strong paw emerged from the dark. "Take this, miladdo."

The fieldmouse wondered who this creature might be. The voice sounded friendly enough yet there was a tone in it that commanded attention and obedience. Twit reached out and clasped the offered paw tightly.

"Now you jump and I'll pull."

Twit jumped and the strong arm tugged fiercely.

Before he knew anything Twit was in the shadows next to the owner of the voice.

"Not too bad were it?" it said. "Now, you seem done in, let's away from this dark place."

The creature pattered away and Twit followed obediently.

Soon they were back on the top deck. What a waste of time, thought Twit. The great chain coiled and snaked its way to a large wheel. But something else caught the fieldmouse's eye, and he turned and jumped with a start. There seemed to be some large animal lurking to one side.

"'S all right," called the imposing voice ahead of him, it's not real! Come on now."

Twit looked more closely at the big creature that he had seen. It was a pig – a wooden pig. He tapped it and it made a hollow sound. What would anyone make a dummy pig for? Twit shrugged and set off after the stranger.

Through dark spaces between decks they went, Twit's curiosity burning in him to find out more about his guide. Yet he was too polite to ask.

Only when they emerged from the darkness and stepped out onto the dimly lit lower deck could he see the stranger properly for the first time.

He was a mouse, of middle age, with white whiskers framing a round face. His eyes were bright and wise. He was stout but could obviously move with speed when required and he looked very strong. There seemed to be an air of something foreign about him as if he had been to far-off countries and adopted some of their habits. This effect was emphasised by a red kerchief around his neck and a shapeless navy blue woollen hat on his head.

"Well," the stranger said, turning to Twit at last. "Welcome aboard matey." He stretched out his paw. "Midshipmouse Thomas Triton," he introduced himself.

Twit took the paw in his and shook it vigorously. "Willum Scuttle, but mostways I'm called Twit."

"Hmmm, well lad you've a look as one who's got a tale to tell. Come with me, back to my bunkhouse. We'll have a sip of something to warm you down to your toes."

Twit couldn't help accepting the invitation. He had an immediate liking for the midshipmouse, for there was something solid and dependable about him.

On the lower deck of the Cutty Sark were great sacks of wool – examples of its former cargoes, and tall screens telling the ship's history.

"Nowt in those sacks," Thomas said in disgust. "I looked, I knows. Fine ship this was once. Now look at her!" He seemed passionate about it.

"I think it's marvellous," replied Twit.

"Well, you speak your mind," the midshipmouse laughed. "Aye, I'll think the better of you for it. But no, this ship once sailed the high seas, felt the salt spray in her rigging and the rolling ocean swell against her hull. Now . . ." he waved his arms about sadly, ". . . permanent dry dock! Proper invalid she is – can't go nowhere, like me I suppose," he added softly. "Guess that's why I live here – two of a kind, her and me."

They walked over the polished floorboards and under glass cases containing models of other ships until they came to a steep flight of steps.

"I bunk in the hold," said Thomas, "Don't see why I should change now after all these years. Can you manage these stairs?"

Twit answered that he could and the two mice descended.

The hold was an eerie place, not as cluttered as the lower deck but long and high, sloping gently and curving round at each end.

It was dark down there, and in the gloom Twit could just make out a row of giant figures on both sides of him. All were staring fixedly ahead. There were gentlemen, painted ladies, two black exotics, hunters, kings and a chap showing white teeth ready to champ. Twit hesitated.

"I ain't goin' in there," he whispered, "there'm gert forms a-starin' with big round googly eyes."

Thomas laughed. "'S all right matey!" He slipped behind a wooden rail and climbed up to the nearest figure, a tall, voluptuous woman with curling blond hair and wearing a flimsy blue dress that was belted with a scarlet sash which matched her lips. Thomas raised a paw and knocked soundly on her.

"They're only figureheads carved from wood," he assured, "friendly enough. Matter of fact I live in one of 'em."

Twit went over to peer at the carvings. He had never seen their like before. In his field, decorations were looked on as frivolous and he knew one or two staunch mice who would go so far as to call them heathen and idolatrous. He tapped at the wooden folds of the blue dress then beamed brightly.

"'Tis amazing," he said.

Thomas Triton led him to a figurehead that was somewhat smaller than its neighbours. It was the image of a maiden, painted a glossy white with a turban of gold on her head.

"This is my princess," he said, "now up you go matey, round the back with you."

Twit peered behind the carving. There was a rich smell of fresh paint close to her and there, where two joints didn't quite meet was a small hole.

"Through here?" he asked.

"'Sright – she opens up inside once you're through."

The fieldmouse passed easily through the hole and into a comfortable room in the middle of the figurehead. A stubby white candle flickered gently, lending the room a warm, cosy glow. In one corner was a bed and here and there, neatly arranged, were Thomas's few belongings: a tiny wooden ship, a lead anchor charm, some pictures of distant lands and maps of continents, and a highly polished sword.

Thomas bade him sit down. Twit found a block of wood and sat on it.

The midshipmouse strolled over to a corner and brought out two deep bowls, he gave one to Twit and filled it with a strange-smelling liquid. He took a wooden pipe off a shelf and stuffed it with tobacco. Then he leant over the candle flame and puffed on the pipe. All this he did in silence, obviously waiting till everything was to his satisfaction and he was comfortable before talk could begin. He sat down on the bed and looked across to Twit, considering him from beneath his bushy white brows.

Twit wondered if he was meant to say anything but the other mouse seemed to be enjoying the silence so much that he kept quiet. Instead, he gave his attention to the full bowl he held in his paws.

He lowered his head and sniffed tentatively.

By now Thomas had filled his own bowl and said, with the pipe stuck firmly in one side of his mouth, "You drink it matey, 's all right," and as if to prove the fact he took a good swig out of his bowl.

So Twit drank too. It warmed his throat in a pleasant tingling way and slowly the feeling spread down to his toes and the end of his tail. It was a thick syrupy drink that spoke to him of exotic fruits and foreign shores, not a bit like the blackberry ferment drunk in his field. He smacked his lips.

"That's rum lad," grinned Thomas. "A good belly warmer to get you goin'. Now what were you doin' outside?"

For a moment Twit collected his wits and put everything that had happened to him and his friends in order. Then he took a deep breath and began, telling of Audrey's first disappearance and the search for her in the sewers; the fight with the rats – Thomas seemed to listen very intently at this stage – then on to Oswald and Piccadilly, how they had set off to find the mousebrass; finally he described how Audrey had vanished from the cellar and how he had followed Arthur up to the attic in search of the bats.

"Up through the roof they flew me," he said, "and out into the night, around towers and hills, oh it were marvless. Then they got tired and threatened to drop me in the river."

"But you ended up here instead," Thomas finished. "Hmm – a good tale young Twit and it makes me wonder."

"About what?"

The midshipmouse puffed on his pipe and gazed abstractedly through the blue smoke that had gathered around his face. "Things are moving matey. I've felt it for some time, a change in the order of things; that's one reason I was on deck tonight –

been fidgety you see, could always smell a storm comin'."

"I just wish my friends were all safe in their homes again," Twit said glumly.

"Well, we can't help that can we? Not at the moment." Thomas got to his feet and paced around impatiently. "Summat's up – or should I say down, as that's where the trouble is. Some retirement this is!" He turned to Twit and said darkly, "I been many places matey. Strange lands I've seen and stranger creatures I've met; I've seen foreign gods and heard the beat of pagan drums in the night. I've slept on a bed of spices from the far Indies and I ain't had such a decent kip since. Once I got lost in the East and folk there were mighty queer, mice wore outlandish masks and claimed to possess certain powers – an' I believed 'em too, but ..." he paused to consider things, "but I say I ain't never come across owt like the situation here. A living god down in the sewers and a blacker fiend you won't find all round the world: everyone's afraid of him, no exceptions – rats, mice, even the squirrels in Greenwich park yonder don't talk about him. The tales I hear would make your tail drop off. Heartless cruel don't come near to describin' him. He's a dirty stain on the land and he's up to summat." Thomas knocked his pipe on the shelf. "Time I found out what. Come on lad!"

The midshipmouse was stirred into action. "Been idle too long – you come just at the right time."

Twit finished the rum in his bowl. "What are we going to do?" he asked excitedly, catching the other's mood.

"Find out what he's up to!"

He ushered Twit out of the figurehead and extinguished the candle flame before following.

"Where are we going?" inquired the fieldmouse. "Will we have to climb down the side of the ship?"

He remembered how difficult this feat was and did not relish tackling it a second time.

"We're off to the sewers, matey," Thomas replied. "And don't worry – there's an easier way than the one you tried before." He led Twit back past the other figureheads once more until they stopped at the carving of a king with a golden crown.

"Neptune, Lord of the Waters," declared the midshipmouse as Twit gazed up. "Yet also a handy doorkeeper. Come see." They circled the carving and Thomas showed Twit a small hole hidden in the King's shadow.

Thomas wriggled through it. "This gap gets smaller every day," he grunted, as Twit followed. Beyond there was a dark passage that smelt of pitch. The fieldmouse thought about his new companion – what an odd character he was! He longed to hear Thomas's tales of far-off lands and his adventures there, but here he was on his way back to the sewers – where all roads seemed to have led recently.

He wondered if Oswald and Piccadilly had found Audrey's mousebrass yet and were safely back in the Skirtings, then he thought of Audrey herself – what had happened to her? A touch of guilt struck him. Should he have left with the bats when she was still missing? Poor old Arthur would have got back to the hall ages ago and now have another disappearance to worry about.

"Nearly there now," Thomas called out in the dark.

A sliver of pale moonlight showed ahead as the two mice emerged from the Cutty Sark.

"Just climb down this bit of rudder," Thomas explained. They managed it easily and were soon standing on the concrete. The ship reared high above them in shapely grace.

"Yes she's a beauty," Thomas nodded in approval.

"Sometimes in the dead of night I catch her out. Maybe it's just the timbers shrinking after a warm day, but there are occasions when I fancy I hear the old girl sighing and sobbing for what was." He pointed to the metal struts supporting the ship.

"Look at these," he said angrily. "Spears in her side! She'll never sail again; no wonder she cries – got a right to."

Thomas reached out and stroked the ship tenderly. Then he shook himself and led Twit to the side of the concrete trench. There was a gutter in the floor and he followed it round until they came to a grate in the wall.

Twit stepped back in alarm.

"The Grill!" he choked.

Thomas looked at him curiously, "Aye, 'tis a grill – nothing more."

But Twit shook his head. "The Grill leads to *him*! 'Tis an evil door, see how it pops up everywhere."

Thomas understood. "Ah, so you have a similar thing in the Skirtings."

The fieldmouse scratched his head.

"No, the Grill there is fancier with leaves 'n stuff, but 'tis the same – can you not feel the dark things lurkin' beyond?"

Thomas had to agree. The air that issued from the grate stirred his mind and whispered grimly to him – he had not felt it before, but Jupiter's realm was growing and his power was spreading.

"Wicked magic fills the air," murmured Twit. "Black thoughts come to you and het you up terrible."

He had not forgotten Arthur's vicious and sudden outburst earlier that night.

Thomas pulled his woollen hat further down. "I'm not havin' this. Everyone clams up tight when *he's* mentioned – well *he* don't scare me! I've sailed with enough rats in my time to know the ins and outs of 'em! A good thump in the face puts paid to any mutiny in their guts. I'm fed up with all this hushed whisperin' – not darin' to say *his* name. Ain't no-one even seen him! If he's 'orrible to look on like they say with two heads an' such – don't bother me any, things I've seen. Friends of mine have been eaten alive by fish with three rows of razor teeth; I've heard the screams of a drowning mouse and fought to the death with Spanish rats. No sewer rat gonna intimidate old Tom." The midshipmouse threw back his head and shouted loudly, "JUPITER!"

The call bounced and echoed around the concrete trough. Thomas sighed and grinned sheepishly when he saw Twit staring at him as if he were a mad thing.

"I needed to do that. Too much whisperin's been gettin' me down; all this 'Hush hush, speak softly or his curse will descend.' Rubbish! Time to act: come on matey. We'll go through this grate and find out somethin' useful."

He disappeared through the large spaces in the grating. Twit hesitated to follow. He knew practically nothing about this retired seafarer who could be as cracked as an old jug: he certainly didn't behave like any mouse that Twit had ever met before, and yet when Twit was with him he felt all his worries brushed aside. The midshipmouse, Twit judged, was fearless and trustworthy. The fieldmouse liked him enormously already. With one last doubtful look at the grate Twit followed Thomas. Inside they trotted along the drains. Thomas was striding, determined to discover what Jupiter was up to. Behind him Twit had to run to keep up, but he felt he would rather be down here with Thomas than outside alone.

"Where does this take us?" he asked timidly.

Without stopping or turning around Thomas said,

"Near to the altar of Jupiter where all the rats live. Better prepare your nose for a bit of a shock, miladdo."

The drain opened into the sewer and they continued along the ledge.

Twit gradually became aware of a power beating against him, willing him back, pulling at his insides, and shaking his stomach, filling it with butterflies. He was more puzzled than alarmed: he was not the sort to panic for no reason.

"Can you feel that?" he asked Thomas eventually.

"That's one of the enchantments here," Thomas answered. "He don't like nosey visitors pokin' around this bit of the sewer. I wonder why? Hush, do you hear that?"

He put his paw to his ear. Twit listened.

Very faintly there was a distant chant – a monotonous dirge with many voices singing hoarsely.

"What can it be?" Twit wondered.

The midshipmouse was uncertain. "Let's find the source of this shanty," he said eventually.

So they followed the dismal sound. Twit thought he had never heard such unhappy voices. The music he had listened to with the bats was sad but beautiful; this was just miserable. It dampened his spirits like a hymn to despair.

They were not far from the source of the song. The funereal anthem rose all about them. The words were difficult to catch but the mood behind them was plain – boredom, misery and the bitter tang of hatred.

"We must be near the altar chamber," Thomas said. "Let's skip around a back way and see what's up."

There was a hole in the wall and the voices boomed through it. Thomas clambered into the opening and helped Twit do the same.

It was only a short tunnel. It turned sharply to the right and after a dozen paces ended abruptly, but on their left the cement had crumbled and a pencil of light shone through.

Thomas put his eye to the peephole. "Blow me," he breathed incredulously. "What are they a-doin' of?"

Twit tugged at his paw. The midshipmouse lifted him up so that he too could see. Twit gasped.

Before them was a tunnel, wide and high, the floor of which was a good deal below that of their own humble passage. It was filled with rats.

Nasty, ugly rats, sneers on their great faces and sweat pouring off their bodies. Twit covered his nose. All the rats were labouring and as they worked they sang. It was a work song, a song to keep them in time with each other. It told of slow deaths, of throttlings, throat-slittings, peelings and roastings.

Every rat had a tool of some kind in his claws: old spoons, sharp bits of metal, anything to dig with. Twit realised that the whole tunnel had been dug by them. There was an army of them straining and striking the ground. Some were actually scrabbling at the ground with bleeding claws.

Older, less useful rats wearily heaved the soil away in sacks and tins strapped to their brittle, bony backs.

It was a hive of bizarre industry, with no rest. The pace was set by the youngest and strongest; the others had to follow. Twit saw one old rat strain at the heavy sack he was struggling with. It was obvious that he had not slept for a long time, and Twit doubted if he had eaten. He guessed rightly that when breaks were given the rats scrambled for the food provided and the weak were lucky to suck the bones after the others had finished.

The old rat pulled at the sack and heaved it onto

his back, his ears drooping and his eyes shot with blood.

He took several faltering steps, staggering beneath the weight and then his heart burst. He fell like a stone to the ground. No-one made any effort to help. The rat gasped, his ribs heaving up and down. He opened his mouth, trying to say something, but the words were lost in the din of work. With agony in his face the old rat's eyes slowly closed and never opened again.

"That's how they look after their own," Thomas said softly in Twit's ear.

Another elderly rat picked up the sack that had been such a burden to the other.

He looked down at the pathetic crumpled body that lay at his feet. The rat sneered and spat in the upturned blank face, then he set off, kicking the corpse aside into the dirt.

Twit looked away, disgusted at the scene that had unfolded before his eyes. Then he turned to Thomas.

"What be they diggin' for?"

He could see no point to it at all.

"Oh there's a reason! Jupiter's got something up his sleeve," Thomas pondered. "Treasure maybe or p'raps some powerful magical thing to make him stronger, Green Mouse forbid." He closed his eyes and turned slowly around. His whiskers twitched and then he said, "If my sense of direction is right, and it always is, I reckon that tunnel they're diggin' runs clear under the park. If they keep this up they'll be under Blackheath soon. Now I wonder what Jupiter wants there."

He put his arm around Twit's shoulders. "Let's get out of this dungeon and take a walk in the fresh air. I've a mind to find out what Jupiter's after."

The two mice left the small passage and the slow chant behind them.

# 8

---

# WHITE AND GREY

Whilst Audrey had waited with Twit in the cellars, Oswald and Piccadilly had run headlong into the sewers in search of her missing mousebrass. Oswald had hurried ahead, but Piccadilly soon caught up with him.

"Hang on pal," he called. "Where's the fire? Stop a minute, will you?" He pulled Oswald's scarf and slowed him to a standstill.

Oswald's pink eyes were wide and round with excitement. "It can't be far now," he panted. "Look at the divining rod: it's twitching like anything."

"Maybe, but we've come too far." Piccadilly gazed at the tunnel they were in. Large *plops* echoed in it as water dripped down from the arched ceiling. "We're not on the right track any more." Piccadilly swept his hair out of his eyes and looked back along the tunnel. "I think I can remember the way," he said.

"Shall we go on then?" inquired Oswald.

Piccadilly nodded. "Why not! Okay, Whitey, lead on."

Oswald coughed. He disliked being reminded how different he was; his friends in the Skirtings made a conscious effort to avoid saying things like "Pink Eyes", "Bino", "Freaky" and "Whitey".

Piccadilly fiddled with his ear. He had seen

Oswald's reaction and he bit his lip. "Sorry Oswald," he apologised. "Didn't mean anything by it, honest. Besides, white suits you."

The other mouse managed a smile. "Oh I don't mind the way I am," he sighed. "It's the way others react that gets to me. Just because I'm tall and have funny eyes. It hurts Mother most of all though; I've often caught her looking at me sadly."

"How do you mean?"

Oswald frowned as he searched for the right words. "Well, I know that she loves me and all that, but I can't help feeling that sometimes she's . . . ashamed of me."

"That can't be true."

"You don't know Mother," said Oswald softly. "Oh I know I'm not what she wanted . . . No, it's true." He sighed and looked absent-mindedly down at his feet. Then he sat down miserably and groaned. "I get the feeling that Mother resents me sometimes. I don't fit in, you see."

Now it was Piccadilly's turn to cough. He was embarrassed by this outburst from Oswald. Nobody in the city had ever bothered to tell him how they felt, and he was quite unprepared to deal with it. He shifted uncomfortably, then sat down next to the white mouse.

"The sooner we find Audrey's brass the better, eh?" He tried to change the subject and bring the other out of his sad mood. "I've had enough of sewers to last me a lifetime. What did she go and lose it for?" He rested his head on his paw and remembered how he had met Albert: it seemed such a long time ago now. Piccadilly had liked Mr Brown. Although he had not known him for very long, a bond had quickly developed between them. With a shudder he relived those last moments in Jupiter's chamber.

Piccadilly closed his eyes and wondered once more if there had been anything he could have done to save Albert. He had been over it many times in his head – something he could have said might have stopped Albert going to listen to Jupiter, or if he had been more alert he might have noticed Morgan creeping up. No, thinking about it didn't help. Albert was gone, and nothing he could do now would alter that. He could dwell on the "if onlys" forever and change nothing. Piccadilly wished Audrey would believe him. He had liked her from the first time he saw her, but she had hated him. Oh, what a mess everything was!

"Come on Oswald!" he said with sudden resolution. "Let's find Audrey's brass and clear off out of here."

Oswald agreed. He picked up the divining rod once again and stood very still, allowing the vibrations to flow through him once more as he concentrated on the missing mousebrass. The rod began to twitch.

"Yes, we're on the right track," he said.

They set off along the ledge at a brisk pace. For some time they pattered quietly down the deserted tunnels, turning whenever the rod jerked them in a different direction. Piccadilly let Oswald lead because the albino's eyes could see more in the dark than his.

Suddenly Oswald let out a shriek and fell over. Piccadilly was so close behind that he too found himself sprawled on the wet ledge.

"What happened?" he asked, stunned a little.

"I'm sorry," Oswald said quickly. "I didn't look where I was walking and yes, there you see, I fell over that piece of wood."

A green, damp, swollen plank lay obstinately behind them. Piccadilly forgave his friend, if only to shut him up. Oswald was a constant apologiser. But the albino mouse soon stopped again.

"What's that?" he whispered abruptly.

"What's what?" Piccadilly could hear nothing.

Oswald cocked his head to one side and listened intently. "There," he said softly.

A faint rumble came from in front of them. It grew steadily louder.

"Oh lumme," breathed Piccadilly huskily. "Rats is comin'."

Oswald clapped his paw to his mouth. "What are we to do? What are we to do?" he yelped.

"Keep calm," Piccadilly urged him. "They can't have seen or heard us yet. So don't go givin' us away."

Oswald nodded and took his paw away, but the occasional stifled squeal kept rising from his tummy as he tried not to panic.

Piccadilly tried to follow his own advice and think calmly. The rats – and it sounded like a lot of them – could come around the corner any time and they would be caught with nowhere to hide. They would surely be seen and chased; he might not be so lucky this time. No, Piccadilly decided they had to hide somehow and let the rats pass by. He grabbed Oswald's paw and dragged him back down the sewer.

"Look for a niche, or hole in the wall – anything," he explained.

"But you know we haven't passed anything like that," Oswald protested.

"Shut up and look!"

The mice groped frantically at the brick wall. Oswald grazed his paws badly in his fright. But there was nothing – neither crack nor gap.

Piccadilly glanced quickly over his shoulder; the tramp of rat feet was very close. From behind the corner came a glow. The rats were carrying torches!

The city mouse knew that they would never be able to hide from them. The torches would reveal them wherever they hid.

He looked across to Oswald, whose eyes were wider than he would have thought possible. Oswald gulped, and the divining rod fell from his hands.

Piccadilly edged back slightly, awaiting the end. Oswald buried his face in his paws and shook uncontrollably. Something brushed against Piccadilly's foot and a splinter pierced his heel.

"Ouch," he cursed and looked down. There was the plank that they had tripped over before. He gave it a vengeful kick. Then a wild idea seized him.

The noise of the rats was very loud now, and the bobbing glow from the torches brighter. Any second now they would turn the corner.

Piccadilly lost no time. He picked up the piece of wood. Telling Oswald to do the same he ran off the ledge.

Before Oswald knew what they were doing they had jumped clear away from the side of the sewer. Then *Splash!* Dark water swallowed them.

The rats burst around the corner. There were twenty of them, all jostling for place as they ran. The fiery torches were held high over their ugly heads. It was a startling sight: their red eyes sparkled in the firelight and shone with the hunger and hatred that drove them. They were all dirty and sweaty; some were scabby; others bald, where fur had been torn out in fights. Leading them was a rat with a patch over one eye: it was One-Eyed Jake.

For some time, Morgan had been keeping an eye on Jake as a possible source of trouble. Jake was too cocky for his own good. He was one of the rats that Morgan felt might one day fancy promotion. Maybe he should arrange it so Jake failed to wake up one

morning. He was getting too popular with the lads, and that worried Morgan. His position as Jupiter's lieutenant was under threat. He would have to see to it personally, of course – he trusted no-one. It would have to be quick too; Jake was younger and stronger. Yes, throttle him while he slept, or better still slash his ugly throat.

But at the moment Jake was laughing and whooping with his mates. He had been ordered by Jupiter himself to go and bring back any mice in the sewers. If there were none there then he had been authorised to find the Grill and grab any girl mice and a particular "grey" from the city. Jake chuckled as he recalled the frosty glare Morgan had given him outside the altar chamber. He was losing his grip, that one, thought Jake. None too in with His Lordship of late, letting things slip. Jake let out a crow of delight. Yes, soon he would take over from the Cornish rat. Things were looking up.

Jake was in a good mood. He had been let off the digging for a while and entrusted with a mission. There might be mouse for breakfast yet.

The teeming rats filled the sewer ledge and sang bawdy songs as they ran. They were in high spirits.

Far below them Oswald was gasping for air. He splashed about wildly in the water. He had swallowed a good deal of it and he gagged and choked at the taste.

Piccadilly had already scrambled aboard the plank, which floated quite well. He used his paws to paddle over to where Oswald was thrashing around.

Above them he could see the rats waving their torches around, and he could hear them snorting and laughing. He hoped they were too engrossed to look down at the water.

Oswald's head disappeared under once more. Piccadilly reached down into the cold, deep water and grabbed his friend's scarf. He yanked it as hard as he could and Oswald followed, spluttering and coughing as he broke to the surface.

Piccadilly hauled the wet albino onto the makeshift raft, where he lay collapsed like a broken doll. His coughing rocked them and water slopped over the edge of the wood. Piccadilly was afraid that they might sink and prayed for the rats not to hear them. He looked up once more.

The rats were still above them. Why was that? Had they seen him and Oswald? No, the rats were still running. Then he realised with a dull, sick feeling that the current of the sewer water was carrying them along at the same pace as the rats above. Piccadilly groaned. They had been lucky so far. No rat had bothered to look down at the stream below – but it couldn't be much longer until one did. Everyone knew that rats were excellent swimmers.

Oswald's breathing eased. He had spat out as much water as he could. He turned over and lay on his back grunting uncomfortably.

"I'll be ill for weeks," he said glumly.

Piccadilly put a paw to his lips. "Quiet!" he whispered, and pointed upwards. Oswald slowly took in the situation. "Oh my," he whimpered.

"I thought you could swim," said Piccadilly softly. "Sorry."

"Oh, that's all right. We'd have been peeled by now if you hadn't thought so quickly. I shall tell Audrey so when we get back."

"If we get back, you mean," corrected Piccadilly doubtfully.

"Don't say that. We've done fine so far, haven't we?"

"Not really. We haven't found what we came for, have we? And here we are, tagging along with a load of horrible rats."

"One other thing," said Oswald miserably. "I dropped the divining rod! We shan't find the mousebrass now."

"There you are then. What a fix to be in."

They both gazed up at the ledge where the rats ran, mouths agape and slobbering. "Ho, Jake," called one rat to the leader. "What we gonna do with a mouse when we get one?"

"Bloodybones 'im," cackled the others.

"That right Jake?"

"Do what you like with 'im Fletchy, so long as you save me a bit," Jake shouted back. The rest of the rats loved this and sniggered nastily.

"Nice an' juicy fleshy hocks."

"Save me the ears. Ooh, luvverly fried and crispy!"

"Boil the head for brawn gravy!"

"Pickle the eyes in rancid fat."

"Oh yes, very tasty."

"Can't we go faster?"

The mice on the raft shuddered at the suggestions. Oswald was shivering anyway. He was cold and wet through – the water seemed to have seeped into his bones. If he ever managed to get back to the Skirtings he would be in bed for weeks with chills and sneezes.

"Just you remember lads," began Jake, "that if it's a mouse wench or a 'grey' then you or me can't have 'em."

There was a groan from the other rats. "Not fair!" they cried.

Jake warned them, however. "Not so much as a toenail, or else! Not that it's me what says that. It's His Lordship, and we don't wanna mess with Him, do we?"

The rats muttered and shook their heads.

"There you are then: anything else and they're ours. But thems for Him first. Got it? The skirt and the 'grey'!"

The rats nodded grudgingly.

Oswald nudged Piccadilly. "He means you," he said appalled.

"And Audrey too," the grey mouse replied.

"But this is dreadful," stammered Oswald. "They're going out of their way to find you – why?"

Piccadilly shook his head. "I don't know – unless Jupiter thinks whatever Albert heard I did too and he doesn't want it to get about."

"But Audrey?"

"I don't know. She is Albert's daughter. Maybe he thinks she knows too. But that's daft."

"I wonder what it could be that he doesn't want to get out," wondered Oswald.

"Well I, for one, don't know," shrugged Piccadilly.

Suddenly Oswald gave a strangled cry of shock. "Oh no!" he gasped. "They must be going to the Skirtings to find you and Audrey."

"You're right! Crikey, what can we do?"

"We've got to stop them," cried Oswald, thinking of the chaos the rats would cause amongst the mice in the old, empty house.

"But how? They're so many – and here we are down here: they could get us as quick as anything." Piccadilly snapped his fingers. "Two more peeled mice won't help anyone."

Oswald gulped. "Maybe we could lure them away though."

Piccadilly agreed. He knew they had to do something.

"How fast do you think you can paddle?" he asked.

"Oh not as fast as you, I'm sure, but we might give them a good chase – for a while, anyway."

"All right then," said Piccadilly. "If we're sure." Oswald nodded back. The grey mouse looked up at the rats on the ledge. I suppose they might have seen us soon anyway, he thought to himself. He cupped his paws around his mouth and yelled at the top of his voice:

"Oi! Slime stuffers! Where's your hankies to wipe your snotty noses?"

The rats stopped and looked around in amazement.

"Maggot brains!" Piccadilly resumed. "Peel me if you can!"

"Yes ... you nasty whisker pullers," added Oswald, a trifle less dramatically. "Me too!"

The rats saw them now. "There they are!" they called. "Two floating mouseys!"

"Wait!" shouted Jake. "One of 'em's a 'grey' – get him lads."

"Twerps!" Piccadilly continued.

"Smelly feet!" It was the worst Oswald could think of.

The rats flung their torches at the raft. Like flaming spears they hurtled down on the two mice.

"Paddle now," urged Piccadilly, and he and Oswald began pawing madly at the water on either side of the raft.

Fortunately, when the rats had stopped, the raft had not and the mice already had a slight lead. The burning missiles fell just short of them. They plunged into the water in a great cloud of steam.

The rats on the ledge howled in dismay.

"Get down there," snarled Jake and kicked one over the edge. Twelve others followed him, gnashing and snarling as they jumped.

"Look!" exclaimed Oswald when he saw the thirteen rats dive into the water behind them. "They're after us!"

Piccadilly put his head down and concentrated on paddling. "Keep up, Oswald," he called annoyed, "or we'll go round in circles."

"I want the 'grey' alive," Jake's voice came down to them. "Do what you like with the other one!"

And then it was Piccadilly who found it difficult to keep up with Oswald.

Behind them thirteen rats swam, their tails thrashing the water like angry snakes.

On the ledge Jake watched the chase in amusement. This was the sort of thing he had missed and he promised himself never to dig in the mine again. The rat called "Fletch" swaggered up to him. He was a tatty, dark brown rat with big yellow pimples on his black nose.

"Not goin' in for a dip?" Jake asked dryly.

Fletch shook his head. "Don't feel like it today Jake."

"'You and water were never friends, Fletch," remarked Jake, trying to avoid the other's bad breath.

"There's plenty down there to catch those two," grunted Fletch. "I thought I'd best stick with you."

"What fer?" asked Jake suspiciously.

"Oh I just like to stick with the winners."

"Think I'm a winner, eh?"

"Well, one what knows where he's goin', then."

"And you wanna come with me, right?"

Fletch grinned and his breath whistled through his sharp teeth. "Where we bound?"

Jake looked down to the water where the swimming rats were gaining on the little raft. "There's still the skirt to catch. You lot!" he called to the five remaining rats on the ledge. "Leave 'em to it. Let's find our own mouse."

The rats cheered and Jake led them away. Through the tunnels they went until they came to the Grill. To their great glee they found there the very mouse they were looking for. Audrey had just sent Twit to fetch Arthur when Jake reached out and grabbed her from behind.

# 9

# TRUSTING TO LUCK

Piccadilly paddled furiously. The water splashed his face and his hair hung in a wet curtain over his eyes. Mechanically his arms rose and fell as if driven by pistons. Into the water – pull – out of the water – over – into the water – pull – out of the water – over . . . He glanced back. The pursuing rats were very close now. One had a knife between his teeth. He could see the shining greedy eyes and the snorting wet noses. It would take a miracle to save them.

The rat with the knife caught up with them and scrambled onto the raft. His great claws tore at the wood and the plank lurched dangerously in the water. Just as the ugly brute was getting his balance, Piccadilly leapt at him and with a startled wail, the rat fell back and landed on one of his comrades. There was an almighty smack and a fountain of water spouted up around them.

Piccadilly hastily resumed paddling. Ahead he saw the end of a pipe jutting out of the sewer wall. He wondered if he and Oswald could reach it and climb inside. He called to him and signalled his plan. Oswald understood and nodded vigorously. Anything to get off the raft!

They steadied themselves on the plank and stood up shakily – clutching each other's paws for safety. The pipe drew near.

"We won't be able to reach it," howled Oswald. "It's too high."

"Well then, we'll have to jump. Get ready."

"Oh no that rat's got us."

"One."

"He's trying to climb up again! Oh Piccadilly!"

"Two."

"Eek!"

"Three."

All at once a number of things happened. Firstly the raft passed under the pipe and Piccadilly jumped, which was fortunate for him because the rat suddenly lunged at him with his mouth wide open. But the most surprising thing came with a fierceness that stunned everyone, rats and all. With a roar of foam and spray a great rush of water flushed out of the pipe above.

The rat got a mouthful of it and was knocked off the raft into the stream – which had suddenly become a raging torrent. He sank to the murky bottom, never to surface. The other rats were cut off by the sudden waterfall and could not cope with its frothing force. They snapped angrily behind the storm, swearing terrible oaths and punching each other.

Piccadilly's luck held. Although he missed the pipe, he managed to land back on the raft just as it was gripped by the new current and was swept away at breakneck speed. Oswald grasped the sides for dear life.

"Ha, ha," laughed Piccadilly. "That did it. Wheeee!" The raft was tossed around like a straw. It was a wild bounce of a ride for the two mice as they shot along.

"I don't like this!" Oswald cried.

"Well, we're free of them anyway," replied Piccadilly, having a great time.

The water surged about them. "Where are we going?" Oswald had closed his eyes.

Piccadilly smiled at his squeamish friend and fixed his attention ahead. The tunnel appeared to come to a dead end. "We're gonna crash!" he said alarmed. Oswald opened one eye, then snapped it shut again. "Oh no," he trembled. Piccadilly had a thought; why would the tunnel end so abruptly like that? Where did the water go?

He strained his eyes to look at the rapidly approaching blank wall once more. There, at the bottom, was a dark space: the top of a submerged archway.

"Lie flat!" Piccadilly shouted to Oswald and he pulled him down. The gushing water crashed against the wall in huge, frothy violent spurts. Piccadilly clenched his paws and trusted to luck again.

The raft burst down the shallow opening.

Oswald's nose scraped against the low brick ceiling until he turned his head to one side slightly, careful that his ears did not suffer similarly.

What a place! They had no idea where they were going. Piccadilly hoped the water level would not rise any more or they would drown.

"I don't like this either," mumbled Oswald.

"I counted seven rats left on the ledge" said Piccadilly. "If they go to the Skirtings then at least there won't be so many of them."

"I suppose so."

"Cheer up Oswald – you're a hero."

"Am I?"

"'Course. They'll sing songs about you."

"Really? Well I never. Gosh, I suppose so. Owch."

The roof of the tunnel had dropped suddenly and the albino had hit his nose. "OOH! Ow – oh, ow," he squeaked in agony.

"I hope we don't get any higher," said Piccadilly. "We'll get scraped to bits before we drown." He flattened himself against the raft.

"Peeled anyway," gibbered Oswald. "Oh ow!"

Still the water hurtled along and the number of cuts and grazes doubled.

They did not know that as they continued their uncomfortable journey, Arthur and Twit were in the hall of the old house wondering what to do while Audrey had been dragged off by Jake and his lads.

The raft raced along, bumping and scraping through the low passage.

Then, with one last bang on the ceiling they shot out into a lofty, spacious tunnel.

The water swirled and eddied as its force was spent. The raft slowed and twirled around calmly.

Piccadilly sat up. "Hooray!" he shouted in relief.

"Oh by boor doze," moaned Oswald feeling his sore snout. "Id's swellid already." He fingered the bruises gingerly.

"Bathe it in the water then," said Piccadilly, glad that his own nose was not as big as his friend's.

"Dad's dasty," came the blocked response.

"It's all we've got. Go on!"

Oswald tenderly dabbed some water onto his nose. "Ooh dad's bedder," he sighed.

The raft bumped gently against the side of the sewer wall.

"How's your conk now?"

"Oh id sbards. Look ad be, vull ov cuds and scradches."

The raft drifted slowly along. "We ought to get off this now," Piccadilly said.

"Oh doh," whined Oswald immediately. "I'b zo dired. Led's waid a bid."

"All right then but I hope your nose gets better soon. I can hardly understand you."

Piccadilly dangled his legs over the side of the raft and splashed them casually in the water, humming quietly to himself, while Oswald tended to his nose and other wounds. What a light, giddy head Piccadilly had! All the fear had drained away. None of those rats could possibly follow them here. He was practically drunk with relief and smiled happily.

The tunnel opened out into three others. For a while the raft moved between them as if wondering which to choose. In the end Piccadilly kicked his feet in the water and propelled them into one of them. The ledges in this tunnel were low, low enough to climb onto in fact.

"Come on Oswald," Piccadilly said cheerfully. "Time to get off."

Oswald stirred and gave his nose one last pat. Piccadilly hauled himself up and then turned to give him a helping paw. Gracelessly Oswald scrambled up onto the ledge.

His nose felt a little better and the swelling seemed to be going down, so he was able to speak more normally. "Oh wait, what about de raft?" he asked.

"Well we can't take it with us and there's no turnin' back so we've got all we could out of it."

"I suppose so," Oswald murmured, as he watched the piece of wood float gently out of reach.

"We've got things to do," said Piccadilly breezily, as if they were going for a picnic. "Come on Oswald!"

Oswald felt glum. He had no idea where they were now. "But what cad we do?" he asked lamely.

"First off, let's try and see if we recognise where we are; then get back to the Skirtings if we can."

"And Audrey's bousebrass?"

"You said you'd lost the divining rod, didn't you

old chum? Pity – I'd dearly like to see her face if we did find it. That'd show her."

"Oh, she won't think you're a coward Piccadilly. I'll tell her how barvellous you've been."

Small tunnels led away from this larger one and the mice chose one that was not too dirty to go down.

"Wait a bo," said Oswald before they set off. He pulled the scarf from around his neck and wrung it tightly, then gave it a good shake.

"It'll only bake be worse," he explained.

Piccadilly sighed. "Now can we start?"

Into the small tunnel they went.

"Doesn't smell too bad in here," commented Piccadilly.

"I woulden doh," Oswald replied. "Can't smell a thing."

But it was drier than most of the tunnels they had been in. Slime did not drip off the walls or lurk treacherously on the floor.

"Wonder where we are now?" thought Piccadilly aloud. "Don't ever remember this place even when I was wandering around before I met Albert."

Further in they strode. "I can see an opening in the side up ahead," said Oswald, his sharp pink eyes scanning the area in front of them. "Shall we take a look?"

When they reached the hole Piccadilly sniffed it to check. "You know," he said thinking aloud, "I don't think this passage is used by the rats very much – if at all. I just get the feeling that no-one knows about this place."

"What about this opening?" asked Oswald. "Do we try it? How does it smell?"

"It's odd." Piccadilly breathed in deeply, filling his nostrils with the air of the hole. He tried to explain it to his friend. "Well it's sort of musty – very dry, salty even, I'd say."

"Ought we to go in then?" Oswald asked doubtfully.

Piccadilly frowned. "It whiffs strange. What does it remind me of?"

"Maybe it's the sea," suggested Oswald. "Master Oldnose says that smells salty – only I can't remember why."

"The sea's not round here," scoffed Piccadilly. "Nearest we've got's the river an' I don't think that's salty. No, I was thinkin' more of . . . yes that's it. Once, when I was in the city I found some of those cringin' rats with a salted fish. Don't know where it came from. It were all dried and brittle – they didn't know what it was. They'd licked it and were gaspin' for water. I gave 'em a good bit of chat special for the occasion." He laughed at the memory of it.

"I don't understand," said Oswald. "What's salted fish doing down here?"

"I only said it smelt like it. Perhaps we've stumbled across someone's secret larder." It was a joke, but Piccadilly did not realise how right he was.

Oswald shivered. "I hope not. They won't like it, whoever it is, if they know we've been there."

"I suppose it must be nasty stuff if it's in the sewers," Piccadilly said slowly. "Rat hoard, most like." He gave Oswald a quick, mischievous look. "Fancy a butchers?"

"No! I don't want to see dried rat food. It might be anything. No, I'll stay here and keep watch."

So Piccadilly cautiously passed through the opening. There was a narrow passage beyond which abruptly opened out into a small chamber, the walls of which were very rough. It had been dug out with claws and teeth. The room was small and it was filled with all sorts of rat booty. Some chocolate biscuits were still in their wrappers; a bag of sticky, fluff-covered boiled sweets lay on the floor; there was a large bundle of dark sacking or cloth in one corner; several bundles of knotted, tangled string; a tall jar with a few shrivelled lumps in it; and a squashy tomato that was gradually acquiring a green fur coat.

Piccadilly looked distastefully at the bizarre collection. The things rats collected: it was peculiar to say the least.

A movement behind made him swing round suddenly.

"It's only me," said Oswald. "I didn't like it out there on my own. Gosh, look at all this crazy stuff!" He gazed around with interest and repulsion. "It's perfectly horrid. Oh yuk!" He looked down at his foot. "I've trodden in something sticky – those sweets have oozed over the floor." Oswald hopped about as he examined his tacky foot.

"There's some cloth or sacking over there," giggled Piccadilly. "I'll get it for you to wipe that off." He clambered over the biscuits, avoiding the mouldering tomato.

Oswald leaned against the wall. "I suppose it could be worse," he said. "I might have stepped in that tomato thing. Oh it's disgusting! Is that what was making that funny smell you were talking about? Shouldn't be at all surprised. Have you found that cloth yet? Fancy us being in a rat's larder, makes me shudder. Piccadilly?"

The grey mouse was standing stock still and staring at the crumpled dark material in his paws. Oswald became concerned. It wasn't like Piccadilly to be so quiet. "What is it?" A hint of fear crept into his voice: there was something about his friend that made him uneasy. "Don't tease."

"Oswald," Piccadilly muttered thickly. "Come see."

The white mouse forgot all about the sticky substance on his foot and hurried over to see what the other had found. Piccadilly turned a drained, shocked face to him. His eyes were wet and his lashes blinked the tears away.

Not knowing what to expect, Oswald fearfully looked down at what Piccadilly was holding.

It was not cloth or sacking as Piccadilly had first thought – it was a mouse's skin. It had been a brown mouse with a splash of white on the breast; the ears were missing and Oswald felt sick as he recalled the rats' passion for them fried and crispy. His bottom lip trembled – what a horrible thing it was! There were holes where the eyes had been and the paws and feet had been chewed off. It was a macabre trophy. Oswald began to weep. "There was a mouse," he stammered through his tears, "who disappeared when I was young. He lived on the landing and he ... they ... they used to call him 'Bib' because of a white patch on his chest." His voice broke up chokingly.

"There's more over there," said Piccadilly quietly. "Mostly 'greys' like me and from the size of two of them, rats as well."

Oswald shook his head in disbelief. "They even do it to, themselves? What sort of creatures are they?"

"The creatures of Jupiter," replied Piccadilly coldly. "Sshh! he hissed suddenly, "There's someone coming."

Oswald's tear-stained face broke into a despairing picture of misery. His lips wobbled with the wail that was about to surface.

Piccadilly grabbed his scarf and shook him angrily. "Look!" he said sternly. "If you don't want to end up like good old Bib in here you'd best come and hide with me, and not a sound, right?"

"But where? There isn't a place to hide in here," Oswald gibbered.

"In there!" Piccadilly pointed at the bundle of dried mouse skins. He dragged his horrified friend towards them.

Morgan came tramping in.

A sack was on his back. "Ach," he cursed. "What now? Why all the way up there?" Morgan looked around the room. This was his own special place; somewhere to think out his dark schemes; somewhere to hide his treasures, creamed off the offerings made by the lads to Jupiter; somewhere for his bitterness to fester. It was a secret – nobody came here.

Morgan dumped the sack on the floor and plonked himself down next to it. He had just been ordered by His Majestic Darkness to go to Blackheath and this sack had been waiting on the altar for him to take along. Things were changing and Morgan didn't like it. His lord was planning something and he couldn't figure out what it was.

Morgan stretched out a claw and dipped it into the putrid tomato. He scooped up a dripping lump, mould and all, then sucked his claw clean.

"Mmm," he grunted contentedly. This was a good place – a private realm of his own where everything belonged to him. He had only popped in for a moment though – just to think by himself with no fiery eyes watching him. What was he going to Blackheath for? He wondered what was in the sack.

Morgan twirled something in his claws. One of Jake's party had returned, drenched and bedraggled. Apparently the water that had gushed from the pipe had drowned most of the rats that were pursuing Piccadilly and Oswald. The survivors then involved themselves in blamelaying, and fighting ensued. Only one young rat had returned to the altar chamber to tell the tale and bring this odd thing with him. Morgan threw it up into the air and caught it again – it was the divining rod!

He cackled. Jake was going to get it in the neck from His Highness for letting that "grey" escape – he wouldn't last long.

Morgan looked doubtfully at the sack again. He was suspicious of that round, heavy lump in there.

He licked his teeth and cast his eyes on the rest of his bounty. His gaze rested on the fluffy sticky sweets. He grasped one and flicked it into his waiting jaws. The sweet squelched and stuck between his teeth, clinging in gluey lumps. Morgan picked at them with his sharp claws amidst appreciative sucking noises. Under the pile of mouse skins Piccadilly and Oswald huddled together, hardly daring to breathe. It was the skins that smelt of salt. It had been rubbed well into the newly peeled flesh to preserve them. So dense was it that when Piccadilly moistened his lips he could taste the salty tang. Oswald had closed his eyes. The thought of their situation was too horrible for him. Here he was wrapped in dead mouse flesh. It was a chilling, gruesome thing; the pawless arms dangled around and touched him so softly that it was like being tickled by the dead and caressed by ghosts. At this thought Oswald nearly jumped out of the skins and shouted, "I'm here! Eat me. I'm here." Anything to be out of them! It said much of Oswald's courage that he did not do this, but the hairs on his neck were tingling and standing on end.

Piccadilly peered out from the mound of the dead. In the deep shadows his eyes twinkled. He saw Morgan and recognised him from the altar chamber. This was the rat who had caught Albert, and here he was feeding his ugly face and sucking his yellow teeth. Piccadilly's jaw tightened. He knew that he would feel no remorse if he killed Morgan – the murderer! In fact the city mouse had no doubt that he would actually enjoy it.

Unaware of the hidden mice, Morgan decided it was time to go. He dared not linger; Jupiter had ordered him and he must obey. The rat swung the sack onto his back, mouthing obscenities at the humiliation of manual labour.

With one last sigh as he glanced around his secret place, Morgan lumbered out, dragging his stumpy tail behind him.

For five full minutes the mice remained where they were in case Morgan should return unexpectedly. They stayed there, crouched amongst the dry skins which crackled like parchment, and waited. Oswald was terrified but Piccadilly was lost in his own thoughts.

It was Oswald who eventually forced them out of hiding. A cramp in his legs suddenly became too much to bear and he shot out of the skins, limping and stamping for all he was worth.

Piccadilly let the furry scraps fall about him. His face was stern and he resolved to kill Morgan – one day that piebald Cornish rat would be his. He promised himself that.

Oswald collected himself. The pins and needles were going now. "I'm glad he's gone, whoever he was," he puffed.

Piccadilly stepped out of the skins. "That was Morgan," he stated flatly. "He gave Albert to Jupiter."

"Oh," Oswald said meekly. "Poor Mr Brown." He glanced back at the skins pathetically crumpled on the floor. Oswald felt terrible for disturbing them and he knew that he would be haunted by nightmares for years to come. "What shall we do about them?" he asked.

"There's nothing we can do."

"Well, we might pray."

Piccadilly balked at that. "Who to? Your precious Green Mouse? Don't bother! I don't want to hear it. Believe all the stories you like, Oswald. Praying to a phoney myth won't bring them back!"

Oswald returned to the untidy pile and folded them neatly and reverently.

"No, you're right there," he said softly, "but it may make their rest easier – wherever they are now." Oswald bowed his head and clasped his paws together. Piccadilly turned away. He did not want to hear Oswald's prayer, but the gentle murmuring words came to him and in spite of himself, the cynical city mouse felt a lump in his throat.

He shuffled his feet and waited.

Oswald completed his prayer and raised his head. "I feel better for that," he said mildly. "I hope they do." He blinked, then stared past Piccadilly.

"Look!" he cried and ran to where Morgan had been sitting. The rat had left the divining rod behind. Oswald snatched it up and flourished it proudly. "See," he bubbled excitedly, "I knew the Green Mouse wouldn't desert us."

"Don't be daft, Oswald. Morgan, not the Green Mouse, brought that." Piccadilly shook his head.

"Well, it's still here," Oswald muttered. He did not want to argue. "Shall we still try to find Audrey's brass?"

"I suppose so – it's a shame to go back to the Skirtings empty-handed now."

Oswald was already holding out the rod, waiting and concentrating. It jerked and jumped wildly. "It must be very close. Look at it!"

Piccadilly cast one last glance over the neatly arranged skins. Oswald had even folded the rat furs. They had all been victims of a horrible death and the white mouse had supposed that that united them in some way and cancelled out whatever wickedness those rats had done in their lifetimes.

Oswald was jumping impatiently now. "Piccadilly, come on!" We can find it and get out of here at last." He ran out of the chamber.

Piccadilly followed him from Morgan's secret place, but in the tunnel Oswald was already a distance away, running for all he was worth.

"Oh no!" Piccadilly cried. A madness seemed to have gripped Oswald. The grey mouse ran after him.

Oswald hurtled along, stumbling and tripping in his usual ungainly manner. He paid no attention to the pain of his toes as they struck sharp stones or skidded in the puddles. His mind was full of Audrey's mousebrass and the divining rod pulled him to it. He had no control over it now. It was all he could do to keep hold of it – how it tugged and wrestled to be free.

"Not long now," he thought. "Then we can go home and Mother can scold me all she likes. I shan't care."

He did not see the passages he ran down or hear Piccadilly's voice calling to him some distance behind. Oswald continued to run blindly on.

Piccadilly panted – he was surprised at how Oswald could run. It was as if all the rats in creation were snapping at his heels. He only caught glimpses of his friend far ahead. He was afraid he would not be able to catch up. Piccadilly was uneasy; he did not know where they were going but he felt it was dangerous – running like a stupid rabbit headlong into peril. If there was a Green Mouse, Piccadilly wished he would do something to help.

Oswald splashed across a murky pool, disturbing the oily scum on its surface. Then he slipped and fell. He cracked his jaw on the hard bricks but did not flinch at the blood which trickled down where a chunk of fur had been scraped out.

The divining rod had been knocked out of his paws and it danced and clattered on the floor like a thing possessed. Oswald chased it, cornering the magic twitching thing as though it were alive, then he swept it up and set off once more.

It was enough of a delay, however, for Piccadilly to catch up. He tried to clutch at one of the ends of Oswald's scarf which was streaming behind him.

But still Oswald ran. He had forgotten about the city mouse, only the mousebrass mattered now. He did not feel his heart thumping madly in his chest or hear his own difficult breathing wheezing in the echoing tunnel.

A piece of rag was stretched across the path, obscuring the way ahead. Oswald did not see it and crashed through regardless.

Piccadilly saw the dirty cloth and a twinge of wariness clutched suddenly at his stomach. He had to follow Oswald though, and he pushed the rag aside and ran on.

They seemed to be in a large chamber, littered with sacks; large bundles on the floor, hanging off ledges, piled in corners. Oswald was in the centre stooping. Piccadilly caught up with him, nimbly hopping over the bundles.

"What are you doing? Are you crazy?"

Oswald stared at him with glassy, heavy eyes. He held his head to steady himself as the mania wore off – the divining rod was limp in his paws. Oswald swayed and came out of his trance. At his feet gleamed the mousebrass.

Piccadilly looked down and froze. Oswald, coming to his senses at last, blinked and gasped.

The chamber they had barged into was the main sleeping quarters of the rats. The sacks they had jumped over were sprawled, sleeping brutes. All about them were hundreds of snoring rats.

Oswald and Piccadilly had run slap bang into the middle of them.

The mousebrass they had come so far to find was clenched tightly in the cruel claws of a large brown rat. Oswald gulped: strapped to the stump of the rat's arm was a peeler. It was Skinner. The sharp talons of his one good arm were twined about the cord that had once held the charm around Audrey's neck. Oswald thought of the skins he and Piccadilly had found and wondered if this creature had taken part in their murders.

He stared at the grunting, snoring beast at his feet, feeling weak and sick. If there had been any colour in him it would have drained away. He turned and saw all the terrible brutes slumbering around them. In all the chilling horror stories whispered around the winter fires he had never heard of anything so dreadful as the situation he had run headlong into. Oswald finally looked back to Piccadilly.

"Pick it up," hissed the grey mouse indicating the mousebrass.

Oswald shook his head, appalled at the suggestion. He didn't want to touch the snoring monster to retrieve Audrey's brass. "Let's leave," he implored.

"Not till we get what we came for."

Piccadilly bent down. The heat from the nostrils blew harshly against his arms. Piccadilly braced himself and gingerly unwound the cord from the claw. A disturbed mumble growled from the rat. The grey mouse paused, waiting to see if the rat stirred, but there was nothing more. Piccadilly resumed. Gently he lifted one of the talons and pulled the cord free. Slowly he passed the mousebrass to Oswald and lowered the sharp talon.

"Now," he whispered, "let's go. One clumsy move, Oswald, and we're rat meat. You'd better let me go

142

first and you tread where I do."

Oswald nodded. He wanted to get out of this frightening place. His instinct was to flee, to run wildly through the rag partition – but there were so many sleeping bodies between it and them that he knew Piccadilly made sense.

He marvelled at the luck which had brought them this far without treading on a tail or whisker and inwardly thanked the Green Mouse. Oswald's admiration for Piccadilly soared as well. He could never have taken the mousebrass like that. He glanced at the gleaming yellow charm in his paw. They had come all this way for this, an anti-cat sign – was it worth it? Oswald was not sure now.

Piccadilly began to pick his way through the rats, showing Oswald where to step safely. With a nervous last look at the sleeping rat, the white mouse followed.

With a painful slowness that made every bone of them ache the two mice edged their way back to the cloth stretched across the entrance. Piccadilly sighed when he reached it and pushed it aside gladly.

Oswald hopped over the last rat – he was a scrawny villain with one ear torn off, and he ground his teeth loudly as he slept. But as Oswald neared the partition an almighty gong boomed throughout the chamber and the rats awoke.

Oswald couldn't move. There were yawns and stretches as the rats prepared for their shift in the mine. The sound of two hundred knuckles cracked in the chamber.

Oswald should have run but his legs wouldn't respond. He stayed there and whimpered, stricken and frozen. Through a rent in the cloth he saw Piccadilly's urgent face calling him, but it was no use. He was rooted to the spot.

Piccadilly cursed his luck for running out here at

the end of their journey when the mousebrass had been found. The rats were sure to catch them. He saw Oswald, bleak and terrified, trembling in the chamber – what could he do?

Oswald grasped the mousebrass tightly. He saw Skinner rub the sleep out of his eyes and then stare blankly at his empty claw.

"Nar! Where's it gone? Who's 'ad me prize – which stinkin' sot's pinched me mouse dangler?" Skinner turned on his neighbour and gripped him by the throat. "Were it you, Spiker?" he snarled. "I'll gut you an' make rope from your entrails."

The rat called Spiker eyed the peeler as it swayed menacingly before his face. "Keep yer bile in," he spat. "Haven't got yer poxy bauble. Mebbe Pokey 'ad it," and another rat was involved in the argument.

So far no-one had seen Oswald. All eyes were on the brawl in the middle of the chamber. The mouse felt life return to his legs and he crept quietly towards the partition.

A claw gripped his shoulder.

"'Ere, who're you then?" the rat with the torn ear growled behind him.

Stammering, Oswald turned round – face to ugly face. The rat grinned; there were bits of rotten green in his long teeth.

"New are you?" he sneered, looking Oswald up and down. An odd light flickered in the rat's eye. "Where'd you get this then?" he said, pointing to the green scarf. "Trophy is it? You'll not get many of them in the mine."

Oswald was totally puzzled. And then he realised what had happened – he had been mistaken for a young rat! His pride was somewhat injured by this insult, but it was hardly the time to complain – he told himself that after everything he had been through he probably did look quite dishevelled.

The rat told him it was time to start and the gong sounded again. "I hates it! That's our shift that is. Look at them over there, most of 'em too thick to tell dung from apples – they do what they're told. What's it all for though, eh?"

He turned to see the fight between Skinner and Spiker.

Oswald shot a glance at the hole in the rag. Piccadilly was bewildered. "It'll never work," the city mouse mouthed.

Oswald pulled a "what can I do" face and Piccadilly mimed to him to hide his obvious mouse hair and ears from view. Oswald quickly removed the scarf from his neck and tied it about his head in a rakish manner, then he tucked the mousebrass under it.

"I'll get help." Piccadilly assured him and the grey mouse turned and ran back down the passage as fast as he could.

The scuffle in the chamber ended suddenly. There was some cheering – others muttered, but Spiker said nothing – he fell dead to the ground, a great slit up his middle.

"I'll finish the job later," said Skinner and he licked his bloody device clean.

"I hates both of them – should have both copped it," mumbled the rat next to Oswald. "Pus-buckets they are." He tore the cloth aside and made to stomp through, but he turned to Oswald and said, "You'd best stick wi' me on yer first day. I'll show yer the ropes. We'll get on fine you an' me – mates together, be old cronies this time next shift. You'd like that wouldn't you lad?" he brought his face closer. Oswald nodded hurriedly.

"Name's Finn."

"Oh . . . I'm . . ." Oswald coughed and tried to sound harsh and croaky like a rat whilst he fumbled for a suitably rattish name, ". . . Whitey."

"Mmm, most like," Finn smiled unpleasantly. "I'll show you the mine, Whitey lad."

Oswald followed the scrawny rat into even greater danger.

# 10

# MAGIC
# ON THE HEATH

The night air was cool and refreshing. Twit quickly recovered from the stifling atmosphere of the sewers as the breeze ruffled his fur slightly and blew away the memory of the cloying, sweaty rat smell.

Thomas had led him back through the sewers a slightly different way to the one they took when they entered them. The two mice had surfaced near to the park where great iron gates kept out unwanted visitors in the night. They ducked under the ironwork and pattered along. Great trees stood black against the sky, looming above them so high it hurt Twit's neck to look. Their new leaves dappled the mice with moonlight as they passed underneath.

"The oldest trees are over the hill there," pointed Thomas when he noticed Twit's upturned face. "Huge chestnuts, ancient and knobbly. Give good feast to the squirrels and Her Ladyship."

"Who's Her Ladyship?" asked Twit curiously.

"The squirrels here are a watery lot by and large," Thomas continued, not seeming to hear the question. "I've no truck with them mostways – 'cept her, she's a grand lady." He gazed about them and scratched his whiskers. "This way matey."

Twit trotted after him. Thomas was striding briskly again. "But if you please, *who* is a grand lady?"

"Why – the Starwife," he replied. "Have you not heard of her?" Thomas tutted at this gap in Twit's education.

There were no lights in the park, and the streets to the right were obscured by the tall trees, so little light from the lamp-posts fell on the sweeping lawns.

"See yonder hill?" Thomas nodded to the dark mass that rose to their left. "The strange domed building that sits on top is for lookin' into the sky."

"Oh yes," Twit said brightly, "the bats told me it was to see the stars, but I can see 'em anyways."

"Aye the stars," winked the midshipmouse. "Oldest navigation points. Hmm, there's paths to be found up there. Lead you far away and back again they can." He cleared his throat and dismissed the urge to roam that was rising in him.

The seafarer shook his head slowly and removed his woollen hat. He stared at the glittering heavens and sighed, "No, you've had my best, I'll not wander again, whatever you tempt me with. I've anchored down at last and nothing can draw me out." Thomas pulled his hat back over his head, covering the white wisps of hair that had been revealed and which waved like seaweed floating in the deep. He smiled at Twit. "It's a strong pull the world has once you've seen it. Well, where was I?"

"The Starwife," the fieldmouse reminded him.

"Yes 'at's right. Well, below yonder hill in their drays an' whatnot live the squirrels."

"I've known a squirrel family," said Twit unexpectedly, "They was all right – though always fussin' about one thing an' another."

"It's the same here, as I said. Wet they are: most of them not worth a candle."

"Except the Starwife."

"True enough. Oh she's wise – an' older'n some of those trees I daresay. Doesn't get about much now though. Has to stay indoors with rheums and warchin' in the bones but she's not gone 'ga ga' like most old dames do. Strike me but she's sharp – need your wits to tackle her. Only met her the once when I first come here: that were plenty."

Now they were walking up the gentle slope of the hill next to the dark road which was only used when the park was open.

"Maybe we should visit her and get some advice," suggested Twit eagerly. He loved meeting strangers and the Starwife sounded intriguing.

Thomas shook his head. "No, it's best when dealing with her to visit only when invited. The other squirrels always get jumpy with other folk about. That thought has crossed my mind, though – I was wondering what she'd make of it all." He paused for a while brooding on the matter. "Summat's not quite normal 'bout her you know, she's got a other world quality – serene in peace, frightenin' in a temper; very like the sea in some ways. Rules those squirrel colonies with an iron rod. No, I don't think tonight's the night for payin' calls. Not a hospitable hour and they're only new awake after the winter."

They had reached the top of the hill where it levelled out into an expansive plateau. The road split into three. Thomas took the right fork.

"Not far now," he said. "Blackheath is just through those gates."

"What do you think we'll find there?"

Thomas shrugged. "Nowt I suppose. I just want a looksee."

The gate was before them: they ducked under it and blinked. A main road lay in front of them. For a moment Twit and Thomas steadied themselves and watched as roaring, wheeled monsters hurtled past. Twit did not like the road. It threw him into such a confusion that Thomas had to hold his paw tightly.

"We've got to cross this nightmare," he called above the tumult. "Wait till there's a break."

So they stood and waited until there was a space between the receding red lights and the oncoming white beams.

"Now!" shouted Thomas and he dragged Twit off the pavement and down onto the road. Quickly they ran. Then up onto the paving at the other side, just as an oncoming engine swept past. Twit panted heavily and Thomas coughed into his hat.

"That was a near thing," he said after a while. They turned to look at what lay before them.

"Oh no," groaned Twit, "another 'un."

They were sitting on a grass verge sandwiched between two roads and the next one looked busier than the last.

The two mice walked through the grass up to the edge of the road. Beyond the dash of bright lights and the rumble of traffic was the heath.

It was a dark place, a vast area of flat grassland surrounded by roads and buildings. A few paths crossed the breadth of the heath but hardly any trees grew there. There was only one small tight clump and this was fenced in.

An old church rested uncomfortably on the brink of Blackheath – it was a disturbing place: nothing stirred and only the stars gazed down on it.

Thomas and Twit waited patiently on the pavement as the noisy engines sped by. They wiped the smoke from their eyes and held their paws over their noses as the fumes spluttered over them. Conversation was impossible so they just sat and waited for their chance. Twit regarded his new friend and wondered what had made him give up the sea. Was it merely his age? Or had something dreadful happened to make Thomas want to forget his voyages? Twit knew that Thomas longed to be out on the rolling oceans. He was such a strong character that the small matter of his age would surely be no problem. But then Twit had seen enough of folk to understand that everyone has a reason for doing what they do even if they can't explain it – even he was going to return home soon, back to his parents, back to the sniggers of some and the pity of others. If the midshipmouse had a reason for staying on dry land then it had to be a good one, Twit decided.

Gradually the number of the machines became few.

"This is it." Thomas jumped to his feet. "Now Twit!" Once more they leapt from the pavement and ran across the road. When they reached the grass they flung themselves down on the ground and caught their breath.

"Let's away from the noise of the road so we can hear ourselves think," Thomas said.

The grass was short on the heath: it only came up to Twit's tummy. As he glanced around he saw a number of strange marks. Here and there patches grew, darker than the rest, only in perfect circles – deep ring patterns. He wondered about this odd occurrence.

"What be these circles Thomas?" he asked.

"I seen 'em too – though I'm blowed if I know. Been at sea most of my days – not up on grass an' such. Reckoned you could tell me, old son."

Twit went up to one of the dark bands. "Strange this is," he murmured. "'Tis actually a deeper colour in the very blade of the grass. And look, toadstools do grow in the circles – nowhere else, only in amongst the dark grass rings."

Tall spindly white fungi were scattered around the circles.

Thomas did not like the look of them. "I had mushrooms once," he said. "Nice 'n tasty they were too, but I wouldn't touch those pale excuses with a bargepole."

He eyed them disdainfully.

"No they don't smell too good," Twit added, sniffing them tentatively. "Poisonous most like." He pulled a face.

"What's in the soil to cause it, I'm thinkin'," Thomas muttered. "On what do they feed to turn out so?"

Twit was staring out onto the heath. Something had caught his eye: it was a small dot of light.

"It's so quiet here," Thomas went on, "hushed and lulled like a sea becalmed. What are you lookin' at, matey?"

Twit pointed. "There! You see that there light a-winkin', 'tis only small."

"Oh aye" said Thomas. "Let's take a peep. Only we ought to go quiet, there's summat about this place makes me tail twitch. Can't put my finger on it yet but that's always a bad sign – last time it happened . . ." He pulled himself short as if he had said more than he meant to. "Come on matey."

They waded through the grass making for the light. Once more Twit was glad to have Thomas Triton with him. They were careful to avoid the dark circles.

The noise of the road sank into the background and the angry lights became small points that streamed in bright ribbons in either direction.

As they neared the source of the light Thomas pulled Twit to the ground.

"We've got to go careful now," he whispered. "Summat's funny about that glow."

\* \* \*

Morgan spat on the ground. He had walked a long way and he was not used to it. Things were not going too well for him at the moment. Madame Akkikuyu had his lord's favour and so had a few others, younger rats bucking for his position. Morgan trod a tightrope of treachery; he could trust no-one. He carried a sack on his back: it was not for him to do manual labour but Jupiter had commanded it and given him certain crazy-sounding instructions. Still, he was the big boss. If Jupiter wanted him to wear ribbons, Morgan would do it gladly so long as he remained the chief lieutenant and could exercise power over the others. Power! What a pleasant sweetmeat that was. Yet he never had his fill, and if obtaining more meant grovelling and scraping to those eyes in the dark portal then he would do it.

Morgan hated being outside. Like every rat his main instinct was to run for the nearest dark and smelly hole. But "Go to the heath!" Jupiter had commanded him, so here he was. He could not afford to displease His Majesty. He had been pushing it of late: too many things going wrong and all the lads at that digging. It was difficult to keep them at it. Rebellious words were being voiced quite openly and it would be him, Morgan, who would be held responsible. His thoughts turned to the last thing that Jupiter had told him before sending him out of the sewers. "I shall meet you there," he had said. Morgan wondered if this meant that he would get to see his lord at last. Many a long year he had served Him without so much as a glimpse of those two heads. The rat afforded himself a quick sly smile as he remembered how he had got this job. He had been younger then, his claws stronger, but still Biack Ratchet had put up a very decent struggle – it had taken longer than he had expected to throttle him.

"I'd best watch out meself." He shuddered at the thought of some usurper dishing out the same fate to him. Morgan licked his long yellow teeth.

His directions had been precise. To the middle of

the heath he had to go. Well, he judged this to be fairly central. He put down the sack: it was fairly light but he could feel through the cloth a round object that weighed more than the other contents. He had no idea what they were. Normally he would have had a good look but at the moment, things being what they were, he dared not.

"Go to the centre and remove the crystal from the sack," had been Jupiter's instructions. Morgan opened the neck and groped round inside. Finally he fished out the smooth, heavy round object.

"Blast it," he cursed. "What'd he want this rubbish for?" It was the crystal ball of Madame Akkikuyu. "Still, he knows best," he said scornfully. Morgan tried hard to remember his next instruction. It was to find a ring in the grass, the largest there was and place the globe inside. What a daft thing to do.

Nevertheless, if Jupiter was going to come in person Morgan did not want to be found wasting time. He looked around him. No, there was nobody about, unless he was hiding, watching, testing. Morgan made sure that he followed the orders to the letter. The crystal was put in a large round ring. Morgan, tempted by the toadstools, popped some in his mouth but even his tainted palate found them impossible. He stuck out his coated tongue in disgust and spat out big brown phlegmy globs. He drew his arm over his dribbling mouth then recalled the rest of the instructions. Morgan stepped out of the ring and said the words he had committed to memory.

"Jupiter, Lord of All, in Darkness' name come forth." He bowed as he had been told to and waited for the creature with two heads to step forward from the hiding place. In that, Morgan was disappointed, but all thought was soon driven from him as a blinding flash seared his eyes.

Madame Akkikuyu's crystal was burning.

154

Morgan peered up. There in the dark ring the glass globe was on fire. No, the flame was within the crystal. It lapped the insides, yet there was no sign of the glass getting scorched and no smoke issued from it. Morgan gazed at it dumbly and then he saw two small points of red amongst the flames. Gradually these grew larger; floating orbs of scarlet brilliance blazing away far brighter than the other fire. Morgan realised that he was looking at two fiery eyes. Jupiter stared out of the crystal at him.

"Oh my Lord of the Night," he mumbled as his knees shook and his legs gave way in fright. What powers Jupiter possessed! Morgan had never dreamed they were this strong.

Morgan remained bowed.

"My Lord?" he ventured. "Can you hear me?" He was answered by a hollow, mocking laugh from the crystal.

* * *

Thomas and Twit had crept silently along the ground until they could see the source of the light.

Twit smothered a gasp and even Thomas the stout mariner was taken aback at what he saw.

The two mice were at the edge of one of the rings, concealed in the grass from the rat standing before them. It was Morgan. Madame Akkikuyu's crystal was held high over his head. Two burning, cruel eyes were suspended in the heart of the globe.

The voice of Jupiter bellowed from the middle of the flames and Twit quailed in his hiding place.

"Mark out the circle, Morgan," it snarled harshly. "The first stage must be completed tonight."

The rat placed the crystal on the ground and moved hurriedly to a bundle of sacking outside the ring.

"Move them inside," hissed Jupiter, "Once complete the circle must not be broken."

Morgan hauled the bundle within the ring. Thomas peered over the grass stems. The flickering light from the crystal licked across the sack as the rat foraged inside.

"Which is it first, Master?" Morgan asked, his snout muzzled in the sacking.

"The bones, Morgan – I have just explained it all to you."

The rat brought out four shinbones and flourished them proudly.

Thomas covered his eyes – they were the bones of mice.

"That's right," Jupiter hissed and the fire rippled softly in the globe.

"Trace the circle around with the notched bone, then place the others at the compass points, saving that one for the North. And take great care if you value your neck."

Morgan carefully drew over the ring. "Am I doin' it right, Majesty?"

"Get on with it."

Twit moved nearer to Thomas. "How do that there ball talk and why do it burn?" he whispered.

Thomas looked worried. "That is the voice of Jupiter speaking through yonder globe by some magic art," he said gravely.

Twit was astounded and terribly afraid: the worst nightmare of all mice was in front of him. "My Lord!" he shuddered.

"Let's hope it doesn't come to that," returned Thomas.

Morgan had completed his first task. Gleefully he smiled and clapped his claws together. He looked to the crystal for further instructions.

"Now the candle," uttered Jupiter.

The rat searched in the sack once more and fished out a short thick candle. It was a dull brown colour and Morgan gave it a cautious sniff. "Here it is . . ." he began to say. "Oh it smells good enough to eat." He licked his teeth appreciatively.

"Do not even try," threatened the disembodied voice. "I have spent a long time distilling the substance from which that candle is made – it is not a common wax."

Morgan sniffed once more and slobbered over it. The wax reminded him of juicy bacon fat and crispy crackling – what a wrench it was not to gobble it down. The wick of the candle was odd too – not the usual string, more like fine plaited hair of different shades.

"Hold it up, Morgan," ordered Jupiter.

The rat did as he was told and waited.

The flaming eyes in the crystal narrowed and the voice became low – too low to hear.

Suddenly the fire in the glass leapt out in a whip of blazing flame. It snaked around a startled Morgan who closed his eyes and cowered. The fire flared above him and in a splutter of sparks the strange candle was lit.

"Observe," said Jupiter. "You may put it to the North."

Morgan took the guttering candle to the edge of the circle and placed it next to the notched bone. The candle gave off a thick pall of brown, evil-smelling smoke.

Not far off, Thomas and Twit had to back away to avoid choking.

"What a stink," coughed Twit.

"Don't breathe any of it in," urged Thomas hastily. "Let's move upwind."

"Now, resumed Jupiter, "return to the sack and bring out the parcel."

Once more Morgan did as he was told. It was a heavy package wrapped around with brown paper through which sticky grease was oozing.

"Remove the contents – carefully."

Piece by piece Morgan tore the wrapping away. "Streuth!" he cursed, "There's a howlin' fume from this. Ach, it makes me wanna honk!"

"Be silent!" growled the voice. "Separate the pieces into four and put them with the bones."

Twit and Thomas could hear Morgan grumbling as he obeyed his master.

"What is it?" asked the fieldmouse. "I can't see what's in his hands."

"You don't want to know," replied Thomas shakily. "I can scarce believe it. This is an awful, evil thing to witness." Thomas lowered his head.

"There Master. 'Tis done," said Morgan wiping his claws on his belly.

"And finally the remaining items."

The rat brought from the sack several lumpy roots.

"Throw them into the candle flame."

Morgan did so. The roots burst into flame and vanished in a cloud of sparks as they passed through the flickering candle.

"Now Morgan, lift me! Lift the crystal over your head and prepare yourself."

The globe was seized in sharp claws and raised over the rat's head.

The fire within shone into the night as the eyes opened wide.

"With fire I summon thee," called Jupiter.

The candle flared abruptly and the smoke became a dark plume above them.

"With mandrake I woo thee."

A scream came from the air. Thomas pulled Twit away. "Come, we dare not linger for this. We must return you to your friends."

"But this . . ." Twit stammered. He did not understand the terrible danger that they were in.

"Pay no heed and stop your ears if you ever want to sleep again, my lad. A curse will fall on us if we don't leave now." He dragged Twit away as fast as he could. "In India I did see summat similar to that but not as powerful – or disgusting."

The mice ran from the middle of the heath with as much speed as they could get from their trembling legs. Nervously Twit glanced back. Whatever had been taking place must have been truly horrible to scare sturdy Thomas. A phrase came to him – something the bats had said – "Thank your Green Mouse that you were blessed with your simple wit."

Yes, Twit thanked the Green Mouse now. He was glad he did not understand what Jupiter was making Morgan do. Sometimes it was a blessing to be simple.

Thomas gripped his paw tightly and they crossed the two roads.

\*　　\*　　\*

Back in the magic circle Jupiter finished his last conjuration.

"And with bone I order thee," he shouted exultantly.

Morgan looked cautiously around trying not to tremble. His lord and master had never asked him to do anything like this before. He wondered where it would all lead. Oh, how he had underestimated Jupiter's powers – they seemed to be growing daily, or was he merely showing his full strength at last. If so why?

There were many things Morgan did not understand. He for one did not know why he had to come to Blackheath on this windy night – couldn't all this stuff have been done in the sewers? That would keep the lads quiet for a while. Morgan stiffened. It was windy. Before there had been a slight breeze but now, how that wind howled! It wasn't natural.

159

The candle flame was blown here and there, battered down by the wind but not extinguished.

"Mercy," the rat thought with round, staring eyes.

The smoke from the candle was snatched and torn by the wind.

"Oh breath of the darkest night," Jupiter began again. "Take the form I have designed. Kiss the final embrace and step down from your throne in the void."

Morgan was nearly knocked off his feet by the rending gale. It stampeded out from the black sky and whirled about the circle.

Above Morgan's head the eyes in the crystal shot beams of red, flickering light upwards and luminous vapours trailed off the glass in great swirls.

Much as he wanted to, Morgan could not close his eyes. "Stone me, what next?" he yammered wildly.

The four clusters of objects that he had placed around the circle suddenly burst into flames and presently there was a ring of fire surrounding him. But the fire was a sickly purple in colour with pulses of red running through, a red that looked like rivers of blood.

"Do not enter here," Jupiter spoke into the wind. "Consume your feast and begin the task appointed."

The thick dark smoke curled about the objects, then it swirled over the flames and rose high into the darkness.

Morgan's stumpy tail swung awkwardly between his legs. Then he heard voices in the air. They whistled and yelled, but they were hollow sounds with no body.

They came from the smoke and worst of all, they called his name.

Morgan cowered down, still holding the crystal aloft. He could hear Jupiter's voice laughing madly inside it.

Despite himself the rat continued to watch the scene before him, as though he was compelled to do so. He began to see forms in the ever-moving smoke – at first he thought it was imagination or madness taking over. Little figures, faint and indistinct darted through the dark cloud. The empty voices grew louder as they found bodies to house themselves in. Soon the smoke was writhing with them.

Morgan bit his lip as he stared about him in terror. The clamour pressed ever closer but now there was no smoke, only squat deformed creatures that flew and billowed thickly overhead. They joined in with Jupiter's laughing.

Wild was the dance around the circle. The figures wheeled in mad frenzies. The purple flames suddenly became yellow and leapt higher. With a yell the creatures raced through them, emerging as yellow glowing things themselves. Faster and faster they span until Morgan's head ached. He wished he had never come to this nightmare place.

"Enough," cried Jupiter above the din. Immediately there was silence and the forms hung foggily in the air waiting for his commands.

"Do your work," he ordered.

Without any further ado they opened their dark mouths and with a shock Morgan realised that he could see straight through them – they were ghostly ephemeral things.

A shout went amongst them all and at once they all dived to the ground sinking into the soil and vanishing with a great hiss like a thousand snakes. The flames around the circle reached up suddenly very high. Morgan found himself inside a raging column of bright fire, and then they too disappeared. The bones and the other items had gone. Morgan looked for them but there was no trace of anything – he had the unpleasant idea that they had been consumed. There was no sign to suggest the ritual that had just taken place. All was quiet and a light breeze swung the rat's earring gently to and fro.

"Is it over now, My Lord?" he ventured warily.

"Yes," said Jupiter. "For the moment you can return to my chamber."

"Did I do well, Your Highness?"

"Magnificently Morgan – my trusted one. Now you must come back to me."

Morgan lowered the crystal. The fires within it failed and the burning eyes closed. It was just a dark glass globe once more with a twist of colours in the centre.

Shaking, Morgan put the crystal in the sack and began the journey to the sewers.

# 11

## DANGEROUS COMPANY

Audrey had fainted when One-Eyed Jake and his lads had pulled her roughly through the Grill. Her unconscious form had been slung over his shoulder and they had slipped quietly back to the sewers.

"What about the rest of the miceys in there, Jake?" asked Fletch. "Aren't we gonna catch a few for breakfast?"

"This is the one we want," replied the leader sternly. "I'm not gonna risk her scarperin' while you lot fiddle with yer peelin'."

Fletch licked his teeth and looked at him for a moment. "Yes, right again Jake – you always know what's for the best." After a while Fletch turned to the five other rats and muttered to them. One of them, a squint-eyed brute known as "Leering Macky" started to grumble loudly.

"You said as how we could have mouse, an' all we get is her. Not right, that ain't. We ought to go back an' grab a few, a whole one each mebbe."

Jake whirled around snarling angrily. He clasped Macky's throat tightly and squeezed until blood trickled down his arm. "Keep it up, Macky lad," he hissed. "You'll do what I say or by Jupiter I'll stick you good and proper!"

Leering Macky swivelled his eyes: they looked out in two directions at once. "You're the boss," he snivelled.

Jake released him and glanced at the others. The rats blinked at him. The shadow of a smile flickered across Fletch's snout.

"Listen all of yer," Jake snarled. "No-one goes back and no-one touches this mouse either – right?"

The rats shuffled awkwardly and Macky wiped the blood from his neck. Fletch bowed his head to Jake to show that he understood perfectly, then he stared at Audrey coldly and said,

"You make a fine wet-nurse, Jake."

It broke the tension and Jake laughed; the others joined in. It was then that Audrey woke from her faint. Slumped over Jake's shoulder she emerged from her dark dreams into a reality that was far worse. Her eye-lids fluttered; she heard the laughter and was confused, thinking that she was still dreaming.

"Look there Jake," nodded Fletch. "The skirt's wakin'."

"Is she now?" Jake pulled Audrey down from his shoulder and set her on her feet.

The mouse sagged to the floor. Jake grabbed her lace collar and dragged her up again. Coughing, Audrey glared at him. She saw his eye patch and recognised him as one of the three she and Piccadilly had found cornering her brother, Oswald and Twit. Audrey almost smiled as she recalled that this was the rat she had bitten on the ear.

"You taste foul," she said acidly.

For a moment Jake was puzzled, then he remembered her too. "So, it was you was it? Well, don't try it again or I'll bite back."

"What do you want with me?" Audrey asked defiantly.

Jake sneered at her. "Well I could tell you what the lads here want from yer: breakfast."

She looked beyond him to the six rats staring at her. She didn't like the look of them at all. Leering Macky rolled his eyes at her. Audrey shuddered under his gaze, and glanced at the tatty brown rat with spots on his nose; Fletch bared his teeth.

"Where are you taking me?" she demanded, determined not to show any fear.

Jake stroked his whiskers and chuckled. "Got some guts ain't yer? A proper Miss Uppity! Let's just say, me dear, you're off to meet someone who's right keen to see yer."

One of the rats laughed horribly. Audrey frowned, trying to figure it out. Why had these rats gone to all this trouble? She was still alive, so they must have a good reason. She pondered on who would want to see her down in the sewers.

"Madame Akkikuyu?" she wondered out loud.

Jake guffawed. "'Tain't that old bag. What made you think it would be her? No, this is someone really . . ." he said the last word delicately, ". . . special."

Again one of the rats laughed.

"Now, we'd best be off." Jake prodded her with one of his claws. "You're fit to walk." He pushed her in front of him and the party set off.

Audrey stumbled ahead of Jake; the thought of him immediately behind was enough to keep her going at a fast pace. Even so, the claws on his long feet would occasionally catch her heels. Fletch followed Jake and behind him came Leering Macky. Behind him was "Vinegar Pete". Pete had a bald patch on his egg-shaped head and a perpetually sour expression on his face as though he was continually chewing lemons – hence his name. Bringing up the rear were three old rats. On their backs they carried sacks which contained provisions: dried meat and a flask or two of potent liquor acquired by Jake for his own personal use. The three rats had lost their youth and the rebellious vigour that went with it. They had accepted their orders and their burdens with resignation. At least they would be fed, and work in the mines, for them at least, was postponed.

Fletch kept turning and talking to Macky and Pete in a hushed whisper, every now and then stealing a sly glance at Jake. The two rats listened to him with grim, set faces.

Audrey was growing tired. The rat march was too fast for her small legs. More and more she staggered and Jake's sharp claws clipped her feet. Often a hard shove thrust her forward until she could go no further. She spun round and planted her feet firmly on the brick ledge.

"I'm not moving one bit until I've rested a while," she said flatly. It was daring, but she was curious to know how far she could push these rats – they were obviously not going to kill her themselves.

Jake was furious. He snatched her up and held her over the sewer ledge. Audrey's legs dangled over the sheer drop. Far below she could hear the sewer water surging and bubbling.

"Listen to me, my lovely little miss," he growled menacingly. "I may not be able to kill you here and now but there are other things I can do – things that will make you wish I had killed you." He shook her violently.

For the first time Audrey was truly frightened. She had gone too far. She could only hope a way of escape would show itself before they reached their destination.

"Put me down," she squeaked – her voice was not as confident as it had been. Jake threw her roughly onto the ledge.

"You've got to learn, miss! I don't take that sort of

chat from no-one – havin' a skirt won't save you. See this eye patch? Wanna know how I got my eye poked out?"

Audrey sank against the wall, shaking her head and breathing in short gasps.

"She were bigger'n you."

Leering Macky snorted with amusement. "Peg-Leg Meg they call her now," he cackled.

"That's right," confirmed Jake. "Tore it clean off in a temper I did – not so pretty now when she hobbles about." For a moment, Audrey saw the hatred burning in his eye.

"I'm sorry," she said.

"Come, come Jake," began Fletch swaggering up. "Let's deliver her and have done, eh?"

Jake relaxed. "Get up," he told her. Audrey obeyed, biting her lip to hold all the insults back. They marched on. The tunnels soon divided into three. The rat party continued straight ahead ignoring the openings that they passed.

Suddenly one of the old rats right at the back gave a shout. There was a moment of confusion – the rat cried out in his thin, cracked voice and above it floated a high surprised yell.

Piccadilly had run all the way from the sleeping chamber where he had left Oswald and on turning round a blind corner slammed into the doddery old rat. Shock and surprise registered on both faces before the grey mouse turned and fled up the tunnel. He never even saw Audrey at the front of the rat pack.

Audrey recognised his voice though, and it brought her courage. She saw the bewilderment of the rats as Jake laid into the one who had let Piccadilly escape. She saw her chance and ran.

But Audrey was not fast enough. Jake bore down on her and caught her streaming hair. He pulled and dragged her back to his comrades.

"It was the 'grey'," said Fletch dryly.

"Were it now?" spat Jake angrily. "So the other fools lost him – wonder what happened to the white one?" Audrey wondered too.

"What we gonna do?" Fletch inquired.

Jake staggered back from his appalling breath and shook his head short-temperedly. "Darn everything!" he cursed.

"Didn't His Highness demand both dainties?" continued Fletch. "The skirt and the 'grey'?" He coughed affectedly. "Are we to chase him?"

"Can't drag this wench on a chase," shouted Jake, shaking Audrey by her hair.

"I would be honoured to watch her whilst you caught the other," Fletch said softly.

"Hah! I bet you would, Fletchy. No, I'll guard her and I think it's best if you stay by me." He looked quickly at the five rats left. "Macky and Pete," he called. "You go get that 'grey' – alive right?"

The two rats whooped and darted up the tunnel after Piccadilly.

"Bring 'im back here!" Jake shouted. He motioned to the three oldsters. "Hey, you fogies: break out your packs. Might as well stay here till they come back."

The old rats pulled the sacks from their backs and sat down, their bones cracking as they slouched over the bags. Jake let go of Audrey's hair.

"I'm faster 'n you are so don't bother," he warned.

Audrey rubbed her sore head. She would not try to run off again. Her ribbon had come loose and it hung down straggly and crumpled. She took it in her paws and smoothed it out.

As she was retying it in her hair Jake reached over and hauled one of the sacks to himself. He opened it, stuck his snout in and ferreted about inside.

Fletch looked bored. "How long we stayin' here?" he asked. He kicked a stone off the ledge and listened to it "plop" in the water below.

"Till they come back an' I say we can go," Jake said into the sack.

Fletch sat down slovenly. "It's cold 'ere and there's a terrible draught whistling round yer ears," he grumbled, wrapping his tail about him.

Audrey felt the cold too but she tried not to shiver with it. Down in the sewers the winter lingered.

Jake raised his head out of the sacks; there were greasy stains round his mouth. "There's wood in that bag there," he mumbled spitting out bits of meat. "The spare torches we brought – use those and light a fire."

One of the rats handed the sack to Fletch. They were glad of a rest, and they watched Jake keenly as he stuffed his face, marking where the scraps fell for later.

Fletch pulled out four pieces of wood. They had rags bound about one end and these had been steeped in fat. He took from the sack two stones and some fluffy material. Fletch struck the stones together near the woolly stuff and waited for the sparks to ignite it.

Presently a crackling fire burned on the sewer ledge. The firelight played over Audrey's delicate features, picking out the chestnut colour in her fur and turning the lace of her collar and skirt a rich gold. Jake looked up from his gluttony and his one beady eye sparkled at her like a fire itself.

Fletch rubbed his claws together and held them near the flames. "Got anything in there for us, boss?" he asked politely.

Jake threw him a lump of gristle and Fletch dived on it, sucking, chewing, gnawing and crunching until there was nothing left. He licked his lips carefully.

The three rats looked miserably at one another. Jake spotted them and tossed them a chunk of something he had found inedible. They fell on it and fought each other for a lick of it – in fact they had more of a meal biting one another than from the sorry lump.

"Gis that sack," Jake ordered Fletch. He was handed the last remaining bag and from it he brought out two large flasks. Jake opened one and poured a thick brown liquid down his throat. Then he belched.

"What's keepin' Pete an' Macky" he wondered.

"Mebbe that 'grey' is givin' them a good chase," replied Fletch. "He's done so before."

"So long as that's all he's givin' 'em! They better not peel him or I'll peel them." It was no idle threat: Jake had eaten rat before now and liked it. He took another long swig from the flask then flung the half-empty vessel to Fletch who gurgled appreciatively and guzzled it down.

The old rats were left to sniff the empty bottle and stick their tongues in at the neck to catch any last dregs.

Jake uncorked the other and offered it to Audrey. "Want some, missy?" he asked. She shook her head. "Warm yer good an' proper – put fire in those veins of yours."

"No, thank you."

"Suit yourself, all the more fer me." He tipped it up and swallowed. "Ah!" he sighed, his wet and frothy mouth glistening in the firelight. "That's better!" He scratched his belly and looked at her fully.

Audrey began to edge out of the circle of dancing light, uneasy at this dangerous rat. A stern tap of Jake's claws on the ground stopped her.

"Don't be so keen to go," he said. He threw the

171

flask to Fletch and leant forward, the orange firelight flickering in his eye.

"Where's your dangler?" he asked. "I thought all you squeakers had 'em." He reached out to the place where the mousebrass should have been.

Audrey flinched from him. "I lost it," she stammered, "when I bit you."

Jake grinned. "Oh, so that's what Skinner found, was it? He kept that close. So what happens to you now?"

"What do you mean?"

"Do you get another one? Wouldn't mind one meself."

"No, we're only allowed one – that was mine." Her eyes looked away from Jake. He unnerved her.

Jake belched again.

"Tell me," he said, "what is it you lot worship – is it our Majesty?"

Audrey looked up proudly and held his gaze steadily. "We honour the Green Mouse," she answered.

Jake tittered. "A green mouse?" he scoffed. "I've seen green mice, well, bits of green mice – wouldn't honour them though. They turn black after they're green."

Audrey turned away from him. It was no good: these were ignorant brutes who would never understand.

Jake spoke softly to her. "Do you know who I honour?"

"I believe so," she said.

"Do you now, I wonder."

"You worship Jupiter in his stinking darkness."

Jake's eye narrowed. "Yes, we do. He is the Lord of All." There was a strange bitterness in the way he said it. Fletch had put down the flask and was listening intently.

172

Jake glanced around him and saw Fletch before the other had a chance to lower his eyes. "We're very near," he whispered. Then he stood up and dragged Audrey to her feet. With his other claw he took one of the burning torches from the fire.

"We'll not be long," he told Fletch. "Stay here and wait for the others."

Fletch set his jaw and his eyes gleamed coldly. He gave the flask to the three old rats. Jake turned the corner that Piccadilly had ran so blindly around, pulling Audrey harshly. He had drunk too much and walked in a zig-zag along the ledge.

"I'll show you what real things there are," he mumbled.

It was damp in the tunnel and moss grew down the walls in sickly pale clumps. Jake strode up to one large patch and drew it aside. He thrust the torch in front of him.

There was a passage beyond the moss, leading steeply down. Jake pushed Audrey inside and followed after her.

The mouse scrambled down the passage and waited at the bottom. She wondered wildly where she was being taken and why. Jake grasped her paw again and her skin crawled at his touch.

"Not far now, lovely," he said.

The bricks were different now. They were older and larger than those in the main sewer. Audrey knew she was walking into a very ancient place.

Marks began to appear on the walls. At first they were meaningless scrawls, but soon she could make out pictures in the torchlight: crude paintings telling of battle and bloodshed.

They entered a great room.

Jake let go of her and bowed before something she could not see.

"Oh Lords and Lady," he said reverently. He

turned on Audrey savagely. "Kneel!" he roared. She fell to her knees, and Jake fell silent for a moment.

"Oh yes," he sighed, "there are still those amongst us – just a few, who remember. My old dad was one – sot though he was. He told me, like his dad told him before."

Audrey raised questioning eyes to him.

Jake flourished the torch and strode to the far wall of the room.

There were three altars, covered in the mouldering remains of some old offerings. Above them, painted in the primitive rat manner, were three figures.

Jake went to the first. It was a crouching rat with no head. At its feet were many heads.

"Before His Highness came, all those years ago," Jake said, with the wide eyes of a fanatic, "there were the three gods! They were not living gods like Him but gods in the true sense. The three gods of the rats – now forgotten by all save a few dedicated ones like meself. We come here from time to time and do what worship we can. Until He goes it won't be safe, see. Oh I does all He asks and show humility but that's just to save me neck."

"Who is that?" asked Audrey. "Why hasn't he got a head?"

"That's Bauchan – the artful one. He wears whatever head he likes – master of disguise he is. A great liar." Jake moved to the second altar.

The picture above it was of a female rat with a tooth necklace and a third eye daubed on her forehead. Tassles hung from her ears.

"This is Mabb – the sleep visitor. She comes in dreams and urges us to war: a dark one she is. Revels in slaughter," Jake laughed madly.

Jake went to the last altar. Audrey gasped when the torch revealed the painting. This was surely the most evil thing she had ever seen: it was a rat with great horns protruding from his forehead and a mass of red hair curled like a mane about him. The tail of this figure was forked and at his feet lay a mass of bloody skeletons.

"Lord Hobb," breathed Jake. "War bringer." He turned to Audrey. "These are the true gods of the rats – fighting and slaughter's what we want. Not diggin' in poxy mines."

"Who makes you do that?"

"His High and Stinkin' Mightiness that's who. Oh those two pairs of eyes He has blazing at everyone. Red and yellow – He ain't our proper lord. It's just that everyone's scared of Him. Well, how long for, eh? A lot of the lads are grumbling against His dirty work. We ain't workers – we want blood on our knives."

Audrey backed away. She had to get out of this terrible place.

Jake placed the torch on Lord Hobb's altar and advanced towards her, an evil gleam in his eye. Suddenly a voice spoke behind her.

"So this is it!" Fletch spat on the floor. "You dirty heathen, Jake."

"Get out!" Jake ordered furiously.

"Nowt doin', said Fletch. "His Mighty Holiness – Lord of all – sent you on this job Jake, but me," he paused reflectively, "He sent to keep an eye on you! Oh yes, He knows all about this crummy dump – just wanted to make sure it were you who led the others. All dead by now by the way – gone to serve Him on the other side."

Jake looked at him stormily. His face was like thunder and sweat broke out on his snout.

"Look at all this dross," sneered Fletch. "What a piffling load of old tat!"

With a wild yell, Jake leapt at the rat, teeth bared.

175

Fletch was ready and dodged aside neatly, then flung himself on top of Jake.

They growled and bit each other. Fur came out in lumps and claws scored out trails of blood.

Audrey jumped away from them. Gradually she eased herself out of the temple, keeping her eyes on the bitter rat fight and wondering who would win.

Fletch gripped Jake by the throat, clearing a space for his teeth to bite out his windpipe, but Jake writhed and thrashed about and knocked him away with his tail. Fletch scampered to the altar of Lord Hobb and picked up the flaming torch, then waved it threateningly before the one-eyed rat.

"I'll put out the other one," he taunted. "Old Blind Jake you'll be, eatin' dung and kicked around. I'm gonna get Morgan's job."

They circled each other warily then Jake sprang.

With his head down he charged and butted Fletch in the stomach. The torch fell from his claws as he was rammed against the altar of Bauchan. The flames sent their shadows high onto the ceiling in grotesque wrestling shapes.

With his head Jake had Fletch pinned against the stone altar and the wind was knocked out of him. As he struggled for breath Jake snatched up the torch and plunged it deep into his enemy.

Audrey turned and fled up the passage. Jake's triumphant voice came to her.

"You'll breathe no more, Fletchy lad. I haven't got time to 'bloody bones' yer for Hobb so this one's for Bauchan!"

He snapped Fletch's head off, and blood spilled all over the altar.

Audrey scrabbled as fast as she could up the steep passage. Loose stones rattled down as she raced upwards. At the entrance she pushed aside the wet moss and breathed deeply, her heart fluttering. She was quite sure that all rats were stark raving mad.

"Jake been 'avin some fun with yer, sweetmeat?"

The harsh voice startled Audrey completely and she yelped. She had been oblivious to everything except escaping that evil temple. Now she turned to find Leering Macky goggling at her.

"Is Fletchy down there an' all?"

Audrey shook her head dumbly. She wondered how Macky would react to the news. "Fletch is dead," she managed at last. "Jake killed him . . ."

Macky nodded. "Thought that would 'appen. Well, won my bet with Pete – knew Jake'd come out on top." He looked past her to the entrance behind the moss. "Finishin' him off down there, is he?" He licked his lips then fixed his eyes on Audrey. "We're bored back there; proper cheesed off we are. That 'grey' give us the slip – blast him."

Audrey sighed with relief. Piccadilly was safe.

"Bah, you lot always stick together – come on." He grabbed her arm and pulled her down the tunnel.

The fire was burning low now. The three old rats had finished off the last flask. One of them was fast asleep, but the other two were giggling stupidly. Vinegar Pete crouched near the fire staring sulkily into its glowing depths.

Macky and Audrey joined them. He kicked the old rats out of the way.

"Little miss sweatmeat 'ere's gonna do some entertainin'," he laughed, pushing Audrey in front of the fire.

"Gis a song!" demanded Pete.

"Oh I couldn't," said Audrey.

"We're not askin' you," rumbled Macky.

Audrey knew now that look in the rat's eye. Hastily she tried to think of all the songs she knew. Her mind was blank. She could remember nothing. Audrey clasped her paws to her chest and desperately searched her memory. She recalled Master Oldnose rapping the walls loudly to wake the lazy young mice. When he had taught her, there was a song she had learnt and was fond of. He had written it himself. It was a sad mouse lament, telling of two young mice who were promised to each other from childhood by their families. The boy mouse loved the girl dearly but she could not return his love and one day ran off with a handsome stranger.

Audrey began. Hesitant and timid, she closed her eyes to see the words more clearly. Her confidence grew and her small voice rose high and beautiful in that grim place.

The two old rats ceased their foolish mirth and listened, and their sleeping comrade had pleasant dreams for once in his sordid life. Leering Macky rocked back on his haunches and Vinegar Pete nearly lost his sourness.

The song continued and the rats began to tap the floor in time. Audrey carried on – the more she sang the happier she felt. She imagined herself back in the Skirtings in better days, when her father was there to take her troubles away.

Macky began to tap faster and Pete followed him. The beat quickened.

Audrey tried to keep up with them. The soft enchantment the spell had worked on her was broken now. Her eyes were wide open as she struggled to race the words out.

The rats began to clap. They smashed their claws together clumsily. A tear welled up in Audrey's eye as she continued to sing in vain.

Macky grinned and leapt to his feet. He took hold of Audrey's paws and whirled her around. At first she thought he was going to hurl her into the sewer water, but then she realised with a shock that the ugly beast was dancing with her. He moved in time to the clapping of the others with great, heavy, lumbering steps. Audrey had to be very nimble to avoid his big feet crushing hers. Macky's tail swayed awkwardly behind him as he hopped about.

"Gis a turn," called Vinegar Pete eagerly.

"Sorry Petey – but it's me next," said a voice in the darkness.

Macky stopped dancing.

Audrey's heart missed a beat as she looked. One-Eyed Jake stepped into the ring of firelight. With Fletch's blood splashed all over his body he looked like a lurid creature of nightmare. He smiled and his mouth was red and wet, then he grabbed Audrey's paws. His claws were sticky with blood, and Audrey cried out at the feel of them. She shook like a new leaf.

"Start yer clappin' again," Jake said to Pete.

The beat began.

Jake twirled the mouse about, then he spun her out and in then they danced round in a ring.

"Faster!" he yelled.

Audrey held her head as far back as she could. She could smell the warm blood on him. It matted his fur down in dark, wet patches. She knew he had feasted on Fletch and she felt ill.

"Faster!"

They were spinning at a tremendous speed now. Audrey's feet barely touched the floor. She whirled round and round, struggling not to be sick. Her head swam, she was uncomfortably dizzy but still Jake went faster.

He held on tightly to her paws as she lifted into the air, stretched out and nearly flying. If he let go she would be dashed to pieces on the far sewer wall.

Audrey could not cry out – everything was a mad blur of fire and blood.

"Leave her alone!"

Suddenly Jake stopped and Audrey rolled into the corner, cracking her elbow on the brickwork.

Jake whisked round at the voice.

"Keep out of this, trollop," he snarled.

Madame Akkikuyu stepped over the old rats, cuffing them about the head as she did so.

"I said leave the mouselet be," she said coolly.

"No-one stops me, you old witch. Get back to your peddlin' and fortune-tellin' – it's all you're fit for now."

Akkikuyu eyed him soberly. "Popular Jake, not so favourite now. Leave while you can."

Jake held up his bloody claws and flicked them before her. "I'll rip out your gizzards, you ditch drab." He jumped at her.

Madame Akkikuyu reached smartly into her bag and threw some dust into his eye. Jake fell back howling, temporarily blinded.

"Come to me mouselet," Akkikuyu beckoned to Audrey. "See what I return to you?" She held up two small silver bells, the same ones she had taken from Audrey as payment on their first meeting.

Audrey ran to the fortune-teller almost gladly, and took the bells.

"Don't just sit there. Pete – Macky, rip the witch apart."

The two rats, who until now had looked on in amazement, edged cautiously forward.

"I think not boys!" said Madame Akkikuyu as the rats looked on nervously. She delved into her bag once more, and this time brought out a handful of herbs. She cast them into the fire.

The flames spluttered and crackled. Bright white stars sizzled in the fire and with a *whoosh* the flames shot up to the ceiling and scorched it black.

Macky and Pete stared fearfully at the blazing column before them.

"She is a witch," Vinegar Pete muttered.

"I have Lord Jupiter's favour," admitted Madame Akkikuyu proudly.

"Look there!" Macky pointed to the roaring, surging pillar of fire. In its centre two circles formed, and shone out brighter than the surrounding flames.

"Mercy on us!" Pete cried. The old rats fell on their faces and grovelled in the dirt.

The eyes of Jupiter were before them.

"Hear me," the rich, velvety voice called to them from the flames.

"Akkikuyu will now complete the simple task I set for you. You have failed me, and I am greatly disappointed in you all." There was a frightening edge to the voice.

"It weren't us fault," wailed Macky. "It was Jake – he made us stop."

The fiery eyes became slits. "Where is Jake?" Jupiter asked softly.

The one-eyed rat came forward. The magic of Akkikuyu had startled him, but his confidence was returning. He wiped the last bit of irritating dust from his eye and swaggered past her. He bowed respectfully.

"Oh Gracious Lord," Jake began. "I was delayed through their incompetence – the lads here are not the able folk I trusted them to be. They wrong me in the blame – it does not lie with me."

Pete and Macky protested.

"Soft," soothed Jupiter, "I hear what Jake has to say. So Jake my lad, it was not your fault – maybe it was Fletch's."

"That's right – yeah the dirty snotbag. It were him."

"And where is he now?"

"Oh, I had to stick him, My Lord. He were a baddun – rotten he was."

"Jake," Jupiter interrupted. "You forget I know all that goes on in my realm: you worship false idols, not your true master. You, Jake, have betrayed me."

Jake fell on his knees. "No, oh Dark Magnificence – it was Fletch not me what went down in that poxy temple. I followed him – that's why I stuck him. I did it for you. I knew you wouldn't like what he was doin' – honest."

The fire ran red and Jupiter roared. "Enough Jake! I have done with you – I see and hear all. I have sentenced you." The eyes looked quickly at the five other gaping rats. "Get you to the mines and work there till you die." The rats fled, falling over each other in their haste to be gone.

Jake swallowed. He was frightened now. He had underestimated Jupiter's powers. Silently he waited for his fate.

Jupiter began laughing softly and Jake shivered at the sound.

"Oh Jake, what have I in store for you?" he chuckled wickedly.

"Am I to serve you on the other side of your altar?"

"What would I do with a rebel like you, Jake? No I have something far more amusing planned. You're something of an old soldier aren't you Jake – and you know what they say don't you?"

"My Lord?"

"Old soldiers never die Jake, they simply fade away." Jupiter laughed again. "Goodbye."

A spark from the fire flew out and landed on the end of Jake's tail. He howled and stamped on it but it would not be extinguished. The spark took hold and burnt into his tail. A bright yellow ring slowly spread around it and began to creep up towards him.

Jake blew and stamped but his tail smouldered stubbornly on. Horrified he saw that where the bright sizzling ring had been only ash remained.

The ash that once was the end of his tail dropped as grey dust on the floor, and still the burning ring advanced.

"Soon it will reach your body Jake – then at last your head. Ha ha ha."

Audrey hid behind Madame Akkikuyu. She buried her face in her paws but the acrid smell of singed fur found her nose.

Bit by bit Jake's tail was consumed. He turned pleadingly to Madame Akkikuyu.

"Help me. You must do something," he begged her.

Akkikuyu stood back. "I gave you a chance to leave, Jakey boy – you pay now for the game you have played."

"No, no!" he screamed. The smoking ring was near his body now, his tail a mound of grey ash on the ground.

"I'll put it out!" he yelled wildly. "I'll get away from you and jump into the water." Jake ran from them and dashed round the corner, away from the fiery eyes.

Audrey peered out between her paws. She hoped Jake would be able to put it out in time.

A sudden last scream echoed in the tunnel and was abruptly cut off. Jake had not made it.

Audrey had no time to feel sorry for him. Jupiter spoke to Madame Akkikuyu.

"Have you the girl mouse there?"

"Yes, she is here. Come out mouselet!" She ushered Audrey before her.

The mouse stared terrified at those eyes that burned in the fire. Nothing could save her now.

"Where is she, Akkikuyu?" asked Jupiter irritably.

"But Lord. The mouselet stands in front of you."

"You lie." The eyes searched for Audrey but were unable to focus on her.

183

"I not tell lie – she is here."

"Shadows gather about her: I cannot pierce them. She must be shielded by some protective spell."

Akkikuyu smacked Audrey on the back of her head. "Stop funny business and let the High One see you."

Audrey was bewildered: she knew of no spell.

"Mousey not so simple as look says," said Akkikuyu.

"Wherever you are!" Jupiter snarled and Audrey knew he was addressing her although he could not see her. "Know that there are no powers to match mine – I have waited long and grown mighty." The eyes flashed, still hunting for her. But the shadows that had clouded over Audrey were too thick. "Akkikuyu, bring the mouse directly to me. This is but an extension of myself. Before my true person, whatever crude charms she has woven about herself shall be broken and her impudence suitably rewarded."

"I obey Lord." Akkikuyu bowed. "I no make error in delivery."

"Make haste." The eyes closed and the fire died suddenly.

Madame Akkikuyu looked at Audrey. "What magic you have?" she asked.

Audrey shook her head. "None, really, I don't understand what happened."

"Hmm," considered Akkikuyu. "Well, my mouselet, there is nothing that can protect you from Jupiter. Rat god will have you: so sad for one so young." She kicked the glowing embers off the ledge into the water below. "You come with me now," she said to Audrey. "Oh mousey mouse, what awaits you?"

Audrey dared not imagine. She meekly followed the fortune-teller around the corner.

184

A long trail of ash stretched before them.

Akkikuyu shuffled through it regardless. "Oh bad boy, Jakey," she tutted, sending up clouds of grey dust.

Audrey held her nose and covered her mouth, trying to avoid inhaling any of it. They followed the ash trail until it ended abruptly. On top of the last, sad little mound was an eyepatch.

It was a gruesome reminder. Madame Akkikuyu stepped over it, then paused. She turned and picked it up. "Never know," she told herself, "may come handy!" She popped it into her bag. "Keep up mouselet," she said to Audrey. "Not far to go."

# 12

---

# HOT MILK AND HONEY

Gwen Brown sat down heavily and hung her head. Silent tears splashed on her lap. Arthur tried to comfort his mother.

"You shouldn't have left her," she said sadly.

"I know Mother, but really, I can't look after Audrey all the time."

Gwen lifted her head and looked through the doorway to Arthur and Audrey's bedroom. The sight of the empty bed made her lip quiver. "What is to become of our family?" she said, clasping his paw tightly. "Are you sure she went through the Grill?"

"There's nowhere else she could have gone."

Mrs Brown sniffed and rubbed her red eyes. "This is terrible. And you say that Oswald and Piccadilly are gone too?"

"Oh, and Twit," Arthur added, his fat round face sagging glumly.

"What are we to do?" How can I tell Arabel Chitter?" Mrs Brown wondered desperately. "She will be so distraught over this. Oswald's a delicate child: the damp is sure to get to him."

"I don't care what she thinks," snorted Arthur. "She'd make a drama about anything – I just hope Oswald will be able to look after himself in a tight spot."

"Yes – oh this is too terrible! Poor Oswald! I can't

think of him in those nasty dark sewers: whatever possessed him? But at least Piccadilly is with him. Our Audrey is alone!" She stifled another sob.

Arthur knelt down in front of his mother and gazed steadily into her eyes.

"What should we do? I could go down after them if you like."

Mrs Brown would not hear of it. She held onto her son tightly and forbad him to go. "No love," she said. "You would be lost too. No, if Audrey can come back then I'm sure she will. You following blindly won't help anybody. We must just trust in the Green Mouse."

Arthur tried to sound brighter than he felt. "If the rats have got her then they'd better watch out," he joked.

Mrs Brown ruffled his head with her paw. "Come Arthur," she said gently, "you must be very tired. You should go to bed. You're very brave. Fancy you going to see the bats. Now go and get some sleep: you need it."

"What about you, Mother?"

She smiled at him weakly. "Oh I'll go soon. I shan't be able to keep my eyes open for much longer."

Arthur kissed her on the forehead and reluctantly plodded off to his room. He knew that his mother would not sleep that night. This was yet another blow to her heart . . . Arthur was sure that she would not be able to take much more.

He sat on the edge of the bed, unwilling to get under the covers. If only he could do something to help. Why had all his friends disappeared and not returned? He began to think that the Grill had come to life and snatched them away. Arthur was now frightened by that metal grating. He had always scoffed when the elders had told fantastic, scary tales of it and the mysterious underworld that lay beyond.

His own experience in the cellar with Twit was enough to show him that there was some foundation in those tales.

Arthur began to wonder if the Grill was alive in some mysterious way. Had Jupiter imbued it with life and thought? Arthur was not sure. A few days ago he would have laughed at such a suggestion, but not now.

He blinked his eyes and shook his head sleepily. A yawn struggled free, and very soon he was lying on the bed and snoring softly.

Gwen Brown busied herself with tidying the supper things: she washed and dried them, then she tidied up the already tidy room. With nothing left to do she sat down and tried to stay awake.

A knock outside the Skirtings brought her up with a jerk. She had nodded off after all. She crossed to the mouse hole but hesitated before drawing back the curtain. Terrible news might be waiting for her: they said bad tidings rode on the wings of night. Taking a deep breath, Mrs Brown pulled the curtain back.

There stood Twit, and next to him Thomas Triton, sword in hand. They had returned from Blackheath via the Cutty Sark where the midshipmouse had paused to collect his old weapon.

"Beggin' your pardon," Mrs Brown," excused Twit hurriedly, "but we got to see Arthur."

"Hello Twit," was all Gwen could think of to say. She looked inquiringly at the stranger in the woollen hat with the kerchief tied around his neck.

"Oh, 'scuse me," Twit stammered. "Forgot me manners. This be Thomas Triton, midshipmouse," he added grandly.

Thomas bowed and snatched off his hat. His white hair waved about like a frothy sea. "Ma'am," he said deeply, "me and the lad here desire to have a word or two with your son – if it pleases you, of course."

"It does not please me," replied Mrs Brown, collecting herself. "Twit, where did you vanish to? And no, I'm sorry, but Arthur has gone to bed and I won't disturb him now."

"It grieves me to hear you say that ma'am," Thomas bowed again. "If I seemed discourteous you must forgive me, but I've seen some rum things tonight and it goes ill with me to stand like a beggar at the door."

"Oh!" Mrs Brown was embarrassed at not inviting them in. "Please," she said hastily, "I am sorry – it's just that so many worries have made me forget myself."

She waved them to seats and began to heat some milk and honey for them. "I really am anxious for news," she said, passing them each a steaming bowl.

Thomas sniffed the milk, thinking that it would not warm him as much as a good tot of rum would.

"Now," said Mrs Brown as she sat down, "I have no intention of waking Arthur until you tell me what you want from him. And you, Twit, I'll ask again, where have you been, and have you seen Audrey?"

"Permit me, ma'am," Thomas broke in politely. "The young lad and me have seen some right peculiar stuff this evil night and none of it seems to make any sense. We thought your Arthur could throw some light on a few things."

"But why Arthur, Mr Triton?"

"Well, the bats spoke to him, and what they told him must have meant something, dear lady. Miladdo here couldn't quite hear what they said to him, so I thought if we asked him to tell us word for word what the bats told him we might be able to work it out." He looked at her pleasantly, his eyes twinkling beneath his frosty brow.

"No, you must forgive me, Mr Triton, but my son

is worn out. He must rest, and I'm afraid I have more important things to worry about than bat riddles. My daughter, you see, is missing." She wrung her paws together in worry.

"Pardon, but . . . dear lady, have you not thought that our two problems are linked? They have a common root, a dark, poisonous canker that must be cut out before it does any more harm. Both our worries are urgent." He frowned, and Mrs Brown was startled at how stern he looked. "Don't dismiss my urgency, ma'am," he continued. "My instincts are never wrong. I have ignored them before and regretted it most bitterly." His voice was dark and grim. "Unless action is taken tonight a calamity will occur and all of us shall be sorry." Thomas stared at her intently, willing her to help.

What a disturbing mouse this was, she thought. She felt that she could trust him, but what could possibly be so important?

"Twit dear," she said, turning to the fieldmouse. "Go and give Arthur a shake, would you?"

Twit hurried from the table and scampered into Arthur's room.

Arthur lay on his side, his nose resting on his arm. His tail dangled off the bed and twitched as he slept.

Twit nudged him gently. "Arthur!" he whispered. "Wake up!" He shook the sleeping mouse a little more roughly.

Slowly Arthur squirmed, then yawned and mumbled. "Go way!"

"Please, Arthur, it's Twit."

"Mmm?" Arthur carefully opened one eye and waited for it to focus. "Hello Twit," he muttered. "Where've you got to? I was lookin' for you."

"I'm here," said the fieldmouse, not convinced that Arthur was really awake.

"That's right!" Arthur yawned again and rolled

over on his other side, away from the Twit in his dream.

Twit folded his arms crossly. "Oh Arthur, do get up."

The fat mouse on the bed snored.

With a wry smile, Twit pinched his friend hard on the bottom.

Arthur yelped and sat bolt upright.

"Who is it? What's happened? Where?" he waved his fists around before calming down.

"Get up, Arthur," Twit laughed. "Someone wants to talk to 'ee."

Arthur's mouth fell open.

"Twit!" he exclaimed. "Where did you spring from? Where did you get to? I looked high and low for you when I came back from the attics."

"I don't think you looked high enough," Twit grinned.

"Is Audrey with you?"

"No she ain't – nor Oswald, nor Master Piccadilly."

"Well, where the heck did you get to?"

"Ah," Twit replied mysteriously, his eyes shining. "I went a-visitin'."

Arthur rubbed his eyes and scratched his head. "Just what have you been up to, eh?"

Twit chuckled and grasped Arthur's paw, tugging him off the bed. "Come see who I done brought back with me."

Arthur got to his feet and stretched. Twit scampered out of the room and, greatly puzzled, Arthur followed him.

Thomas Triton drained his bowl of hot milk and stroked his wiry whiskers dry. Arthur stared dumbly at the midshipmouse.

"Arthur dear," began Mrs Brown, "this is a friend of Twit: Thomas Triton."

"Midshipmouse," Twit added.

"How do you do lad?" roared Thomas, his eyes sparkling beneath his bushy white brows.

"Very well, thank you sir," Arthur replied, eyeing the stocky mouse doubtfully.

"Yes, I can see that," Thomas grinned, glancing at Arthur's stomach. "Well, sit down boy – I won't eat you."

Arthur looked questioningly at his mother. Mrs Brown nodded encouragement. He shuffled to the table and sat down.

"Well now!" Thomas bent his head forward and stared at Arthur for a while. "Now matey, I believe you went to see the bats."

Arthur nodded. "That's right."

"Well, I'd dearly like to know what they said to you. There's many an evil thing I've seen this night and it's time I had some answers. There are questions reeling in my old head and makin' it spin."

Arthur tried to remember all that the bats had told him. "I didn't really understand what they meant," he said. "It was all in silly riddles and stuff."

"Just try your best dear." Mrs Brown gave his paw a quick squeeze.

Thomas leant back on his stool as far as he could. "In your own time lad," he said gently, "but in the bats' words."

Arthur closed his eyes and concentrated. He thought of the bats high on the broken rafter and the puzzling words they had uttered.

"It was all about Audrey," he stammered. "They kept mentioning her – not by name but by description: 'she is the mouse who has lost her brass' – that sort of stuff."

"That would be your sister?"

Arthur nodded. "They said she made dolls and that she was going to be wearing silver – how can she do that?"

"Them bells I gave her were silver," piped up Twit.

"But she never made a doll in her life," protested Arthur. "You see, it doesn't make any sense at all."

"No, no," said Thomas. "None of this is relevant. Did they mention Jupiter at all?"

Mrs Brown gasped at the open mention of the name. Arthur thought hard.

"They talked of a fiend that lives below. That must mean him, surely?"

"And what did they say of him matey?"

"That I was to be wary of him, but that Audrey should be especially careful; she was the one in real danger: 'threefold the life threats' they said." Arthur searched his memory. "'How shall he be vanquished? By water deep, fire blazing and the unknown path.' What can that mean?"

Thomas frowned. He did not like it. "Fire and water, that's a pretty way to die – are we to roast Jupiter and throw his carcass into the sea?" He drummed his fingers on the table. "Why do I get this feeling the time for action is now?" He stood up and paced around impatiently, slapping his strong paws together as he thought.

Arthur looked across to his mother. Mrs Brown shrugged. Twit seemed about to speak, when in a whirl of clucking and wailing, Mrs Chitter barged in.

"Oh Gwen! My Oswald hasn't come back yet. Have you seen him? Arthur, you must know where he is." Then she saw Twit and howled at the fieldmouse: "Where is he? Why are you here? You should be in bed too. Where's my Oswald? What have you done to him – your own cousin?"

"Madam!" A strange, stern voice stopped Mrs Chitter in mid-moan. She had not noticed Thomas Triton when she crashed in. Now she considered the stranger; her eyes slid swiftly to Mrs Brown and her brows rose sharply.

"I'm sorry, I'm sure, if I'm interrupting anything."

Mrs Brown sighed. "Sit down Arabel," she said softly.

Mrs Chitter sat down. She pursed her lips and eyed the stranger.

"This is Thomas Triton. He is a friend of Twit."

"That doesn't surprise me!"

"Madam." Thomas bowed stiffly but Mrs Chitter turned away and rounded on Twit once more.

"Where is Oswald? You know and won't tell me. After all the kindness I've shown you, welcoming you into my own home after the shame your mother caused me. This is how you repay me."

Twit stared at her open-mouthed. She was too frantic to reason with, and ranted on and on.

"MADAM!" Thomas roared, slamming his fist on the table and making all the bowls jump in the air. Mrs Chitter jumped with them.

She turned to the midshipmouse, ready to give him a piece of her mind.

Thomas held up his paw to stop her. "Enough. I will not have you cackling like a stupid hen when more serious matters are at hand."

Mrs Chitter was outraged, but Arthur hid a quick smile.

"Your pardon, madam, if I appear a little brusque," said Thomas, "but time is running out. Your son is, I believe, down in the sewers."

Mrs Chitter gasped.

"He is very brave and, let us hope, safe – for the moment. The daughter of this worthy lady is also in the sewers. Maybe the two have met there. The question is, what are we going to do about it?"

For once, Mrs Chitter had nothing to say. She had never suspected that Oswald would be in the sewers, and faced with it suddenly, she was dumbfounded. She thought of her poor child in the darkness, in the nightmare world beyond the Grill, and her eyes began to water. "Oh my," she cried at last, and began to wail again.

Gwen put her arm around the sobbing mouse and patted her silvery head.

"There now," she soothed. "Calm yourself Arabel."

Thomas cleared his throat. He had been astonished by Mrs Chitter's behaviour and remembered one of the reasons why he had gone to sea in the first place. He had always found hysterical ladies difficult to cope with. Now he stepped forward and said briskly, "Arthur, how many mice are there here who would follow me into the sewers?"

Arthur thought for a moment, but the question was answered by Mrs Chitter.

"None, you fool. No-one here is as mad are you obviously are. Why, there's not one mouse prepared to go through the Grill."

Thomas eyed her coldly. "And yet through that same grating has your son gone, madam. I wonder where he gets his madness from?"

Mrs Chitter spluttered but could not think of anything to say.

"I'm afraid she's right," said Mrs Brown sadly. "We're all too frightened to go near the Grill. When we are children we are told how dangerous it is to even go into the cellar. There are powers, you see, enchantments that dazzle the senses. You lose your head, and before you know where you are, you're lost in the sewers."

"And the peeler gets you," added Mrs Chitter knowingly.

Thomas twitched his snowy whiskers. "There must be someone who'll come with me," he sighed, tapping his sword on the floor.

"I will," chirped Twit cheerfully. "The Grill do frit

me but I'm willin' to go sewerin' again." The fieldmouse had grown to respect and trust Thomas so much that he would have followed him anywhere.

"I knew I could count on you matey," laughed Thomas, clapping the fieldmouse heartily on the back.

Arthur glanced quickly at his mother. Mrs Brown looked at him fearfully but before he could say anything a grey storm crashed in on them.

"Stop! Stop!" it cried.

Piccadilly had run hard. He had dodged Leering Macky and Vinegar Pete and dashed up to the Grill. Hastily he scrambled through the rusted gap and darted across the cellar floor. Up the steps he jumped and then bolted into the Skirtings.

The other mice were startled but waited for him to catch his breath. Mrs Brown heated up some more milk and honey and he drank it thankfully.

"It's Oswald," he gasped eventually.

Mrs Chitter gripped the table for support, stood up then sat down again.

Gwen ushered the city mouse to a seat. "What about Oswald dear?"

"He's been caught – oh it'll never work, he's sure to be found out and then . . ."

"Now now lad," Thomas interrupted. "Who has got Oswald and what won't work?"

Piccadilly tried to explain. "Rats have got him!"

Mrs Chitter began to wail. "Oh my baby – my poor darling Oswald, eaten by rats."

Thomas threw her a despairing glance.

Piccadilly shook his head. "No, he's not been peeled – not when I left him anyway."

Thomas's eyes narrowed.

"That's mighty queer: ratfolk usually eat owt – there's nothing nicer to them than a young tender mouse."

Piccadilly found it difficult to make himself heard above the lamentations of Mrs Chitter. "But that's just it! You see, the rats don't know he's a mouse – they think he's a young rat and have taken him to dig in a great big mine. It can't work – they'll twig sooner or later. What'll he do when they find out?" Piccadilly's anxious face looked from Thomas to Arthur.

"Well, that's a tale and no mistake," said Thomas. "I'd be interested to find out anything Oswald may have learned in those mines. Are you willing to venture down there again?"

In a grave, faltering voice Piccadilly slowly replied, "If we could help Oswald then I'll go down again."

"We may help many," mused Thomas darkly.

Mrs Chitter, who had not really been listening to the conversation, suddenly exclaimed, "Oh save my baby." She drummed her paws on Thomas's chest and flung back her silvery head. "Oh Oswald. Save him someone."

The midshipmouse untangled himself from her and handed her to Mrs Brown.

Twit shook his head. It was hard to believe sometimes that his mother and Mrs Chitter were sisters. He looked up to Thomas expectantly. A plan was brewing. He could tell that the midshipmouse had made up his mind to do something.

The seafarer gripped his sword with one paw and placed the other on Piccadilly's shoulder. Solemnly he stared at the city mouse. "You're a brave lad. You've seen a lot of bad things that one your age shouldn't have seen, and still you're keen to go into the sewers again. One last time to save a friend. We'll find Oswald – or avenge him, and the young lass too."

"The lass?" Piccadilly did not understand. He looked about them. For the first time he realised that

Audrey was not with them. "You mean Audrey's down there?"

Mrs Brown nodded.

Twit jumped up. "When we off, Thomas?" he asked excitedly.

"I'm off now matey – if you're still of a mind to come you'd best find something to defend yourself with."

Arthur turned to his mother. "I can't stay here," he told her gently; "not while all my friends are in such danger – please Mother, understand."

For a moment Gwen's eyes met his and Arthur wondered what she was thinking. Suddenly she made the slightest of gestures with her head. He had her permission. Then Mrs Brown turned on her heel and ran to her own little room.

Thomas watched her leave. "A fine mouse, your mother," he said to Arthur. "But now we must leave – there's no time to waste. Find a weapon, each of you, and follow me."

Arthur searched around until he found two heavy sticks. He passed one to Piccadilly and smacked the other into his paw experimentally.

"Right, let's be off." Thomas brandished his sword and made for the hall.

"One moment," pronounced a voice behind the sober group.

They all turned. There was Mrs Brown. All emotion was drained from her – she was like a statue of cold, hard marble. No soft gentle light flickered in her eyes. She was resolute and determined like a warrior going to war. In her pink paws she held a long rapier, and around her neck, alongside her own mousebrass, hung Albert's.

Thomas began to protest but Mrs Brown took no notice. "All my family have gone, Mr Triton. If Arthur is to go then there is nothing left for me here. I have made up my mind and no-one, not even you, will prevent me."

The midshipmouse realised that he could not dissuade her and consented to her joining them, although he grumbled all the way into the cellar.

Mrs Chitter watched the party disappear behind the cellar door. She had never gone near it herself and marvelled at how they could pass through into that dreadful place. Even now, with her son's life at stake she knew that she could not bring herself to join them. Mrs Chitter did not reprove herself, she was not made to be brave. The quality that makes a mother stand and fight extreme dangers to protect her children was not present in her. She may have regretted this but tried not to show it – how could she change?

All alone, without even the cold company of the moonlight, Mrs Chitter sat outside the Skirtings and waited. A great, silent tear welled up and slid down her cheek. She bent her head and prayed.

# 13

## DARK REWARDS

Finn passed Oswald an old bent spoon. "'Ere Whitey, use this to dig with," he said.

They had marched into the rat mine. The entire shift had poured through a small door set into one of the mine walls. It had then been locked behind them. The mine shaft was immensely long, and wound and twisted gradually upwards. Burning torches were fastened on the walls and lit the way with orange tongues of light. All around were the signs of labour: makeshift shovels, pieces of sharp glass, sacks full of earth. Evidently there had been cave-ins, for the roof was supported here and there by crude wooden struts.

The air was stale with the rank smell of sweat and blood. With horror Oswald noticed several bodies amongst the rubble. They were old, wizened rats – too thin to be of any more use. They were kicked out of the way and lay in the dust with their noses in the dirt. The albino mouse felt very sorry for them, but he tried to remain ratlike and displayed no emotion.

Finn rubbed his claws together, spitting on his palms. "Another slog," he sneered, "and not enough in me to keep a bluebottle goin'."

Oswald was avoiding the evil stares that some of the other rats were giving him as they brushed past. He heard some of them sniggering.

"How yer keepin', Finn?" asked one with amusement.

"Stick it!" rapped Finn.

"What's that then? A piece o' chalk?"

Oswald blinked, but said nothing.

"It's death warmed up." The rats were laughing at the albino, and their jeers stung him deeply.

"Ho, Wishy Washy."

"Like yer head scarf."

"What a pasty milksop!"

Oswald gritted his teeth against the remarks and insults but every one of them found its mark.

"Freak face."

"Dolly eyes."

"You don't pay no mind to 'em! Snot-gobblers they are," said Finn. "No, it's the likes of 'im you don't wanna bring yerself to the attention of."

A huge rat had gone by. He was strong and his coat was a sleek dark brown. Oswald looked at the newcomer's face and gasped.

"His mouth . . ." he stammered.

Finn hushed him quickly. "Look as though yer doin' summat, 'fore he sees yer."

The rat moved on. His great claws were long and sharp, his thick, mighty tail swished behind him. But as for his face . . .

The rat had a permanent ghastly grin which showed all of his cruel teeth. It was a frightening expression that he could never change.

"That's Smiler, but don't you let him hear yer call him that. One of the best diggers he is – uses 'is bare claws: that's why he stays up at the front at the mine face."

"But what happened to his mouth?" asked Oswald appalled.

Finn smiled twitchingly. "When 'e were a youngun he lied to Morgan so the old stump had his lips sliced off. Bet he regrets it now though, seein' as how Smiler turned out so big an' strong. Doesn't half give Morgan dirty looks when he goes past. Yer should see the Cornish goon tremble. No, keep to yerself, Whitey lad, don't go makin' no trouble fer yerself."

Oswald stared at Smiler's broad back as he stomped away. The world of the rats was a nightmare of vicious backstabbing. Oswald could not believe that he was stuck in the middle of it. He wondered how long his disguise would last. How many hours or days would he be able to keep up the pretence of being a rat?

The gong boomed and echoed through the mine.

"Start diggin', lad," said Finn, throwing a sack over his bony shoulder. "I lug the freshly dug stuff away from the face. See yer later. Just keep yer head down." Finn tramped away.

Oswald struck the ground with the spoon. He made no impression on it whatsoever. The soil was hard and stony. He pushed the spoon and bashed it on the floor but nothing gave. He looked around him. All the others were working busily, striking the ground and gouging out the earth. The slow work song began. It was so dismal that Oswald was lost for several minutes in its melancholy words. As backs bent and arms toiled the chant flowed like a poisoned stream that wound in and out of each of their hearts.

Faces were scrunched up in exertion as stones were dislodged and tangled root knots were loosened and cut away.

At the mine face Oswald could see Smiler on his knees, slashing out great clumps of earth with his claws. The rat was like a machine: nothing got in his way, and even large chunks of brick were excavated and tossed aside like pebbles.

Amongst the many sweating rats Oswald spotted

Skinner, using his peeler to plough deep into the ground. Oswald patted his head where he could feel Audrey's brass beneath the scarf and hoped it would not fall out. He prayed that Skinner wouldn't recognise him. He had no wish to end up like Spiker.

"Work lad!" Finn had come up to him. The sack on his back was full now and he staggered under the weight of it. "You'll feel the bite of the whip if you dawdle like that."

"Where do you take all that soil?" asked Oswald.

"We dumps it into the water – right at the beginnin' of the mine shaft there's another way in. It don't have no door on like the one we come through, but yer can't get out that way see. There's only a narrow ledge out there an' water swirls all about, and there's summat worse to stop yer scarperin'. Some of 'em tried once – nobody tries any more. That's where we dumps this stuff – right into the water. Well, yer can't eat it can yer?" Oswald felt sure that Finn spoke from experience. The rat turned and plodded off down the tunnel.

Oswald returned to the spoon, thinking of this watery entrance. He wondered what was so dreadful out there that frightened all the rats. He hacked at the ground. A small stone showed signs of budging, so he gave this his full attention.

The end of the spoon dug into his soft paws till they blistered and bled but at last the stone moved. It popped out of the ground and hit Oswald on the nose. He rubbed it and moaned – his poor nose had seen a lot of punishment lately.

It was a while before Finn returned. He trotted up with his now empty sack flapping behind him. "That's right, Whitey," he said, "no slacking."

Oswald could not make Finn out. Could he trust him? The rat certainly seemed to be helping him – but why? From what Oswald had seen no rat helped another unless he was going to get something out of it. Oswald could not see what Finn's motives were. Maybe he was being too suspicious and had stumbled across the only friendly rat around. But this he doubted. There was something creepy about Finn – an edge to his voice that made Oswald shiver and go goosepimply. No, he could not work him out at all.

He drove the spoon into the ground.

Minutes dragged by sluggishly. The endless chant droned on – hours slipped by and still the chant was the same. Oswald learned the words quickly but would not utter them. He was shocked at the way the rats glorified death and sang about it in this way – murders, stranglings, guttings and roastings, all sorts of barbaric cruelties were chanted. Oswald grew very tired but the pace showed no sign of slowing.

Smiler was still thrashing at the mine face relentlessly. Oswald had to marvel at his strength. He had himself managed to dig out a small heap of soil and he gazed at it proudly. But the others were still going strong. The earth they threw up was shoved into sacks and tins by the older rats like Finn and carted away.

"That's a neat little pile, Whitey lad," said Finn. "Put yer back into it a bit more though – that just ain't good enough. Morgan'll be here soon to see how things are going – you'd best have more dug by then."

Finn was about to leave with another full sack when Oswald asked the question that had been troubling him all along.

"What are we digging for?"

Finn cackled grimly. "Well, not heard the rumours, Whitey? No, maybe you wouldn't. Some say one thing, others summat different. The way I guess it is

206

that old Jupiter is after some treasure or other. Must be a fortune too for Him to go to all this bother to find it. Years we've been doin' this, although they say it's not long now till we finds whatever it is. 'Bout time too, the trouble there's been with this poxy mine, roof falls an such. Must be a mile or longer now. Just hope it's worth it." Finn trudged off.

Oswald felt his paws. They were callused and blistered, and the dirt had got in them and stung. He felt that he would never be able to escape. Everyone seemed to remain at their posts all the time and if he began to wander he would certainly be challenged. He wondered when the next shift would start and theirs could end. By now he was very hungry – his tummy growled and rumbled. The lateness of the hour was getting to him too. Outside it must be nearly dawn. He had not slept since the previous night and his pink eyes had large grey circles around them. The dust blew into his face and clung to his fur. It clogged his skin and made him feel dirty and unkempt. He did not know how the rats could bear it.

On several occasions he heard Skinner mutter to his fellows. He was obviously grumbling about the work and moaning at the loss of freedom to wander and murder.

Oswald resumed his feeble digging, anxious about the prospect of Morgan coming to inspect the work he had done. He thought of the peeled mouse skins that he and Piccadilly had found in Morgan's secret larder.

"That ain't big enough to bury yourself in," Finn remarked behind him. "Won't do, yer know. I saw Morgan comin' up – 'e's not in a good mood either." Finn winked and continued on to the face.

Oswald kicked and bashed at the ground, frightened at what Morgan would say. Maybe he would be discovered as a mouse and eaten on the spot. He had not made much difference to the ground when Finn returned, his sack bulging.

"None too good, is it lad?" tutted the rat, eyeing Oswald's poor efforts.

"He'll string you up he will, an' you on yer first day – won't make no difference to 'im though. Should see the stuff Smiler's diggin' out – takin' six of us to keep up with 'im an' even then it's hard goin'." A sly twitch flitted over Finn's face. "Tell you what, Whitey boy. As it's yer first day on the job, and as I've got a heart soft as pig muck, I'll help yer."

The rat took the sack off his back and emptied the contents onto Oswald's small heap of soil.

"There, that's a decent size, Whitey. See, told you we'd be old cronies after our first shift."

"Thank you," said Oswald.

"Nowt to it lad, but if you could give us an 'and later with a load or two I'd be grateful."

"Of course."

"There now, that's real pals we are." But Oswald did not like the smile that lit the old rat's face. "Here comes stump-tail now. Catch yer later."

Finn bounded over to Smiler again.

Morgan walked up the tunnel scowling and shouting. "Stop loafing you louts!" he yelled. "You're not supposed to be tickling the ground. Look lively there."

The rats wiped their mouths and hissed into the backs of their claws.

"Come on, you lazy scum lickers! Let's see some real work done. His Lordship wants this diggin' to end soon."

"So do we!" an anonymous voice called out.

Morgan squinted in the direction the voice came from. Skinner looked conspicuously innocent.

"I said His Lordship wants to end this diggin' so's

'e can concentrate on greater things – which we shall
be part of. Great rewards will be ours lads. Not far
now. The work's nearly at an end."

Everyone had heard all this before. Nobody was
impressed. The rats gazed about in a bored fashion.
Morgan clicked his tongue dryly. "All right, I want
to see sweat pourin' off yer!"

The piebald rat beat his stumpy tail rapidly on the
ground. Every day it was getting more difficult to
talk to the lads. They were tired and bored of the
work, but what could he do? If only Jupiter would
order them personally or show them a fraction of his
awesome powers, it would save Morgan a lot of
bother. The lads were no longer listening to him –
they were turning to the likes of One-Eyed Jake – or
Skinner there. They wanted fun, and Morgan was
afraid they would rebel at any time now. They
needed to be kept happy or held in check. He sighed.
If only they had been on Blackheath to witness the
ceremony earlier that night, then they would not
dare to be so outspoken. Morgan turned and noticed
Oswald. The mouse was fumbling with the spoon,
aware of the rat's scrutiny. Morgan waddled up to
him.

"New are you?"

Morgan observed the pile of soil next to the mouse.
"Not bad – on yer first day too. We could do with
more of the likes of you," he said loudly so that
Skinner could hear him. "Although it is strange," he
continued more quietly, "how the amount of dirt
heaped there fails to tally with the size of the hole
you've dug."

Oswald's heart sank. He had not foreseen this at
all.

"Arrhh, Mr Morgan sir," greeted Finn hurrying up
to them. "Isn't Whitey shapin' up well? You should
have seen the mound of hard stony lumps that was

'ere before. That Smiler couldn't be bothered to move it, but Whitey 'ere's done it in double quick time."

Morgan looked at Finn doubtfully, then slowly he said to Oswald. "Have a care, white one. Finn 'ere's a crafty old codger. Just you wonder why 'e's so chummy."

But Oswald was already pondering on that.

When Morgan had gone Finn spat on the ground. "Yah, 'e's not gonna last much longer. It's time for a new sidekick for Jupiter. 'E's ad plenty of 'em and 'e'll 'ave plenty more." He flashed a smile at Oswald. "Must be off – another load to dump. But you will remember our bargain, won't you Whitey? Tit for tat: you help me with some of my loads later?"

Oswald nodded uncertainly.

The work continued – in the world outside, the stars were fading and a grey morning began to dawn.

Oswald's limbs ached: he had never worked before and his mother made sure that he did not over-exert himself. Now his head throbbed and beads of perspiration trickled from under his scarf.

Even Smiler had slowed down. His great arms rose less frequently and the amount of soil behind him took longer to pile up. Surely it was time for another shift to take over.

Skinner slouched over a heap of earth and yawned loudly. "This work stinks," he cursed. "A pox on this barmy mine." Several other tired rats joined him. They threw down their tools and talked sullenly. They wanted to know what they were doing all this digging for and what they would be getting out of it.

Oswald listened to their grumbles but pretended to work.

"Always the same questions," Finn said suddenly behind him. Oswald did not like the rat's habit of creeping up like that. "They all want summat out of this dump. Expect too much, they do. Nah, we're lucky if we find the odd worm or beetle down here, and there's not so many of those now." He watched Skinner's group for some time, his beady eyes flicking from left to right. "They'll gab on till the end of the shift now. Useless great lumps. Here's me breakin' me back with this lummackin' great sack of dirt." Finn pulled a pained expression and allowed the sack to fall on the floor.

"No good, can't lug it one step more!" He looked at Oswald craftily. "Do us that favour now, Whitey chum. Carry this 'ere load down for us – just this once."

Cautiously Oswald picked up the heavy sack. It nearly knocked him over when he heaved it over his shoulder.

Finn watched him and something like a triumphant smile spread across his face.

"That's right Whitey! You an' me, old mates now. This way."

The rat set off down the mine and slowly Oswald followed.

Past the shovelling, raking rats the albino mouse laboured, the load on his back weighing him down horribly. Finn was always just ahead, urging him on, encouraging him excitedly. So eager was he that he gradually began to walk faster and compelled Oswald to keep up with him until Finn was virtually skipping along.

Oswald felt he could not take much more. He lumbered as fast as he could but his legs were wobbly and his back ached with the weight of the sack.

"Gettin' too much, is it Whitey?" inquired the rat, rubbing his one ear gleefully. "Good job I'm here then. I knows a short cut! Just round the corner there. Cuts the traipse by half."

They rounded a bend and Oswald noticed a small passage leading off from the main tunnel. It was dark and empty. He did not like the look of it. He shook his head.

"No," he gasped, wary of Finn. "I think I can make it."

Finn laughed. "Don't kid me, Whitey. You look all done in. That scarf o' yours is heatin' up yer head too much. I'll take it off for yer."

Oswald coughed in panic. The other rats in the tunnel were looking at them now and without his scarf one of them was bound to recognise him as a mouse.

"No ... I'll go with you down there," he stammered quickly.

Finn grinned widely. "Thought you might. This way – not far." He entered the small passage and Oswald followed.

It was dark. No torches burned on the walls and the air was cold and stuffy.

Finn's voice echoed along the passage to him. He seemed far ahead.

"Come on, Whitey lad."

Oswald gulped. He felt like a small fly stumbling into the heart of a dark web and Finn was the spider. Nervously he plodded on, his heart fluttering.

Suddenly he crashed into a solid wall – the tunnel was a dead end. Blindly he groped around, panic bubbling up inside him.

Where was Finn? Why had he led him away from the others? Oswald turned his back to the wall and saw two pale points of light approaching. They were Finn's eyes, lit with a mad hunger. He had doubled back and waited for Oswald to pass him in the dark and be trapped.

"Oh Whitey boy! I've been so patient with you. Yes, Finn's not so daft as he makes out. I saw your little mousey ears when I woke up. They had my mouth waterin', they did. Oh crispy mouse ears – gorgeous! But them lot would have had yer an' poor Finn would get none, so I waited and waited."

Oswald cried out in terror. The two pale circles drew closer. Finn was smart: he had lured his prey away from the others where no-one could hear him and at the same time worn him out so he could put up little resistance.

A cold gleam of metal flashed as Finn pulled out his knife. The blade glittered icily as he threw it from claw to claw, taunting his victim.

"Oh spare me! Save me!" yelped Oswald, covering his face.

"But I have saved you, Whitey boy – for myself!" the rat laughed horribly. "I won't eat you all at once. Don't want to be greedy. No, I'll keep what's left here and come visit yer whenever I'm peckish."

Oswald shrank down in despair.

Suddenly the ground shook and the passage trembled and quivered.

"Another blasted roof-fall," said Finn. "Still, they'll be runnin' round like ants for ages in there now. Gives me time to have a nice relaxed breakfast. But first I gotta peel yer . . ."

The circles narrowed and Finn lunged forward, knife held high and ready to strike. Oswald dodged and Finn cursed passionately. "Damn yer stinkin' hide," he said, flourishing the knife once more. But the albino ducked and the blade smote the wall with a scrape of sparks.

Finn's free claw scrabbled around to catch Oswald and keep him still.

Oswald nipped here and there, trying to get past the rat and escape. But Finn was too wily.

"Gotcha!" A claw snatched at him and gripped the mouse tightly by the throat, pinning him to the wall.

"I oughta squeeze yer good an' slow till yer eyeballs pop out on their stalks. Stop yer squirmin'."

The sharp talons bit deeply into Oswald's neck, but he was too frightened to feel the pain. In a mad frenzy he kicked Finn on the shin and reached for the knife arm. He bit it hard.

"Aaarrcchh!" cried the rat in surprise and the knife fell clattering to the floor where it got wedged, blade upwards, between two stones.

"You damn maggot – I will squeeze yer!" Finn thrashed out with both his claws in a wild rage, screaming oaths and snapping his jaws together.

Oswald tripped over the full sack of dirt and sprawled on the floor. Finn jumped on top of him and gouged three long lines in his side. Oswald howled and smashed his elbow into Finn's stomach. The breath whistled through his teeth and he staggered to his feet wheezing in agony. Seizing this chance Oswald gave him an almighty shove. Finn staggered, then tripped over the sack, landing on the upturned knife. He screamed as the knife pierced his ribs. For a moment he writhed in agony and then was still. Oswald had killed him.

The mouse was distraught. He had not meant for that to happen. All he wanted to do now was get away. He ran down the passage, leaving Finn in a widening pool of dark blood.

Out of the gloom Oswald ran, out of the small passage and into the mine shaft. Everywhere was confusion and noise. Rats ran here and there with torches. The cave-in had happened just where Oswald had been digging. With a shock he realised that Finn had probably saved his life by leading him away when he did.

"Twenty snuffed it!" the rats were saying.

"Didn't get Skinner though. He's still twitchin'."

"I'm not stickin' around for the rest of it to fall in."

"Nor me."

"Not worth it, this diggin'. Might be any of us next."

The cry was taken up by all the rats in the mine. Their minds were made up: no more work for them.

Oswald crept down the tunnel. He knew that no-one would notice him in all the confusion. He decided to make for the entrance where the soil was tipped into the water, as the way he had come in was still locked. Anyway, it was too near the rats' quarters for his liking. If he had to swim, then he was sure he would be able to splash to the far side well enough. He had forgotten that the rats were afraid of something that lay beyond that entrance . . .

The rats behind him were shouting loudly now and had begun marching down the tunnel behind him. Oswald scampered along as fast as he could to avoid getting caught up by them.

The mouse ran as fast as he could but the mine was very long. He belted round a corner and ran smack into Morgan.

Oswald fell back. The Cornish rat's face was grim and frightening to look on. He glared down at Oswald. "Get up, Milksop!" he snarled, giving him a spiteful kick. Morgan stared beyond him up the tunnel where the ruddy glow of torches bobbed nearer. "Insurrection is it? Is that what's in their wooden heads? Well no more! They're gonna feel the bite of His Lordship – He's ready for 'em now."

Oswald noticed that Morgan was carrying a sack in which a strange round object bulged. The rat patted it thoughtfully. The mouse got to his feet and edged away.

"Get back in there," Morgan hissed at him, "if you want to save yer fur!"

Oswald scrambled back along the mineshaft. There was something terrible about Morgan. He seemed cloaked in a shadow of evil power that made him seem taller than before. His eyes were like cruel spears and they stabbed out ferociously.

Oswald was trapped between a hundred angry rebels and this malevolent servant of Jupiter. Yet he felt that he would rather face the mutinous rats that marched towards him, their torches held high and their tempers flaring.

"What's this?" they cried as they saw Oswald stumbling towards them.

"It's Wishy Washy."

"Where you off to Pasty?"

Oswald stammered and pointed down the tunnel. "Morgan's coming!" he exclaimed.

"Oh, is he now?"

"Ain't we lucky lads?"

"Old patchy's comin' to see us – that's considerate of him."

"Pull him to bits."

"Rip his head off."

Smiler the giant was amongst the mob and he grinned more than usual.

"Yesshh," Smiler drawled in his awkward, sploshy way. "I'll rif hisshh tongue out and eath it."

"Stick 'im proper – all these years 'e's lorded it over us an' we took it – no more! 'E's 'ad it now!"

The rats waited expectantly and fell silent. Oswald edged past them: they had forgotten him for the moment.

Morgan turned the corner and strode up to the silent mob.

"Well lads – not workin'? It's not time to lay off yet, the shift's still yours." As he spoke he paced up and down looking at each of them menacingly.

Oswald could see that Morgan was not frightened at all. The mouse hid at the back, not wishing to be seen by those evil, beady eyes that darted to and fro.

"We ain't doin' nowt," said a solemn, steady voice.

"That so? Now lads, if you know what's good for yer you'll do as I say or there'll be big trouble."

The rats all cackled, thinking this the most ridiculous and idle threat that they had ever heard.

But Morgan did not flinch. He stood his ground coolly and waited for the guffaws to cease. One by one the rats fell silent. Even Smiler stopped laughing. This was new to them. Morgan had never been brave – or stupid. They wondered why he was so confident. When all was hushed Morgan spoke softly so that they had to strain their ears to listen. He had their full attention.

"How dare you threaten me," he sneered. "Remove those thoughts of revolt from your addled brains and bow down before the Black Prince of Nightmare. Beg His forgiveness! I am His right hand, His servant. Raise a claw against me and you challenge Him. He is Lord of All – do you think He hides in the dark portal idle and ignorant! His eyes are everywhere – all around – all-seeing and all-knowing.

The rats considered this uneasily. Morgan pushed past them like a high priest speaking to the pagan rabble.

"Beware your thoughts!" he continued. "For Jupiter will read them and you will be sent to serve Him on the other side of His altar."

A faint murmur rippled through the rats. He had nearly won them over.

"Return to your places and be honoured that the work you do is for His greater glory."

"A pox on the stinkin' work," shouted a raucous voice.

Morgan looked over the crowd. Approaching them was Skinner. He looked shaky – bruises covered his body and cuts marked his face – his tail was broken in three places and trailed limply behind. The rats turned to him to see what he had to say.

"We choke and die in roof-falls – for what?" he spat bitterly. "We break our backs – for what?" He punched the air with his fists and some rats began to mumble with him. "I'll tell you what for," continued Skinner. "For some fat freak who sits in that chamber laughin' his whiskers off at us. The work keeps us busy – that stops us askin' too many questions like 'Who is Jupiter?' and 'Why won't he come out?' I'll tell you why – because he's a fraud, some old codger who's got it good."

The crowd nodded at that and began to grumble once more – soon they were all waving their fists in the air angrily.

Oswald dared not move. He cowered down and wondered how long the argument would continue before it turned really nasty. Skinner seemed to have the upper hand at the moment but Oswald still reckoned that Morgan had a surprise left.

The piebald rat regarded the mob in disgust. "You fools," he cried. "You know nothing of the power of Jupiter." He pointed at Skinner. "But you are the biggest fool of all." Morgan reached into his sack and brought out Madame Akkikuyu's crystal.

The mirth that the sight of this brought quickly died away as flames flared inside the globe and two eyes of red fire blazed out.

The voice of Jupiter boomed over their astonished heads.

"I AM YOUR LORD."

The rats fell on their faces in terror. They had never witnessed his full wrath before, or his powers. Oswald trembled and sank to his knees, stricken with horror.

"I am your Lord!" Jupiter called again. "I have been generous and lenient in the past but now you have angered me. I should bring a terrible doom on you all."

Morgan raised the burning crystal above his head and the light from it shone out blindingly.

"Without me you would revert to sucking the slime from the walls as you did when I found you. I have blessed you with the thirst for blood and murder – yet you would rise against me," Jupiter laughed. "I know who the ringleaders are. Behold my vengeance."

Skinner looked nervously around him. In his wildest imaginings he had not thought Jupiter was this powerful.

A halo of white fire suddenly formed around the crystal, then shot out in an intense stream of death.

Skinner screamed as the white inferno consumed him. The rats around fell back in fear.

Skinner crackled and sparkled, writhing and waving his arms about in agony. His squeals filled the mine and echoed long after he had died. Abruptly the fire vanished and a smoking, charred skeleton collapsed on the ground. The peeler fell on top, smashing the brittle charcoal bones.

Gasps of horror spread through the crowd.

"Now I tell you to return to your work before I have to demonstrate my anger further. Do not fan the flames of my wrath."

As one, the rats jumped to their feet and scurried back to their posts.

Morgan chuckled. Now he had the power he had always craved. No-one would dare challenge his position now. The fear of His Lordship would keep them in check. For the first time in his nasty life, Morgan felt secure and safe.

The rats worked quickly. The roof-fall was quickly cleared away and the suffocated bodies flung to one side. Smiler charged at the mine face with renewed vigour and the dirt flew up around him.

Oswald picked up his spoon and dug speedily. He dared not believe what he had just seen and his mind was reeling. Surely nothing could defeat Jupiter. Morgan remained on his lofty vantage point observing the work. The crystal was still in his claws and the eyes continued to burn brightly.

"Do not think this is a profitless task," Jupiter boomed. "There will be rewards for all of you at the finish. Once the tunnel is completed, the treasure that lies under Blackheath shall be yours to enjoy for ever." He chuckled wickedly. "Morgan, return to me at my altar. Another problem approaches, one which I shall crush with the utmost pleasure."

The crystal became dark as the fires within died. Morgan jumped down off the brick and made his way through the mine. He was pleased to see how the rats bowed reverently and saluted as he went past. He had achieved his life's ambition at long last and he revelled in the feeling of joy it brought.

Oswald was troubled – he had heard Jupiter's words about the treasure and they worried him, though he did not know why. He dug away thoughtfully. Somewhere a nagging doubt was tickling him and would not go away. He scratched his head and wondered.

Smiler smashed through the soil, his great claws ripping out vast clumps of earth. Then one of his claws snapped and flew off. He cursed and inspected the rough soil before him. He picked out some stones and wiped some dirt away. Hastily he withdrew his claws. "Acchh, it sshhtingsshh," he said, examining his skin. It was growing red and sore.

"The sshoil burnsshh!" he exclaimed.

Several rats went up to him and peered at his burns, then they stared at the mine face.

"Smells queer," sniffed one of them.

"Oohh, it burns me nose," yelped another after having a good whiff. He rubbed his snout.

Get tools and see what it is," they suggested.

Oswald watched them as he racked his brains. He knew the answer was there if only he could find it. Something in the soil that burned . . .

He tried to think back to when he was younger and Master Oldnose had stood before him and the rest of the class of young mice. He had told them of something terrible that had happened many, many years ago. Something to do with Blackheath, but what?

Oswald bit his tongue forcing himself to remember.

The rats meanwhile had scraped some soil away with spoons and revealed a large white boulder. It was the biggest they had yet come across.

"Lever it out," they called and pushed their spoons underneath it.

There was something very strange about the boulder. It was perfectly round with odd, wiggly lines marked into it.

"Heave," the rats cried. They all pushed down on their spoons. Nothing happened.

"Again!" The stone budged slightly.

All at once Oswald remembered. Blackheath – of course! Long, long ago there had been a terrible plague – the Black Death. The bodies of the dead had been buried under Blackheath and covered with horrible, burning quicklime. It was this that was burning Smiler's paws.

"Stop, stop," cried Oswald to the rats. "You don't know what's happening – we'll all die – stop."

"Shut it Pasty. Heave lads," cried the rats. With one last effort the boulder moved, the soil rattled down around it and the great white object rolled out.

It was a grinning human skull.

222

A violent rumble shook the mine as the face gave way and other skulls and bleached bones fell free. Rising with the dust of the disturbed earth was a yellow mist.

It billowed out, curling through the empty eye sockets and seeping through the gaps in teeth. In the dense fog there were ugly spectral forms.

Jupiter had made the Plague a living thing with his black arts and the mist was writhing with evil life. Oswald shrieked and fled.

Panting heavily he charged down the mine.

Smiler looked at the bones dumbfounded. The first skull teetered on a chunk of brick, rocking from side to side as though it were shaking its head at him. Then he saw the mist and the wicked faces that formed there. His eyes opened wide as the fog swirled around his legs and stole up behind him. Two smoky arms reached out from the pale ghostly sea and transparent fingers covered his face. Smiler cried out and tried to pull the creature off but his claws simply passed through the smoke. Higher the phantom writhed until Smiler was staring into unclean eyes full of unquenchable hunger. He could not struggle. The Black Death overpowered him, and he fell to the floor, the fiend seeping down his mouth. Smiler's mighty tail gave one last thrash before he died. It smacked the skull and sent it spinning down the mine.

How Oswald ran. All the rats were looking up in bewilderment. They saw an eerie vapour slowly creep along the ground, engulfing, enveloping, soaking into nooks and niches.

When the mist reached them they tried to step out of it but it clung to them stubbornly and would not shake off. Then they would choke and gasp and fall down, their faces black and swollen. The fog flowed over their bodies.

Down came the skull, crashing and rolling, bouncing off the walls and flattening the rats who dithered in its way.

Oswald heard it rumbling behind him and he looked over his shoulder in terror. He saw the skull gaining, its grisly face turning as it spun. Teeth chipped and smashed when it struck the ground. As it passed beneath the torches the flickering light seemed to make it wink maliciously.

Oswald tried to run faster. The insidious mist was not far behind and the plague spectres rose from it like foam on the sea. He heard the chokes and desperate strangled cries of the rats as the plague touched them. He knew that this was the eternal reward Jupiter had promised.

The other entrance to the mine appeared ahead and Oswald took heart at the sight. He was very weary, his energies nearly spent. Only the thunder of the skull chasing him kept him going. Vaguely he recognised the small passage that Finn had led him to as he raced by. The yellow fog would seep in there and cover the rat's body.

*CRASH!*

The skull bounced on a rock and snicked Oswald's tail as it landed. He put on an extra burst of speed.

The entrance was close now. With one last leap Oswald jumped clear of the mine. He landed clumsily and struggled to keep his balance.

Oswald was on a narrow ledge. Below him water surged thickly. He turned to face the skull, which seemed to laugh as it rushed towards him. An almighty thud rattled the ledge.

The skull had plugged the entrance completely. Not a gap or chink was there to be seen around it. The demonic mist would not be able to escape. Oswald breathed heavily in relief and bowed his head – he was safe.

He glanced upwards and froze. On the adjoining wall of this large chamber was the altar of Jupiter.

# 14

# THE DARK PORTAL

A hot sulphurous wind began to blow through the sewers of Deptford. It blasted down long-forgotten passages and buffeted the hanging weeds.

Audrey hurried along behind Madame Akkikuyu. The warm, dry air made it difficult to breathe. "It's so hot," she gasped. Her ribbon was damp and dangled limply around her neck. When she touched the sewer wall next to her she drew back in alarm. "The bricks are hot!" she exclaimed. "What is happening?"

Madame Akkikuyu replied without turning round. "He is growing, mouselet," she said knowingly. "His fiery claw reaches out – the Prince, he make ready."

Audrey was afraid. Her palms were sticky and she nibbled the edge of her lace collar nervously. What doom was she going to? Jupiter himself awaited her, and she felt so small against him. There seemed to be no way out for her. She could not escape: something was guiding her small, delicate feet towards him. It was as if this meeting had been decided long ago, fated since before she had been born. Now she was merely carrying out the part set for her.

The sewer ledge was getting hot now. Audrey had to hop around to keep from burning, and the silver bells on her tail jangled wildly. Madame Akkikuyu showed no signs of having noticed the rise in temperature. Audrey glanced at the rat's large feet and saw how leathery and covered in calluses they were. It would take a long time for the heat to work its way through them.

As they drew near to the altar chamber it became even more stifling. Surely the legends about Jupiter breathing fire were true, thought Audrey. He must be belching out flames like some demonic dragon.

The sewer water had even begun to steam, and wisps of it curled up and rose into the hot air, gathering about the tunnel ceiling. Damp sizzled in the brickwork and moss withered on the walls. Soon even Madame Akkikuyu loosened her shawl and mopped her face with it.

"Like when Akkikuyu very young," she said. "Now mouselet – we nearly there."

The fortune-teller passed through a small arch, and following, Audrey found herself cramped in an ante-room. It was dirty and smelt dreadful. A pile of old straw in one corner showed that someone occasionally slept there. Madame Akkikuyu's crystal was there too, nestling in the straw like some magical egg.

"Master Stumpo kip here," Akkikuyu said. "The old spotted one has to be near the High One at all times. But for how much longer? Akkikuyu wonders."

The fortune-teller paced over to the crystal and popped it into one of her bags. Then she stretched herself to her full height and puffed out her chest, bursting with her own importance.

"I have the trust of His Majesty. He learns me dark secrets and I deliver you to Him, so bargain is kept. I am worthy of the black knowledge." She smiled for a brief moment, happily contemplating the power that would be hers. When she broke out of her reverie she looked down at Audrey with something approaching pity.

"Oh poor pretty mousey," she sighed heavily and blinked her coal black eyes. "Why you get mixed up in things too great for you?"

Audrey considered the rat and this new mood that had seized her. Carefully she said, "You could let me go. It's not too late."

Madame Akkikuyu shook her head sadly. "Oh no my mouselet, too late it is. Roads only go one way – no back turns allowed, never." The rat gazed into space. "Akkikuyu could never return – no," she whispered softly to herself. "Paths are made and you must walk them. Akkikuyu know this. Akkikuyu done many things in life, many bad things. The way back is locked for me. Happenings happen: you cannot have say in all you do. Make best with what you got."

Audrey broke in cautiously, "Or the worst."

"Don't be wise," the rat snapped, flustered by the large staring eyes of the little mouse before her. "Little do you know of Akkikuyu, you in your cosy hole with gentle mamma. What you know of ratlife? We not like you mouseys, we different."

Audrey shook her head. "I don't think you're so very different."

The fortune-teller backed away disconcerted. "Akkikuyu is rare creature – none like her. You tiny mouselet do not know what turns in her head." She faltered, her thoughts far away in the past, reliving old moments. Her first tentative steps to love and the sneering ridicule she had received had stung like a whip and crippled her heart.

"What would you do if you could have a place to settle, a home, dignity?" Audrey continued.

Akkikuyu paused and wondered. It was a long time since she had contemplated such things. They had always seemed to be a luxury that she would never have. But now this mouse stirred all these old neglected dreams and she savoured them. Were they out of reach even now? Could she not repent all her wickedness and cast aside all her ambition? The seeds of a new life embedded themselves deep in the rat. If only she could find somewhere safe and peaceful. Slowly she nodded as the idea shone in her mind like a chink of light amongst the old spiteful shadows.

"Mouselet," she said hurriedly. "You, me – run away. Leave dark places, hide and be happy in summer sunlight." She clutched Audrey's paw in excitement and smiled nervously. Her heart became lighter, and many years of toil and misery seemed to fall from her shoulders. Akkikuyu looked young again. Yes, she would leave all this behind; her evil past would be a dim memory blotted out by joy; there would be those who could forgive her. She would have friends – someone to tell her worries and fears to, someone to confess her doubts to, someone to share special moments with. Madame Akkikuyu had never had any friends before: there had been many suitors when she was young, but none of them had lasted for more than an evening by the creek. A friend was something she really longed for. She could see that knowledge of dark powers was no substitute. This was her one last chance to decide.

A shadow fell on them.

Morgan stood in the small archway rubbing his claws together. Madame Akkikuyu stiffened and the eager hope left her eyes.

"Found 'er then, did you witch?" snarled Morgan, staring at Audrey. "What's so special 'bout 'er then? Looks nowt from 'ere."

Madame Akkikuyu bowed her shoulders. Suddenly she looked older and more weary than ever before. She knew now that there would never be any turning back for her. Croakily she said, "This mousy very special. Keep your claws off."

Miserably she looked at Audrey. "Nice dream, my mouselet. But you must see, paths do not turn back. Akkikuyu must follow hers, though she hate it, wherever it leads. And you I must deliver."

"Get on with it, witch!" growled Morgan, pushing her out of the ante-room. "His Lordship's waitin' an' 'e's in a foul temper: the mine's collapsed and summat's wrong."

The fortune-teller threw him a withering look and slowly led Audrey to the altar chamber of Jupiter.

"Bah!" spat the Cornish rat. "She's barmy."

\*       \*       \*

Oswald crouched under some sacks on the adjoining wall. The ledge on which he trembled was far below the altar. He was too afraid to move from his hiding-place although he was nearly fainting with heat and fatigue. Through a hole in one of the sacks he could see the altar of Jupiter clearly. The candles burned steadily, but beyond their pale flames all was dark. Oswald wondered if the rat lord was aware of him. Nothing had happened since the skull had jammed in the mine entrance – surely Jupiter must know about that?

Something moved in the corner of his eye. Oswald gulped in dismay: it was Audrey, and beside her walked an ugly rat woman. What was she doing on the altar ledge?

Without thinking Oswald stood up, scattering the sacks that had hidden him and shouted up to Audrey.

\*       \*       \*

Madame Akkikuyu urged Audrey on. "Pray it will be swift, mouselet," she whispered.

The bricks on the altar were scorching, and

beneath them the water seethed and bubbled.

Audrey's mind was filled by the dark portal. Never had she imagined a darkness so deep, a blackness so eternal. The most terrifying depths of night were locked in that pitch void.

A small voice that sounded vaguely familiar drifted up to her. But she was now enchanted by the spells that Jupiter had wound around his lair and could not answer.

Madame Akkikuyu stepped over the soft, warm wax that dripped from the candles, and like one drugged, Audrey did the same.

Together they stood before the black archway and gazed into the louring darkness.

"Most High Majesty," called the fortune-teller. "I have delivered what was promised."

A distant echo rumbled out of the void as Jupiter approached. Two dim points of red flickered in the dark distance and advanced.

Audrey felt weak and giddy. She staggered backwards and would have fallen over the edge if Madame Akkikuyu's arm had not flashed out and grabbed her.

"My thanks, Akkikuyu." The soft, rich voice of Jupiter rumbled out of the darkness. "So this is the mouse who would upset my grand design and trample me underfoot," he laughed coldly.

"It is as I saw in the crystal." The fortune-teller bowed low.

"I see you now mouse," taunted the voice. "Here in the heart of my realm all powers succumb to mine. How did an insignificant creature such as you dare to challenge me?" The voice quivered with impatience at her impertinence.

Audrey tossed her head defiantly. She wasn't going to give Jupiter the satisfaction of watching her grovel.

"I am Audrey Brown," she shouted proudly, "and I know nothing of spells or dark magic: I place myself in the protection of the Green Mouse! Whatever you do to me I know that I shall be received by him."

Jupiter laughed. "Akkikuyu, leave us and make sure we are not disturbed. I will send for you when I have dispatched Miss Brown to meet her Green Mouse."

The fortune-teller bowed again and then glanced quickly at Audrey. Then she lowered her eyes guiltily and hurriedly set off back to the ante-room.

Alone, Audrey faced the Lord of the Rats.

"You have irritated me, Miss Brown – you and that white fool who seeks to hinder my plans. I shall deal with him in due course, but first, come up and serve me on this side of the candles."

"Never!"

"But you must," murmured Jupiter. "My will is yours. Climb up, I command you."

In horror Audrey saw her feet begin to move of their own accord. She shuffled nearer the portal and Jupiter chuckled to himself.

\*       \*       \*

Oswald had made himself hoarse with shouting to Audrey. Now he clapped his paws over his eyes, and fell to his knees sobbing. He knew that Audrey was doomed and that he was powerless to save her. The awful sound of Jupiter's mocking laughter filled the chamber. Oswald wept bitterly.

"Oswald!" whispered a weak voice close by.

"Oswald!" it repeated softly, only this time it seemed to be calling from far, far away.

Fearfully, expecting some trick of Jupiter's, the white mouse peered through his paws.

Amidst the rising steam and shimmering heat-haze he could see a dim and vague shape. It glowed with a pale, watery green light. Very faintly, Oswald could make out the form of the Green Mouse.

The vision blurred suddenly and nearly went out. At the centre of Jupiter's domain the powers of the Green Mouse were feeble.

"The mousebrass, Oswald," called the ghostly figure. "She needs it now."

A great hiss of steam engulfed the figure and the green light was extinguished. The Green Mouse had been banished from the chamber.

Oswald quickly removed the scarf from around his head and using it as a slingshot he whirled the mousebrass over his head several times and catapulted it though the air.

It shone and sparkled, spinning like a wheel of golden fire. With a loud "ching" the charm clattered on the ledge just behind Audrey.

Her feet ceased their steady advance and she shook her head free of the unwholesome spells.

"No!" she yelled into the blackness. "You'll have to come and get me yourself, you two-headed monster."

Jupiter let out a thunderous cry of rage and frustration. "How dare you! I am Jupiter! Dark Lord of All. I am The Mighty One, The Evil One, The Father of Murders. Who are you? A petty mouse – beneath my contempt. Verily I shall come to you. Gladly shall I tear you to pieces." The force in his voice shook the whole chamber like an earthquake and mortar cracked and rattled down as he bellowed.

"Behold the majesty of Jupiter and die!"

Audrey staggered back as the evil demon began to leave his lair for the first time. She screamed in terror.

Below, on his ledge, Oswald saw the great long claws appear from the darkness. A colossal fist, covered with matted ginger fur followed it.

A horned shadow fell on Audrey as Jupiter

brought his enormous head through the portal. Oswald's mouth fell open in a silent scream of naked terror.

Out crawled Jupiter.

As the candlelight shone on the monster, Oswald found his voice and a howl of fright echoed around the chamber.

All the rumours, all the legends, and all the horror stories were wrong. But the reality of the dark god was much worse. Jupiter did not have two heads: his one, huge head was nightmarish enough.

The Most High Satanic Majesty was a monstrous cat!

So massive and bloated was he that he could barely squeeze himself through the archway. His hideous face was covered with repulsive warts, and everywhere poisonous boils poked through his ginger fur. A squat purple nose sat in the middle of his face and bulging rolls of fat hung heavily beneath his open mouth. Slowly he pulled his humped back under the arch.

Audrey stepped back as far as she could, her arms flailing in the air as she balanced precariously on the edge of the altar. But as she did so her feet touched something cold. She glanced down, and there before her she saw her gleaming mousebrass. With one movement she swept it up and held it tightly to herself.

Jupiter's iron claws dug into the bricks as he hauled himself forward.

"Yes," he gloated. "All these years, all this time I have lain hidden and secret from my subjects. Think of it – a cat worshipped as a god by rats!"

Audrey covered her face to shield herself from the stench of his dreadful jaws. And then Jupiter lowered his head.

Audrey saw a rush of red as his gaping mouth

descended towards her. Instinctively she flung up her arms and with them the mousebrass.

The anti-cat charm sparked and flashed, then blazed out like a green beacon in the altar chamber.

Jupiter reeled back. The green light seared his eyes and blinded him. He shook his huge head and roared. His claws shot out and he pounced on Audrey.

From out of nowhere a small furry bolt fell towards the mouse on the altar. It swooped down and snatched Audrey out of Jupiter's reach and into the air. Held tightly in Orfeo's grip she soared higher, the mousebrass still shining brightly in her fingers.

Jupiter heaved himself out of the portal completely and grasped the narrow ledge. He screwed up his face and breathed in deeply. Suddenly he breathed out a shooting stream of fire. One rumour at least was true.

Orfeo dived to avoid the flames, but singed one of his ears.

"Oho! Old master puss!" he cried. "Not that time – try again."

Audrey stared at the giant beast squatting awkwardly on the altar. And then she noticed something else. A small figure was advancing determinedly towards the bloated horror with a sword in his paw. Another fiery blast scorched the wall as Orfeo spiralled high out of the way. And then Jupiter hissed angrily as something pricked his side: Thomas Triton had stormed angrily into the altar chamber. Piccadilly had found the small passage that he and Albert Brown had first discovered. Grimly they had marched up it and looked on the terrible scene unfolding before their eyes. Now Thomas stabbed and swiped at the monstrous cat with his small sharp sword. Jupiter's flesh was tough and there was too much of it for the thrusts of

Thomas to harm him, but the jabs infuriated him.

The corpulent monster's tail flicked dangerously near.

Gwen Brown rushed out of the passage brandishing her rapier and drove it deep into him.

"Get back!" Thomas ordered her. Arthur pulled his mother back along the ledge. It needed both him and Piccadilly to hold her.

A rush of leathery wings startled them as Eldritch landed behind them. With a quick smile at Twit, he brushed past them and flew into the chamber. Beating his wings in Jupiter's face he called to Thomas, who was desperately dodging the thick ginger tail.

"Ho, seafarer!" hailed Eldritch. "Hold up your paw." He plummeted down and caught hold of Thomas. Then up they flew and circled around Jupiter's head where the midshipmouse's sword deftly pricked and stung the angry cat.

Meanwhile Orfeo flitted down with Audrey and she ran to her mother's arms.

From the ante-room came Morgan and Madame Akkikuyu, eager to see what all the noise was about.

The fortune-teller shrieked when she saw the mountainous cat lashing out on the altar. So this was the Mighty One: her hope and future lay in the claws of a cat. She shook uncontrollably and began to gibber idiotically.

Morgan was confused. He ran over to the huge creature and stared up at it, his beady eyes blinking in astonishment.

"My Lord!" he cried. "Is that you, oh Dark One?" The Cornish rat felt cheated and betrayed. Jupiter's reply was instant. His tail fell like a tree trunk on top of Morgan. With a wail he scrabbled at the ledge, but the ginger mass knocked him in the stomach, bowling him over and flicking him out over the precipice. Into the gulf Morgan fell, calling for mercy until he crashed into the water and was sucked under.

This was too much for Madame Akkikuyu. Her mind could not take the enormity of the horror in front of her and it snapped. She fell silent and ran from the chamber, waving her arms about madly.

Twit ran onto the ledge and cheered Thomas on as Eldritch fluttered before Jupiter's malignant face. Thomas sliced into one of the pulsating boils, and a gush of thick, yellow poison spurted out.

"How's that, moggy?", he jeered.

Blind with rage, Jupiter lunged at him, but overreached himself and tottered on the brink of the altar. His massive stomach slumped over the edge and dragged him with it. Jupiter fell from the ledge.

Twit cheered louder and Eldritch flew down. "That's 'im seen to," said the fieldmouse.

"Don't speak too soon," cautioned Thomas looking over the edge. "Come see."

Jupiter had stretched out his thick arms as he had fallen, and his strong claws had bitten into the wall. They scraped and screeched down until they snagged on the chain of a sluice gate.

For a moment he hung there, stunned and silent. But gradually his strength returned, and he gripped the chain more securely. Grinning triumphantly, he began to climb.

His claws slashed out footholds in the brick as he crept upwards. The chain clattered as he put his full weight on it. Slowly it started to move. Through the rusted metal hoops that held it the chain ran, and bit by bit, inch by inch, the sluice gate opened.

Water rushed into the chamber as the gate yawned wide. The level began to rise.

The mice on the altar stared down at Jupiter.

"He's climbing back!" exclaimed Mrs Brown.

Twit grabbed the sticks from Piccadilly and Arthur and flung them down. They bounced off, and Jupiter laughed. Then he took a deep breath.

"Stand back!" warned Audrey as a great blast of fire shot up towards them. The bricks of the altar blackened as the sheets of flame blazed over them. The mice huddled back behind the candles next to the portal.

A plaintive voice rose above the tumult of the water.

"Look," shouted Twit, pointing down to the adjoining wall. "It's Oswald! He'll be drownded!"

The water level was rising quickly. Soon it reached Oswald's chest.

"He can't swim," said Piccadilly anxiously.

Orfeo rose into the air, and just as the water was filling Oswald's ears the bat fluttered over him.

"Put up your arms, pale one," he cried.

Oswald obeyed and was carried out wet and dripping onto the altar.

Two ginger ears appeared over the side of the ledge and Jupiter's great head reared over it. He laughed at the small creatures who had dared to challenge him. Especially the girl: even now she was staring at him defiantly, completely disregarding the danger all around her. Smoke curled out of the corner of his mouth and he spat flames at the mice on the altar.

Audrey faced the terrible cat god alone. "You don't frighten me any more," she said coldly. "Before I die, I curse you with all my strength and all my faith in the Green Mouse. You are an abomination in nature. Choke on my bones!"

Jupiter smirked at her, and a gutteral rumbling came from his throat as he started to purr. His pink tongue slid out and licked the corner of his mouth.

Audrey felt the fumes from his jaws on her face:

the thought of the pain of being crunched and ground between his teeth flashed through her mind. With a last effort she cried, "This is for my father!" and flung the mousebrass towards the beast.

For a moment the charm glittered in space as it turned over and over. Then it hit the ugly great head with an explosion of green fire. Emerald stars burst out, dazzling everyone. The chamber became a turquoise green as fire caught hold in Jupiter's fur. Jupiter squealed in pain.

The green flames licked his huge face and he shook his jowly face to put them out. His huge arms reached up and flayed about, and slowly he began to topple backwards.

With an almighty roar of disbelief he fell. Down he plunged, too far from the wall this time to cling to anything. He writhed in the empty air, his burning fur tormenting him, and then hit the water with a tremendous crash. A giant waterspout reared up and touched the ceiling.

"Look!" said Piccadilly.

Jupiter was not finished. He struggled in the surging water, green fire crowning his monstrous head. Waves lashed at the ledge, nearly sweeping Audrey clean off. Piccadilly grabbed her and pulled her away as the water smashed over them.

Slowly Jupiter struggled to the side.

"He's going to make it," shouted Piccadilly over the tumult.

"Oh don't let him," Mrs Brown cried desperately, and her paw closed over Albert's mousebrass.

Jupiter reached his mighty arm out of the water and grasped at the wall.

"You cannot defeat me," he screeched, digging his claws into the brickwork.

But, deep in the water, something else was stirring. Faint blue lights began to appear around the struggling monster. They glimmered underneath the waves, steadily growing brighter.

Audrey rubbed her eyes. "What are they?" she asked, but when she turned to the others it was obvious that none of them could see them.

"No!" cried Jupiter suddenly. "It cannot be!" Slowly he sank deeper into the water.

Audrey stood transfixed by the sight she was witnessing. Ghostly blue arms rose out of the depths, and small paws clutched at the ginger fur. Every mouse that Jupiter had tortured and devoured had returned from the other side to claim him. With the strength of death they pulled him down.

Surprise and panic showed in his face and he thrashed about with his enormous tail. Mewing harshly he spluttered and choked as the water flowed into his mouth.

"He's going under," said Piccadilly hopefully.

"He's drowning, he's drowning," shouted Arthur.

Twit danced for joy around Thomas. Oswald sneezed and sighed, knowing he would be in bed for weeks with a terrible cold. He wrung out his scarf miserably.

Staring up at the mice on his altar, Jupiter lost his struggle with the shades of his victims. He foundered and the water closed over his head. Great bubbles exploded to the surface and ruptured as his vast lungs were spent. It was a gruesome sight to behold, but Audrey could not take her eyes away. She had to be certain that Jupiter was dead.

Soon the bubbles ceased. Jupiter was no more. His immense bulk sank slowly down into the deep.

Thomas laid a paw on Twit's shoulder.

"It's Davy Jones's locker he's gone to! The world's a cleaner place for it; a dark and nasty stain has been removed."

Arthur and Piccadilly shook paws and laughed

happily now that the dangers had passed. Mrs Brown hugged Audrey tightly.

Orfeo and Eldritch alighted on the ledge gracefully.

"The beast is drowned deep," said Eldritch.

"As are his subjects and his evil plans. The plague will never leave the mine now," said Orfeo.

"A neat piece of work, seagoer," congratulated Eldritch, but as he said it he exchanged an odd look with his brother.

"Come on home," Mrs Brown said tenderly to her daughter.

"Yes, we must leave this foul hole," agreed Thomas. "Back to light and air and the smell of the river!"

"Buds are burstin' out there," chirped Twit, yearning for the countryside.

Only Audrey stared down at the dark water as it calmed and stilled itself. She saw a patch of shimmering blue rising to the surface and she caught her breath as the light took shape. From beneath the waves the shade of Albert Brown smiled at her. A thousand words passed between father and daughter. Then, as if called away, the shimmering phantom lowered his loving eyes and vanished.

"Oh Mother," gasped Audrey, clutching Mrs Brown's arm for support.

"What is it, love?" asked Mrs Brown kindly.

Audrey stared over the edge and closed her eyes. Tears streamed down her face. Then she looked into her mother's mild, brown eyes and cried huskily: "Father's . . . dead."

"I know dear, I know," sighed Mrs Brown, glad that her daughter had finally come to terms with the truth. She held onto her daughter passionately. Audrey's sobs racked both of their bodies.

Thomas put his arm around Oswald's shoulder.

The albino was very tired and weak.

"I know just the thing to warm you up," laughed the midshipmouse, winking at Twit. The fieldmouse giggled at what Mrs Chitter would say. Piccadilly joined them and they left the chamber.

Arthur caught up with his sister.

"Phew, what a terrible week it's been, and after all this you still haven't got your mousebrass. Algy won't believe any of this."

Audrey sighed and glanced back at the altar chamber. Her eyes were raw, but she could see Eldritch and Orfeo huddled together and gazing at her strangely. All she wanted to do was to get back to the Skirtings.

"Goodbye and thank 'ee," said Twit, waving to the bats.

Orfeo lowered his foxy head behind his wings.

"Until the summer . . ." he said darkly.

**ROBIN JARVIS**

Look out for more exciting titles by
Robin Jarvis:

THE DEPTFORD MICE SERIES
The Dark Portal
The Crystal Prison
The Final Reckoning

THE DEPTFORD HISTORIES
The Alchymist's Cat
The Oaken Throne

THE WHITBY SERIES
The Whitby Witches
A Warlock in Whitby
The Whitby Child
  (*available in October 1994*)

All these titles can be bought from your
local bookseller, or can be ordered direct
from the publishers. For more information
about Robin Jarvis books, write to *The Sales
Department, Campus 400, Maylands Avenue,
Hemel Hempstead HP2 7EZ.*